D0984534

HEARTS ON THE WIND

HEARTS ON THE WIND

LESLEE BREENE

FIVE STAR
A part of Gale, Cengage Learning

GALE
CENGAGE Learning™

Detroit • New York • San Francisco • New Haven, Conn • Waterville, Maine • London

GALE
CENGAGE Learning™

LIBRARY OF CONGRESS CATALOGING-IN-PUBLICATION DATA

Breene, Leslee.
    Hearts on the wind / Leslee Breene. — 1st ed.
       p. cm.
    ISBN-13: 978-1-59414-716-6 (hardcover : alk. paper)
    ISBN-10: 1-59414-716-7 (hardcover : alk. paper)
    1. Railroads—Fiction. 2. Scandinavian Americans—Fiction.
3. Middle West—History—19th century—Fiction. 4. Domestic
fiction. I. Title.
    PS3602.R443H43 2008
    813'.6—dc22   2008026751

First Edition. First Printing: October 2008.
Published in 2008 in conjunction with Tekno Books.

Printed in the United States of America
1 2 3 4 5 6 7 12 11 10 09 08

In memory of three honorable and courageous men:

My dad, who always believed in me.
Orville Kermit Carlson

My grandpa, who held his family together
during the Great Depression.
Ernest Thure Carlson

My great-grandfather, who farmed his Minnesota land
and laid the tracks on the early Northern Pacific
in 1871.
Olaus Jahr

ACKNOWLEDGMENTS

Hearts on the Wind, a five-year labor of love, evolved from the tales about my Scandinavian-American ancestors. Long was the road and many obstacles in the path, yet its muse guided me through to completion. Ingrid Johansson and Andreas Eriksen insisted their story be told.

Two nonfiction books proved to be invaluable sources of my early research: *Borghild: A History of Pioneer Days in Clay County, Minnesota,* by Mrs. Henry G. Melbye, and *Twin Cities: A Pictorial History of St. Paul and Minneapolis,* by Lucile M. Kane and Alan Ominsky.

Materials from the Minnesota Historical Society contributed to my knowledge of the fascinating role the rail baron played in rescuing and extending the Northern Pacific Railroad to the Canadian border.

Many heartfelt thanks go to the following individuals:

My editors, John Helfers at Tekno Books and Tiffany Schofield at Five Star Publishing.

Author and editor Denise Dietz. We share a history in and gratitude for the Rocky Mountain Fiction Writers.

Sisters in romance: Colorado Romance Writers and the "Five Star" author team.

Friends in Unity for their encouragement along our spiritual journey.

Mary Schonberger and the water aerobics gang at Bally's South West. You are the greatest!

Education is not the filling of a pail,
but the lighting of a fire.

—William Butler Yates

CHAPTER ONE

Eden Valley, Minnesota, June 1876

In her favorite corner of the barn loft, Ingrid Johansson lingered over the last paragraph of chapter three of *Ivanhoe,* a book borrowed from her younger brother Jens. Stumbling across a long word, she muttered a curse he had taught her. *How will I ever teach if I cannot learn this new language?*

"Where is Ingrid?" her father shouted from down in the yard. "We will be late for the wedding."

She snapped the book shut and hurried over to the loft's open window. Below her, Hans Johansson stood tall and impatient next to the team of horses, his tawny beard contrasted against his reddened face.

A resistant shudder went through her. *I do not want to go!* The last person she desired to see would surely be there.

Her father's angered glance in her direction, like an arrow, pierced her with guilt. "Coming, Papa," she answered, slipping the treasured book under a hay bundle. She scrambled down the ladder.

His loud complaint reached her ears even before she entered the side yard. "You have been reading those English books again, and not helping your mater."

Jens and her sisters Marie Lisbet and Briget waited in the back of the wagon. With eyes downcast, Ingrid took a basket of freshly baked bread and a smoked ham from her mother and loaded it behind the seat. Wrapped in blue-and-white checked gingham, two apple pies peeked out from the top of another basket.

Marie Lisbet held the family's gift to the bride and groom, a finely sewn quilt. Ingrid had apprenticed with the quilt after her chores, watching her mother Sigrie's work-worn fingers make each tiny detailed stitch.

"The Lindstrom wedding will be the biggest celebration of the summer," her mother declared from the front seat as they headed out of the yard. "The Lindstrom boy is a good catch."

Her father gave a short laugh. "*Ja,* his folks own the only hardware store in town."

Hilda Grinvold may be a lucky bride but there are few, Ingrid thought. I will not be tied down to this hard life. I will move away and become a teacher first.

"The Lindstrom nephew will be the best man—a railroad man from St. Paul," her mother went on.

"And a Norskie!" her father groused, his tawny beard quivering. "If he crosses my path, he will have to explain why they charge me a fortune to ship my grain to the city! I hear they do not pay their workers a living wage."

"Do not worry, Papa," Ingrid placated, hoping to keep his temper in check. "We have no interest in anyone who works for the railroad."

A flock of blackbirds soared above the wheat field stretching southward from the house as the wagon creaked along the narrow trail. Young green stalks rippled in the morning breeze. Alongside the road, cherry-red hollyhocks brushed against the wheels, bees humming in the air above them.

It was a perfect day for a wedding, Ingrid had to admit, despite her vow not to marry until she was at least thirty. By that time, she would have earned her education and become the first teacher in the Johansson family.

When they neared the Grinvold farm, the road in both directions was clogged with arriving guests. Ahead she saw their neighbors, the Pederson family, and her stomach twisted.

Her father pulled the horses up to the Pederson's team of oxen under a clump of shade trees. Alighting from the wagon with her brother and sisters, Ingrid greeted the Pedersons politely. When she saw their eldest son, Daxe, standing near the oxen, she turned away. Her father had hired Daxe for the summer to help with heavy work around their farm. She soon discovered he was a randy oaf.

Yesterday morning, he had come up from behind when she was milking. He had snaked his large hand around her and roughly squeezed one of her breasts. Sudden pain and embarrassment flooded through her. Her hands had shaken so badly that she squirted some of the cow's milk down the front of her apron.

Swinging around on the wooden stool, she had challenged his bold smirk. "Daxe! If you come near me again, I will take the pitchfork to you!"

Now, her attention shifted to the young man just reining in his horse and buggy downhill by the lake. He drove a fancy new rig upholstered in shiny black leather. The buggy had a gold-tasseled canopy over the seat and large spoked wheels. The driver got out and assisted his riding companions, the Lindstroms.

"He is the nephew." Sigrie spoke low in her ear. "I hear his *pater* is a big stockholder in the St. Paul & Pacific Railroad."

Ingrid tilted her violet blue, lace-trimmed bonnet and smoothed some of the wrinkles from her best summer dress as she watched the handsome guest stride up the grassy hill. "He looks like he is from the city," she murmured.

The smart bowler hat he wore at a jaunty angle set the stranger apart from the farm boys. Except for full sideburns, the young man was clean shaven. Ingrid guessed him to be in his mid-twenties. A rich man's son.

When he reached the crest of the hill, he tipped his hat.

"*God morgon*," she said with a hesitant smile.

Hans shuffled by carrying their food baskets. "Come now, you women, into the house. Do not waste the day gawking at the Norskie."

Ingrid stared after him, wondering if he was just envious of "the Norskie's" riding buggy as were Daxe Pederson and a few of his friends. Exchanging glances, the young men loitered around the buggy until Mrs. Pederson shooed them away.

The Lutheran wedding ceremony took place in a pine grove on the hill behind the Grinvold's log house. When the groom kissed his bride, half on her mouth and half on her rosy cheek, she flushed as pink as a wild rose.

If only time could stand still, Ingrid wished, and this glowing moment never end. If only matrimony did not mean endless back-breaking toil in the fields and the home, a baby arriving every other year, followed by the constant fear of life-threatening childhood disease.

Beneath the maple trees, she helped the women lay the long table with so many food dishes it should have collapsed. She glanced across the yard, her gaze taking unwitting advantage of her view of the new man. He stood surrounded by half a dozen gushing women.

She saw the way his suit jacket fit snugly across his broad shoulders, the strong outline of his nose and chin, the curl of dark hair behind his ear. When his gaze met hers, firework sparklers flashed between them. She quickly averted her eyes.

"Ingrid is blushing," an elder woman teased.

The Norwegian broke from the group of female admirers and walked in Ingrid's direction. Her knees shook beneath her skirt, and she was powerless to stop them. Had he noticed her staring?

"I am Andreas Eriksen, the groom's cousin." His smile was warm, his manner confident. "Do you live in Eden Valley?"

His eyes looking down into hers were the color of the lake in the morning light, the clearest blue. Words tripped over themselves on their way across her tongue.

"*Ja*. I live a mile from here," she said, "just past Swede Grove."

Behind Andreas, the bride's father ushered the pastor to his rig. Soon afterward, he returned to the party and shouted in a jovial voice, "Come now, you sinners. Let us have some dancing!"

One of the bride's uncles got out his seasoned fiddle and played a lively Scandinavian tune.

The bridal couple started the Old Country spring dance. Other couples joined in. Some of the women danced together, foolish expressions on their faces. Ingrid tapped her foot, yearning to give it a try.

With a daring smile, Andreas took her arm. "Miss Johansson, from the look of your foot, I'd say you would like to join them." He whisked her into a hop-step that took her breath away.

Ingrid held onto him as they swirled and bobbed. "Where did you learn this dance, Mr. Eriksen?"

"From family friends. They call it a polka."

He twirled her around until her bonnet, only attached by its loosely tied ribbons, flew from her head and flopped at the back of her neck. She tried to follow his unfamiliar footwork but finally stepped on his toe and fell against him.

He laughed and caught her around her waist. "I wondered what your hair looked like, tucked up inside your sunbonnet." His eyes were admiring. "How do you get it so tightly braided?"

Out of breath, Ingrid touched her hand to her braided

coronet. "My mater and I do each other's hair."

"It is the color of spun gold," Andreas murmured softly.

She was unable to prevent a warm flush from spreading through her limbs. "Do you always say what you are thinking, Mr. Eriksen?"

"I meant no offense, Miss Johansson."

After Andreas went to get them some punch, her father walked past, a glowering look in his eye. "Be careful the railroad man does not trip you up, girl."

She gazed across the yard at the Norwegian. "Leave me alone, Papa," she said under her breath.

When Andreas returned, they watched the others from the shade of an oak tree and sipped the punch. Ingrid felt a strange queasiness in her stomach. Was her father watching?

She had already defied him this morning. Knowing his resentment of her desire to learn English, she had hidden her brother's book, *Ivanhoe,* in the barn loft.

Continuing the conversation with Andreas, she asked, "Will you be staying with the Lindstroms for long?"

"About a week. I will help my cousin build his new house." Assuredness shone in his azure eyes. "Now that I have graduated the university, I am going back to St. Paul and learn the railroad business."

She eyed him suspiciously. "So, you are going to be a railroad man."

He nodded. "My father says the future of the country will depend on the railroads."

"And the farmers."

Andreas' dark brows lifted. "It will take both railman and farmer working together." Raucous laughter interrupted their conversation.

Over by the barn, Daxe Pederson swaggered among a group of young farmhands, drinking and joking. She guessed their mugs were not filled with cider. Just the sight of him repulsed her.

As sunset fell, Ingrid and Andreas strolled along the footpath toward his buggy. Escaping from the adult's sidelong glances was a relief. A fading crimson ball lingered behind the trees on the far side of the lake.

"The sun is saying goodnight to the lake," she murmured. Instantly her face flushed with heat. Why had she said that?

How foolish Andreas Eriksen must think her. But he merely nodded at her observation, a hint of amusement in his eyes.

His buggy gleamed in the soft, dusky light, the upholstery as rich as black satin. Ingrid reached out and touched the front seat with shy fingers. She had never smelled new leather before; a sweet heady smell it was.

"Would you like to go for a buggy ride, Miss Johansson?"

His offer caught her by complete surprise. "Oh . . . I do not think I should . . ."

Andreas stroked his horse's mane, rays of bronze highlighting his hat and fine dark hair. "Only a short ride."

What could it hurt? Her parents were out of sight, enjoying the celebration with the other guests. "Well, why not?"

She accepted his offered hand and hopped onto the smooth buggy seat.

Andreas Eriksen gave the reins a smart little snap and off they went. Around the lake, shimmering in the last light of day. The black pranced along as if on clouds. An easy breeze teased her bonnet. Seated next to her, Andreas' strong masculine length was disarming. Was this what it felt like to be "courted"? She was afraid she liked the exhilaration far too much.

Breaking her reverie, he asked, "Do the farmers welcome the railroad here, Miss Johansson?"

She shifted uneasily. "They do . . . but I have heard some say the shipping charges are too high."

His intent eyes met hers. "I appreciate your honesty, Miss Johansson."

His gaze lingered on her face, causing an unfamiliar flutter in Ingrid's heart. She steadied herself against the seat.

The ride was over too soon. He assisted her down with a flourish never shown by any farm boy she had ever known.

From behind them, the hulking frame of Daxe Pederson and two other youths slipped out of the shadows. "And this is the fine riding buggy of Mr. Eriksen." His companions snorted at Daxe's remark.

Raising an eyebrow, Andreas turned.

Reeking of alcohol, Daxe brushed roughly against Ingrid's shoulder. "Got yourself a new dandy?" he rasped into her ear. "Why, ain't the Swedes good enough for you?"

She recoiled against his choice of words and glared at him. Before she could respond, Daxe swaggered up to Andreas.

He pointed a stubby forefinger at Andreas' face. "You think you are a fancy pants?" Sneering, Daxe gestured toward Ingrid. "Maybe you would like to sample what is in her drawers?"

Anger flared in Andreas' eyes. "You are a drunken fool!" he snarled, drawing himself up several inches above the brutish Daxe. The other two youths hovered; one spit, the other snickered through teeth set wide apart as a picket fence.

Ingrid stared at Daxe, afraid of what might happen next. Where was Papa? Where were the other men?

"Go back to where you come from, Norskie." Lunging, Daxe threw his full weight against Andreas, knocking him backward onto the ground. His bowler tumbled off into the grass.

"Stop this!" Ingrid cried out. "Go get my *pater*," she urged a red-faced farm boy. Dutifully, he raced back to the wedding guests. Then rough hands grabbed her from behind and she struggled to break free.

Andreas leaped to his feet and rolled up his shirt sleeves,

revealing bare muscular arms. Silently, she urged him to give Daxe the beating he deserved. The two men faced off. "Get the Norskie!" someone hollered. The air grew hair-trigger tense.

Brawny farmhand and agile railman shuffled in a slow circle. Two young bulls with fire in their eyes. Ingrid held her breath.

Andreas landed the first punch in the middle of Daxe's face. Daxe bellowed like a stuck sow, his nose spouting blood onto his bedraggled shirt. Daxe threw a jab to Andreas' stomach. Grimacing, Andreas doubled over. Recovering quickly, he slammed Daxe on the jaw.

Daxe stumbled, then swung wild in blind fury. One fist struck Andreas just below his right eye.

Andreas dived for Daxe's legs. Dust swirled up around the beefy farmhand as he thudded, face forward, to the ground. The air wrested from his lungs in one long "Oooph!"

Mounting him, Andreas took a fistful of Daxe's straw-colored hair and yanked the hired man's head back until he yelped in pain. "Apologize to the lady!"

Daxe whimpered. Blood trickled from his injured nose down into his open mouth.

Andreas gave Daxe's head another hard yank. "I said apologize to her. Now!"

Daxe exhaled through gritted teeth and mumbled his apology.

Ingrid looked at Daxe squinting up at her, unable to move, and felt a rush of victory. This Norskie had just humbled the brash bully and given her at least partial satisfaction.

"Hey—what is going on here?" her father called. The Grinvold clan chased down the hill on his heels.

His eyes glazed, Daxe got to his feet.

"Papa!" Ingrid ran to his side. "Daxe picked a fight with Mr. Eriksen—"

One of Daxe's comrades bulled his way forward. "That ain't

the way it happened. The Norskie started the whole thing."

Her father shook his head, his mouth set tight above his beard. "Well, Daxe?"

Averting his eyes, Daxe muttered something coarse. He swiped his bloody nose on his ragged shirt sleeve, then shouldered through the onlookers and stomped off.

Instead of addressing Andreas Eriksen, her father sent him a glacial stare. He would waste no time hearing the outsider's story.

Andreas's smudged shirt hung open to his waist, exposing his tight-muscled chest. He bent over and retrieved his bowler, dusted it off, and climbed up on the buggy seat. His unreadable gaze found Ingrid's, then dropped to the reins in his hands.

For reasons she did not understand, her heart sank.

"Come, daughter," her father called from behind her in a stern voice. "We are leaving now."

Dejectedly, she went back along the path to join her brother and sisters.

Sitting in the rear of the wagon with the others, Ingrid stared out at the darkening sky. Men. Why did they always have to fight things out? That damnable Daxe! Andreas Eriksen must have thought she ran with a pack of wolves.

"I do not think we will be seeing the railroad man around here again. You see what trouble he started." Her father darted a glance over his shoulder from the front seat, daring her to challenge him.

"He never started the trouble!"

"And, there will be no more English books in the house," his voice boomed above the creaking wagon wheels. "Reading is unnatural for a woman. You will help your mater with the farm chores."

Ingrid's eyes misted in anger. There was no good reason why she should not see Andreas Eriksen again.

And not even her father could keep her from reading and learning. He might as well take away the air she breathed or the sun that shone across the wheat fields. Her destiny waited on the fragmented horizon—far in the distance—yet as close as her heart wished it to be.

She was no longer a child. The day would come when she would leave the farm, leave the family she loved, and pursue her dreams.

CHAPTER TWO

Ingrid climbed to the hayloft after finishing her morning chores. Two days had passed since the Grinvold wedding. Her father's harsh words and the unprovoked fight still rankled.

At least here she could escape into her book *Ivanhoe* for a while before she was missed. Stooping, she searched under the hay bundle in the corner. To her surprise, her hand came away empty. *Gone.* The book was gone!

She stepped to the window and stared out at Jens and her father mending the fence along the road. *He had taken it.*

No more English books, her father had said. Her face heated with anger. Well, she would just find the book.

With a troubled sigh, she turned to the stack of hay and the pitchfork leaning against the wall. She went over and picked up the long handle and started tossing some of the hay into the stable below. Feeding the horses was Jens' job, but she had to have something to do.

As she worked, her exasperation with her father blended with the vision of that sneering Daxe Pederson and his knife-edged slurs, goading her as they had all weekend. How had he dared spoil such a beautiful day by picking a fight with Andreas Eriksen? She lunged at a pile of hay and pitched it across the floor.

Her father had dismissed the chivalrous guest without any attempt to listen to his explanation. He had immediately sided with Daxe. Her jaw clamped in fierce rebellion.

Daxe's taunting face floated before her eyes, his straw-colored hair shooting out around his head, just the way it had when he accosted her in front of Andreas. She lifted the pitchfork high above her and forcefully jammed it down into the hay.

Jolting pain seared from her right foot up her leg to her chest. An animal sound leaped from her throat. She stared down in horror. The razor-sharp prongs had pierced her foot right through her high-topped shoe! She yanked the pitchfork free. Blood oozed from the fresh punctures and spread onto the hay-strewn floor.

"Oh no!" *How could I have done this?* The pitchfork slipped from her hand and hit the floor with a thud.

Ingrid limped over to the hay bundles stacked against the wall, her right foot leaving a scarlet trail. Propping her foot on top of a bundle, she frantically attempted to undo the shoe's laces. But it was futile. They were tied too tight.

Shooting pain splintered from her foot up her calf. Stars shimmered in front of her. She wiped her hand across her perspiring brow and choked back the gall rising in her throat.

She dragged herself to the loft window. Near the fence stood her father, Jens, and a third man, his back to her. Her vision wavered. "Papa! Jens!"

Hobbling to the edge of the loft, Ingrid swung her leg over the ladder. She stepped onto the first rung. Then the second. Waves of nausea overwhelmed her. Her knees buckled and her foot slipped. She fell downward through empty space into strong masculine arms.

Close to her ear came a masculine voice. "I've got you."

"Andreas?"

Then her father's voice commanded, "I will take her." Rough hands pulled her away.

Then, darkness.

Ingrid awoke, her foot pulsing with pain.

"Here, drink this." Sigrie gently raised Ingrid's head and held a tablespoon of brandy to her dry lips. The alcohol seared the back of her throat.

She wheezed, then coughed. "I fell off the ladder . . . and the Norwegian caught me."

Averting her eyes, her mother said, "Papa carried you in from the barn."

Ingrid's face flushed with heat. "But, I remember Andreas' voice." She pushed away the covers and coaxed her legs over the bed side. "Did he come to see me?"

"He said he was just passing by."

"He will be back." Defiant, she got to her feet and winced.

"You cannot walk on that foot!"

"I must do my share of the work."

Her mother held her firmly by the shoulders. "You will do no such thing. Back to bed, now."

By the end of the second day, the pain in Ingrid's foot increased until she could not walk, even if she tried. She unwrapped the bandage and was shocked. Her foot had swollen, the flesh around the wound an angry purplish red. During the night, fever overtook her.

Blackness surrounded her. She felt waves of heat, then icy chills, then heard voices, blurred—but always the blackness. Even when trying to pull free, or force it away, it suffocated her.

Time was meaningless. Sigrie fed her hot soup and poured a bitter liquid down her throat. "Goldenseal . . ." her voice whispered. When Ingrid's foot throbbed in pain, Sigrie changed the dressing and applied clean bandages.

Once Ingrid dreamed she awakened to the touch of small, cool hands exploring her face. Two young elves, one small and fair-haired and one tall and dark, gazed at her curiously. Were they the beloved twins, coming to her now as angels? It couldn't be. They resembled her living sisters but spoke in strange voices.

"Will Ingrid die?" one asked.

Fear tightened its claws around her chest. "No!" she pleaded, gripping the sheet on the sides of the straw mattress. *I have so much to do. To learn . . .*

The next morning she heard two people talking outside the door. She recognized the voice of the county horse doctor who had visited only last month.

"Keep cleaning the wound with carbolic acid and warm water. We're lucky her fever has broken."

"She seems to be in shock. How long shall she stay abed?" her mother asked.

"As long as you can keep her."

Her fever had broken. She would live after all. There would be no new gravestone in the family cemetery. She exhaled a weary, thankful breath.

Lifting her head, Ingrid focused on the chest of drawers by the open window. On its top, a vase overflowed with bright rainbow colors: honeysuckle yellow, sweet William red, cornflower blue. Their fragrance soothed her.

She drifted away again into dreams. A tall, young Norwegian came to see her. Her father stood at the front door, blocking his entry.

As the sun rose over the wheat fields on a late June morning, Ingrid finished pouring the breakfast coffee. She piled hot buttermilk biscuits onto one platter and slabs of ham onto another, and brought them from the wood stove to the table. It was the first time in a week that she was up and around. The swelling had gone down in her foot, but she did hobble some.

"Thank the good Lord, she got no lockjaw," her mother said. Her father nodded and poured fresh milk in his coffee cup.

"The Norskie came by the other day to ask about you, Ingrid," Jens said.

Her father scowled. "*Ja*. He wasted no time."

She set the biscuit plate down on the table with a clatter. "What did he have to say?"

"We talked about the railroads," her father stated in an important tone. "I told him I helped lay the ties to Breckenridge on the St. Paul & Pacific in '71."

Ingrid looked at him with surprise. Had he temporarily suspended his stubborn opinion of the railroad man?

He forked a slice of ham onto his plate. "They worked us as hard as their coolies. Nearly broke my back."

Her mother wagged her finger at Ingrid. "Watch out for a railroad man! He is never at home."

"They think they can come up here and charge us a fortune to ship our crops to the city," her father complained. A complaint she'd heard before.

Flaxen-haired Briget grinned up at Ingrid and reached for a biscuit. "He brought you some flowers."

Ingrid smiled at her little sister, in spite of her mother's warning and her father's grousing. It was clear they were wary of outsiders, especially railroad men. Yet Andreas knew how to please a girl. She remembered waking to the fragrance of wildflowers on her bedroom chest. And when she had fallen from the loft, he'd caught her in his arms. She still remembered their strength.

Eight-year-old Marie Lisbet began clearing up the earthenware plates. Her self-assured expression and her neat cinnamon-brown coronet belied her age. "Daxe told Papa he did not start the fight with the Norskie."

"I was there," Ingrid corrected her, "and I saw him provoke Mr. Eriksen."

Glancing over at her father, her mother laughed. "Daxe is a jealous Swede."

"He will keep to his chores if he wants to keep his job." Her father pushed his chair away from the table, the chair legs scraping across the floor, and went out to the barn.

His curt warning surprised her. Maybe her father was beginning to see Daxe's tarnished armor.

She had held her tongue about Daxe. It was best her family didn't know about his fondling her in the barn. The Pedersons and the Johanssons were close friends, and Daxe would be needed to help with the summer harvesting. She would keep Daxe at a safe distance.

When she and her mother washed the breakfast dishes, she silently scolded herself for being so clumsy as to injure her foot with the pitchfork. At least when she became a teacher, there would be no danger from pitchforks.

At that moment, lanky Jens burst into the house. "Come out to the apple orchard, Ingrid," he blurted. "Someone wants to see you." Then he raced outside again.

She dried her hands and hobbled across the room to snatch her straw hat from the peg beside the door. Her mouth had gone suddenly dry. And inside her rib cage, tiny hummingbirds collided crazily.

"Do not be long," Sigrie called.

She started up the hill behind the house, ignoring the light throbbing in her foot.

Dozens of wild crab apple trees adorned the sloping hillside, discovered years ago by Grandpa Johansson before the family claimed their free land from the county. In the fall, Ingrid and her mother would make spiced cider and tart applesauce. As she climbed the path to see her visitor, her thoughts of cooking were left behind.

Drawing nearer, she saw Jens and Marie Lisbet playing tag between the trees.

Nearby, Andreas lifted four-year-old Briget up to sniff the pink blossoms on a branch. The little girl grabbed a handful of petals and jumped from his arms to join the others. Golden rays of sunlight burnished his fine dark hair.

She tilted the brim of her straw hat, picked up her skirt, and, with only a slight limp, hurried to meet him.

Was it the sudden exertion or the twinkle in Andreas Eriksen's blue eyes that made her heart pound so rapidly? "Thank you for the flowers, Mr. Eriksen," she said.

"Please, call me Andreas." Wearing an engaging smile, he stepped toward her. "How is your foot?"

"It is much better, thanks to Mama and her home remedies." She looked out over the pasture at the fawn-colored Jerseys grazing in the emerald grass. "When will you go back to the city?"

"I have to return day after tomorrow."

She felt a pang of disappointment yet was pleased at the hint of regret in his voice. "And, will you be driving that fine buggy?"

His face turned the color of the apple blossoms. "No. I have to confess—the buggy was a gift from my uncle to my aunt."

"It is your aunt's?"

"Yes. My uncle won't let her take the reins by herself. A woman should never be unaccompanied."

"I see." She frowned, trying to control her rising annoyance. "Why do men always want to overprotect their women when they are perfectly capable of driving themselves?"

His dark eyebrows shot up, a mischievous grin playing at the corners of his mouth. "Oh? You feel women should be more independent?"

She tossed her head, dismissing his patronizing tone. "I think women should be able to express their opinions—the same as men."

His demeanor became serious. "I can see you driving your own buggy one day."

A sidelong glance from beneath her straw brim verified that

he was not jesting. She observed the Norwegian's strong facial features, admiring his generous sideburns and his cleft chin.

"We are going down to the barnyard to see the new kittens," Marie Lisbet called. The children scattered, chasing each other downhill.

Reluctant to leave, Ingrid led Andreas to a nearby apple tree. They sat beneath its umbrella shade. She rested back on her elbows, breathed in the sweet air, and listened enviously to Andreas speak of his city life.

But when he spoke of his family obligation to work on the railroad, Ingrid's stomach tightened. The railroad will take him away before we even get to know each other, she thought. She was glad when he changed the subject.

"My stepsister will be home from her eastern finishing school by now." He made a face. "And my stepmother will expect me back to welcome her."

"A finishing school?"

Andreas gazed at her, half-smiling. "It's just an expensive residence for willful, spoiled young women."

Ingrid wrinkled her nose.

Andreas reached up and broke off a sprig of fragrant blossoms, and tucked it into her coiled braid. When she raised her hand to touch the small flowers, his hand brushed hers. Heat fanned her cheeks and she looked away.

Recovering her composure she said, "I have hopes for the future. I want to learn to speak 'the English' well, and then teach school."

"That is admirable." He smiled, leaning closer. "You would make a good teacher."

His nearness disconcerted her. "But Papa is dead set against it. He does not want me to read. He says I should keep to women's work and not have unnatural ambitions."

A frown creased Andreas' forehead. "You should follow your dreams."

Follow your dreams? She liked that. No farm boy had ever given her such advice.

The brass bell in the yard clanged, and Ingrid heard her mother calling her. "I have to help with the chores."

Andreas placed his hand beneath her elbow and assisted her to her feet. An inner tingle danced up her arm to her shoulder.

They started down the hill. "I'm sorry if I've kept you too long," he said.

She shrugged. "I am glad we could talk about the future." Inwardly, she wondered if there would be any future for her with Andreas.

Approaching the house, Ingrid saw Daxe with Marta, the hired girl. Up to his old tricks, he wrapped his arm around the girl's stout waist as she carried a basket of vegetables from the garden.

Ingrid stared after Daxe with contempt.

"I see your hired man is no stranger to the ladies," Andreas remarked, his tone as taut as a leather glove pulled over a steel fist.

"Papa had better not catch him."

Well, Daxe, she thought, I think you will not be bothering me anymore.

At his rig, parked in the front yard, Andreas asked, "I would like to call on you again, Ingrid. Would your father object?"

She smiled, crossing her fingers behind her back. "Oh, no. He will not mind." But she prayed Papa would not hold him accountable for every railroad sin.

She bade Andreas goodbye, aware that curious eyes could be watching.

"Until then," he said, his eyes holding hers for a moment longer than necessary.

Hummingbirds still fluttering behind her breastbone, she watched Andreas' fancy rig retreat down the road, then she hurried into the house.

Finishing her chores later in the day, Ingrid made a trip out to the corn crib. As she gathered the dried cobs in a hemp sack, her fingers touched something smooth and flat. Pushing aside the cobs, she spied the black cover. *Ivanhoe!*

So, this was its hiding place. She snorted with victory, which was quickly replaced with disgust. Her father was so narrow-minded, set on keeping her as uneducated as her mother and sisters. The Old Country ways were ingrained in him. He was the head of the house, and this was the way it had always been.

She brushed away the yellow dust from the book's cover and held it to her bodice. Now it was her turn to do the hiding. Somewhere where he could not find it.

Then she recalled Andreas' intent to call on her. She must swallow her anger for now if she wanted to see him again, possibly seated at her family's table. Papa's stubborn nature would have to be stroked. As the eldest daughter, she had learned a way or two to do just that.

But as far as her future ambitions, she would need strong support from someone outside her immediate family. Mama was on her side, but she alone would not be sufficient.

Mulling over her prospects, Ingrid tucked the book deep inside her skirt pocket. Tonight she would write a letter to her favorite cousin, Nettie, in Minneapolis.

Nettie was her only hope.

CHAPTER THREE

The steam engine of the St. Paul & Pacific gave a mighty blast. The whistle shrieked. Seated in the coach car, Andreas Eriksen, felt a quick intoxicating thrill shoot through his veins. The train lurched forward on the tracks, leaving the Eden Valley station behind.

Andreas handed his ticket to the portly conductor then settled back in his seat, his legs sticking out far beneath the seat in front of him.

He was anxious to get back to St. Paul. The sooner he could talk to his father about the railroad, the better.

He stared out the window at rolling green farmland, mingling with the sapphire-blue lakes of northwestern Minnesota. Sapphire-blue. The color of Ingrid Johansson's eyes.

Instantly he was carried back to that fragrant apple orchard and the comely face of the Swedish girl. The merriment dancing in her eyes. The tease of her heart-shaped mouth. And, her hair. He wondered how Ingrid's hair would feel beneath his fingers, unfettered from its neatly woven braid, set free in a flowing fall down her back.

A golden bounty!

He visualized her figure in the summer calico dress, so lithe yet holding the promise of ripening sensuality.

There was an assuredness about Ingrid; she'd said she wanted to teach one day. An admirable goal for a young woman. He mused over the image of her driving her own buggy. That would surely raise her father's hackles.

He liked her family. They were so robust and lively. But her father, stalwart and opinionated, presented a definite challenge. To him, Andreas was an outsider. A Norwegian suitor from the city. A cause for mistrust.

"So you're going to be a railroad man," Ingrid had stated, a flash of curiosity in her eyes, as if she found him an enigma.

Was he ready to become a railroad man? His parents assumed that he would be groomed for a high position on the board of directors of the St. Paul & Pacific. But with the endless stock manipulation and mismanagement the small railroad had suffered since the financial Panic of 1873, Andreas wondered if even a miracle could pull it out.

The railroad's uncertain future, and his father's ill health, had weighed on his mind. All the more urgency to solicit his father's advice. He needed to establish a career direction. A desk job would not suit him. A management position was more to his preference.

Using his suit coat as a pillow, he reclined against the upholstered seat and closed his eyes.

The whistle's blare jostled Andreas awake as the train approached the new St. Paul depot. He was impressed to see workings afoot for an eventual terminal system between the twin cities. Nearby lowlands had been filled in along the Mississippi. An accomplishment of the respected shipping magnate and general agent of the St. Paul & Pacific, James J. Hill. His father had mentioned Hill's name in conversation many times, and Andreas hoped to meet him one day.

Eager to get home, he gathered up his luggage and debarked the train.

"How are you, my boy?" Adolph Eriksen glanced up from his watch and greeted Andreas at the threshold to the parlor. The senior Eriksen's punctuality had become a familiar trait. One he had practiced for the past twelve years as vice president of the St. Paul First National Bank.

The two men shook hands.

Andreas noted his father's limp handshake and unusually pale complexion beneath his silver hair. He must encourage him to cut back on his long hours at the bank. "I'm well, Father. I hope you are, too. Do you have any news of the railroad?"

"Yes. We should talk after dinner. But first, tell us about the family and the wedding."

"The Lindstrom wedding was a crowded outdoor affair, the bride was heavenly, and one of the guests knocked me on my ear." Andreas added the last with a sardonic grin.

"Someone knocked you down! Whatever for?" a feminine voice asked from across the room.

Seeing his father's wife Emma seated on the brocade sofa, Andreas moved to her and dutifully kissed her cheek. She wore a dress of a stiff black fabric with fussy ruffles at the neck; the smell of her heavily perfumed handkerchief assaulted his senses.

In answer to his stepmother's question, he said, "Poor fool obviously had had too much to drink." He smiled. "And how are you, Emma?"

Since his father's remarriage, try as Andreas might, calling Emma "Mother" was beyond him. His own mother had met a tragic death in the delivery of a stillborn baby girl five years before. Even now, he carried the pain of it. He had been her only child and they had cherished each other.

Emma's dark features lit up for a moment, her alert brown eyes studying him with interest. "I'm just fine. But tell us more about this skirmish."

Lingering behind the threshold, Dagmar Eriksen observed the three adults in the parlor. Beneath her costume of London-smoke silk and camel's hair, she quivered with excitement. She focused on the tall young man conversing with her parents. Andreas! His tanned face amplified a look of the outdoors above his beige frock coat and blue silk bow tie. His broad-shouldered physique projected confidence. Her heartbeat pulsed rapidly at her throat.

Indeed, her stepbrother had become a handsome specimen in the last three years. With his confident demeanor and social status, he would make someone a fine marriage partner.

Dagmar swiftly gathered up the fringed skirts of her newest dress and hurried to join them.

As she entered the room, her mother turned. "Dagmar, Andreas has been informing us of the Lindstrom wedding in Eden Valley." Emma boasted to Andreas, "Dagmar just graduated from Madame de Beauville's Finishing School in Chicago."

"Yes, I heard." Andreas' smile caused an unmistakable stirring beneath Dagmar's corset.

Andreas observed his stepsister. He was amazed at how much daughter resembled mother. Aside from several inches in height and twenty pounds in weight, the women were definitely cut from the same cloth. Dagmar reminded him of a sleek dark cat. At any moment, he expected her to hunker down and, without warning, pounce on him.

Instead, she held out her tapered hand and smiled coquettishly.

Amused, he shook it, thinking this was what young women learned at finishing school.

"Andreas!" she purred, "how long has it been?"

He drew a blank. How long had it been? He shook his head.

"Don't you remember? Mama and Papa Adolph's wedding—the fall of seventy-three. Just before I went off to Chicago."

Chagrined, Andreas touched his forehead. "Of course. How could I forget?"

Now he remembered her, the scrawny, young girl with the catlike features. At the time, his lingering anguish over the loss of his mother and the shock of his father's marriage to a St. Paul society woman, whom he hardly knew, had fully occupied his mind.

Dagmar angled her head, gazing up at him through long dark lashes. "Andreas, would you like to take a stroll with me? We can catch up on everything that's been happening in the world these last few years."

Although Andreas preferred to stay in the parlor rather than accompany his stepsister, he didn't want to appear rude. "Some fresh air before dinner sounds like a fine idea."

"Don't be too long," Emma said. "Gertrude likes us to be seated when dinner is ready."

Dagmar glanced over at Emma. "Of course, Mother." She snaked her silken arm around Andreas'.

He looked down into her guileless face and for an instant knew a strange sense of foreboding. He wished that it was Ingrid he was about to escort through the garden. Ingrid with her simple country charms, her fly-away bonnet, and her golden braids.

"Tell me about the university, Andreas," Dagmar coaxed as soon as they were out the back door. "Especially about all the parties you went to."

Andreas shrugged. "There weren't so many parties. There were only eight in our graduating class this year."

Incredulous, Dagmar stared at him. "You mean you were just an old stiff your senior year?" She couldn't imagine this tall, attractive man walking next to her could be a dullard.

He laughed. "I guess I did tip a few."

They entered the garden, with its fragrant blooming roses and pansy-bordered path. She saw his dark brown lashes brush his cheek as he looked down at her hand still clinging to his forearm, and thought him romantic. "Are you engaged . . . to anyone?"

"No," he responded emphatically. "I have career commitments to concentrate on."

"If you tell me what you did at your parties, I'll tell you what we did at ours," she said coyly, hoping to steer him away from the boring subject of commerce.

But she debated on just how much to reveal to Andreas of the last social event her school had sponsored with a Chicago men's academy. She and a young man had ventured into a side room, and she had let him unbutton the bodice of her dress and fondle her breasts. The memory now made her blush, thinking of how she would have allowed the fellow even more had not a snoopy chaperone discovered them.

From the corner of her eye, Dagmar glimpsed her mother watching them from the parlor window. How irritating! Emma had pecked at her like a fussy mother hen ever since she'd returned home. It rankled. After all, she was almost twenty-one and deserving of some privacy.

"Oh, there's Mother at the window," Dagmar observed, feigning surprise. She waved brightly and pulled Andreas along. A marvelous idea had popped into her head about the Centennial celebration this weekend. And, she wanted to propose it to Andreas.

They strolled farther along the pansy-bordered path.

Andreas was confounded. Just one short walk in the garden and his stepsister had gotten him to commit to being her escort for the Fourth of July weekend festivities. The last thing he'd wanted to do. Well, he could fix that; he would invite several of his university friends so that he wouldn't be held hostage to her inane chatter.

35

His mission in returning home did not include Dagmar, but the direction his career would take.

Now, the family seated themselves in the dining room around a long, richly laden table. Burgundy damask draperies at the far windows kept daylight from the room and closed out the view to the street. Whenever Andreas joined his father and stepmother in this oppressive room, he'd always been struck with the urge to tear the claustrophobic draperies from the walls and let the sunlight come flooding in.

Fortunately, when Gertrude served an excellent roast beef, he forgot about the draperies and the meal passed agreeably.

After coffee and a rich custard dessert, his father pushed his chair back from the table and said, "I know you want to hear the latest railroad news, son. If the ladies will excuse us . . ."

Emma frowned. "We want to hear it too, Adolph," Emma admonished.

"Yes, Papa," Dagmar echoed.

Andreas nodded. "Please give us all the details, Father."

Adolph cleared his throat. "Well, James Hill has a plan to incorporate the St. Paul & Pacific with the Northern Pacific. Hill and his Canadian friends want to extend a line from St. Paul to the Red River Valley, and upward to Manitoba."

Warming to the subject, Andreas sat forward in his chair. "The Canadian farmers will welcome land transportation for their crops, rather than having to ship them downriver to the city."

"But, can we trust those Canadians?" Emma asked, her stiff skirts rustling around her. "Not so long ago, the bonds fell from a thousand to only forty dollars of their face value!"

His father glanced at Emma with a patient smile. "With all due respect, dear, I know the bonds came to us through your late husband. I'm also aware that his Dutch bankers are holding fifteen million dollars of railroad securities, while we bondholders are left dangling."

His stepmother rolled her eyes toward the cut-glass chandelier. "True. If something isn't done, we could lose everything."

Adolph patted her hand. "My banking contacts tell me Hill's investors are a respectable group of fellows."

Emma harrumphed into her handkerchief. "We'll see what those highbrows come up with."

Andreas nodded in agreement. From across the table, Dagmar's glittering gaze bore into his, leaving him uncomfortable and slightly puzzled. He'd felt her watching his every move in the last half hour.

Adolph rose from his chair. "Let's discuss this further in the study."

Andreas jumped to his feet. "Just what I was thinking, Father."

He couldn't wait to resume the railroad discussion. All decisions regarding his future were at stake.

After dinner, Dagmar changed into a dressing gown in her room, her heart pumping with elation. She must tell Emma her exciting news. Gliding along the hall carpet, she approached her mother's room. The door stood a few inches ajar. What Dagmar observed made her stop in her tracks.

Emma stood before the mahogany bureau holding a small silver flask, which she now lifted to her lips and downed a hearty swallow. Ah, yes, Mother's headache remedy. After taking another sip from the flask, Emma carefully returned it to its hiding place in the top drawer. She smoothed back a stray hair into her topknot and moved to the bedside table, where a grouping of daguerreotypes were displayed in silver frames.

Dagmar stood transfixed, watching. Which photograph would she favor?

Emma focused on one in the front, a young, wavy-haired boy lying in eternal repose. Toddy—Dagmar's late, younger brother.

A tremble shook her mother's hand as she picked up the photograph and caressed it with loving fingers.

Instinctively, Dagmar felt a knotting in her stomach. She doubted Emma ever gazed upon her photograph with such tenderness. But then, she was alive. Toddy, as well as her dear father, had succumbed to the dreaded tuberculosis. Ever since, Dagmar had been sent away to stuffy finishing schools so that Emma could dwell in the world of the deceased.

Dagmar pinched her cheeks, then swished into the room. "Mother! I thought I'd find you here."

Emma jumped at the interruption and clutched the silver frame to her breast. "Oh—you startled me, dear. You look like such a wild thing . . . You really should tame your hair with some pomade."

Dagmar shook her dark hair, letting it fly freer. "Sorry I disturbed you, Mother. But I have something I must tell you."

She watched her mother carefully replace the daguerreotype among the others on the table. *Tod, always Tod.* She had always favored him. But Dagmar would not allow her mother's simpering nostalgia to spoil her news.

"Earlier this evening, I asked Andreas to be my escort at the Fourth of July Centennial celebration next weekend at City Park—and he's accepted."

Emma's jaw slackened in surprise. Then, seeming to compose herself, she said, "That's nice, dear, but what about the other available young men who'll be there?"

"Oh really, Mother!" Dagmar shrugged impatiently. "Andreas stands head and shoulders above the rest. Why should I want to . . . ?" The questioning look that stole into Emma's eyes made Dagmar stop in midsentence.

"You know that Andreas is family," her mother cautioned, "and we wouldn't want the appearance of any impropriety."

"To hell with impropriety."

"Dagmar!" Emma looked astonished. "Is this what you learned at Madame de Beauville's?"

Dagmar pressed her lips together in defiance, then reconsidered. When push came to shove, her mother could be just as stubborn as she, and nothing should interfere with the sweet anticipation of attending the Centennial with Andreas. She swallowed her rising anger and returned Emma's scolding gaze with one of contrition. "Of course, you're right. Perhaps we could all attend the celebration, as a family."

"Yes, that would be a better idea," Emma said.

With a subservient little bow, Dagmar pivoted and glided from the room. Let her mother think she'd had the final say. Let her scurry back to her hidden flask for another sip of the remedy. Dagmar would still find a way to get Andreas all to herself this weekend.

Andreas entered the study, welcoming the coolness of it and a return to their earlier conversation. He sank down in a high-backed leather chair across from Adolph in front of the fireplace and let his eyes adjust to the semidarkness.

For a moment they sat quietly. Adolph lifted his favored pipe from an ashtray, added tobacco, and lit it. Andreas took comfort in the woodsy aroma of the pipe smoke combined with the smell of furniture polish, and the manly furnishings about the room. His father's large walnut desk sat in one corner, the papers and writing pens on its top neatly arranged.

Shelves behind the desk were filled with books on banking as well as fiction and poetry. Ibsen, Dickens, and Browning were some of Andreas' favorite authors among his father's collection.

Adolph leaned toward him. "As we know, Jim Hill is planning a takeover of the St. Paul & Pacific." He took a puff on his pipe. "In March, he went up to Ottawa to raise money for his coffers. Now he's back, sending out feelers to the Dutch bondholders—what price will it take to dispose of their holdings?"

Andreas listened carefully, always fascinated by his father's analytical observations. He waited for him to come to his point.

Adolph ran a finger around the inside of his starched collar. "Hill has a vision for the railroads in the state and for a railroad that will stretch farther west to the coast. The country is ready for it. Hill has his dream. You can too. Your future could be as unlimited as his."

Andreas saw the enthusiasm in Adolph's eyes and felt it himself. Some color had returned to his father's cheeks and he was visibly perspiring. Andreas sat straighter in the chair. "Where would be a good place to start?"

"The Red River Valley. The hundred miles of track coming down from Canada can become self-sustaining. And new settlement up there supports the need for more extension." He set his pipe back in the ashtray and unbuttoned his collar. "This is where you should start."

Andreas thought of the Red River Valley. A train foreman's position there might appeal to him. And, he would be closer to Ingrid.

Adolph continued, his voice urgent. "I can get you a job through my railroad contacts. But, it will be a challenge. You'll have to get your hands dirty. They will no doubt put you in a . . . lowly position."

"I don't mind. I'm ready to roll up my sleeves."

Adolph groaned, clasping his hand to his chest.

"Father, don't you feel well?"

"Just . . . slight pain . . . tightness."

"I'll get you a brandy." Andreas strode across the room to the liquor cabinet. He quickly poured the brandy into two snifters and set the decanter down on a silver tray.

Behind him, a gurgling sound made Andreas spin around.

Grimacing, Adolph fell forward in his chair.

"Father!" Andreas bolted across the room to catch him as he crumpled to the floor. "I'll get your doctor."

Adolph choked out the words. "No time . . ."

Fear clenched Andreas' heart. "Oh, Dad. What can I do?"

Adolph weakly grasped Andreas' arm. "The brandy . . . We'll drink . . . to your future with the railroad."

Sweat dampening his face, Andreas gently propped his father against the chair and raced for the brandies. He held one of the snifters to his father's lips, but Adolph only gasped for air.

"Emma and Dagmar . . . take care of them."

"I will, Father."

The blue in Adolph's eyes faded as he stole one last breath and died in Andreas' arms.

His world crashing around him, Andreas wiped back tears from his face and bowed his head. The rebuilding of the railroad truly did lay on his shoulders now.

CHAPTER FOUR

"Happy Birthday, Ingrid!" Marie Lisbet and Briget's voices chorused.

Sigrie set the *smor kringler* cake, made with generous amounts of butter and cinnamon, on the Johansson's dining table. The cake was Ingrid's favorite. "You are eighteen. Almost a woman," her mother whispered.

Candles glowed in their glass lanterns about the room. An inner glow filled Ingrid with joyful expectation. She opened homemade gifts from her family, and her heart was full.

"Don't forget this one." Jens offered her a parcel postmarked Minneapolis. "Papa and I picked it up at the train station."

Eagerly, Ingrid tore open the outer brown covering and lifted something silky from layers of tissue. "A lace shawl! How beautiful. There is a note." She recognized the loopy signature. "It is from Nettie."

Ingrid read the note silently. *Please enjoy the shawl, Ingrid. You must come and stay with me in Minneapolis,* Nettie enthused in her carefree way. *You can wear it when we go downtown to the theater and go shopping. I have a plan for you to attend St. Agnes with me, too! More later. Love, Nettie.*

Ingrid sighed and tucked the note back inside the box. If only she could enroll at St. Agnes. Money was so difficult to come by for her and so easy for Nettie, an only child, whose father owned a dry goods store in the city.

"What did she say?" Marie Lisbet begged.

"We don't need to know about that now," Ingrid's father interjected. "Tonight, we celebrate Ingrid's birthday."

With a twinkle in his eyes, Hans placed his sturdy hands on her mother's waist and steered her toward the old piano in the front room. "Sit down, Sigrie," he coaxed, "and play for us."

Her mother played the old tunes with vigor, her fingers dancing over the keys. The family sang together until the grandfather clock struck twelve. Then Jens climbed the ladder to the loft, the girls crowded into their bedroom, and her parents retired to their room at the rear of the house.

Ingrid laid the shawl in the chest of drawers Grandpa Johansson had made from a cedar he had cut near the lake. "This shawl is too lovely to wear on the farm," she murmured to her sisters.

Briget crawled into her cot in the corner and made no further sound. For some time after Briget slept, Ingrid and Marie Lisbet, lying beneath the bedsheet, spoke in low voices about Nettie's letter.

"Will you go to the theater with Nettie?" Marie Lisbet wondered.

"*Ja*. I would definitely want to go to a big theater."

If she had her choice, Ingrid thought, she'd rather go on the arm of Andreas Eriksen.

As if reading her thoughts, Marie Lisbet snuggled closer. "How would you feel if Andreas kissed you?"

How would she feel if he kissed her? A warm flush spread from her neck downward beneath her nightgown. She gave her younger sister a playful shove. "Oh, go to sleep, you silly goose."

After Marie Lisbet turned away and drifted into the steady sound of slumber, Ingrid tossed about on the straw mattress. Her mind tumbled with pent-up excitement. Could she ever go to the city? Go to the academy with Nettie?

Imagining it filled Ingrid with such exuberance, such longing as she had never known. But how would she find the money for her fare and tuition? She had never been away from the farm before. Already, she knew what her father would say. A young woman wanting to have an education? A foolish thing.

Still, it was a delicious thought.

To see that tall, handsome Norwegian, Andreas Eriksen, again was also a delicious thought. And, dare she wish it? To kiss him? Sleep did not come easily.

When Ingrid opened her eyes on Sunday morning, she was the only one in the room. Sunlight filtered through the curtains at the window and played across the vacant side of the bed. Next to the wall, the cot stood empty. They had let her sleep late this one day of the year.

She lay staring at the rough, beamed ceiling for a few minutes, then swung her bare feet to the floor and sat up on the edge of the bed.

I am eighteen now, she thought. Eighteen and ready to begin my woman's journey. I will talk to Mama and convince her I must go away to the city and become a teacher.

"Watch yer ass, Eriksen!" McPhergus, the road foreman, shouted over the din of the locomotive.

The 4-4-0 standard engine spouted a geyser of steam and heaved backward, its gears, wheels, and rods flailing. Behind it a line of freight cars waited, loaded with harvested grain. Moving slowly, but now with more grace, the engine closed the gap with the lead car.

In his job as brakeman, Andreas stood poised above the heavy steel coupling, the pin raised in his hands like a dagger, ready to meet its mark. He felt a shiver of terror in the instant before the engine was supposed to slow down. If the engine moved too fast, Andreas could be crushed, or lose a hand. But the engineer's timing was right and the locomotive slowed as he hit the air brakes and eased in toward Andreas' car.

Andreas braced himself against the shift in momentum. Sweat poured from every crevice of his body. He timed the last yards, counting beats. Then, just as the metal members of car and engine hooked together, he rammed the pin down into its slot, secured it, and jumped clear.

"Good job, Eriksen!" the stocky foreman yelled from across the yard.

Andreas waved in acknowledgment to McPhergus. Right, he thought, I did a damn good job. He looked down gratefully at his grease-blackened hands. I've got all ten fingers to prove it.

At a signal, the engine emitted another cloud of steam, shuddered, and rolled forward, with its cargo in tow. Andreas watched the train move out through the Breckenridge freight yard, headed for the mills of Minneapolis.

He crossed the yard in the direction of the main building, stepping over the cinder-strewn grid of rails and ties. His shift was over. He'd been at it since six that morning. For his twelve-hour shift, he had earned the princely sum of one dollar and fifty cents. This week he'd worked four days, and he had six dollars coming to him. Today was payday.

Waiting to pick up his wages at the paymaster's office, along with the other men, Andreas could not ignore his aching back and blistered palms.

He had a sudden vision of Ingrid Johansson: she was gazing at him from those midnight-blue eyes. How he wanted to be near her, but how could he touch her sweet flesh with these ravaged hands? He tried to focus on what he would do after work tonight, not on Ingrid and not on his measly pay.

Most of the crew in this North Dakota border town were single men like himself. Many were new emigrants. Swedes, Italians, Scotsmen, and fellow Norwegians worked beside him in the yard. Some of the men had wives and babies at home. He sympathized with them. How could they feed more mouths than their own on a railroad wage? Andreas' job of brakeman was the lowest tier on the railroad ladder and paid the least. But a fireman or conductor's wage was only a few dollars more a week than his.

His father had said he would have to start on the low end. Andreas hadn't counted on it being this low. But, he had made his promise and he would keep it.

"Hey, Eriksen!" a stout Norwegian and fellow brakeman, by the name of Nordberg, called to him. "Join us for a beer."

Andreas fell in beside the man and several others on their way to a nearby tavern. He had not revealed his privileged background to any of the crew, although he suspected they had heard of it. Some had not yet accepted him as one of them.

The tavern was noisy and packed with grimy trainmen. Andreas' companions ordered beers all around and sat down at a table in the back. Seated next to him, Nordberg started telling a story of a near-disaster he'd had that week.

"*Ja*, I vas running between the cars to unhook a coupling, and I stumbled and fell. Almost lost my leg under the vheel."

He gave out an uproarious howl of laughter and the men around the table chortled with him, taking hearty swills from their mugs.

A tremor of fear, much like what he'd experienced in the first few weeks of his training, clutched at Andreas' gut. Were these men crazy—or just getting drunk to ward off the same fears he felt?

The big Norskie slapped his right hand on the table for emphasis. Andreas stared at the man's mangled fingers. Only three nubs remained between thumb and smallest finger. He winced at the sight.

Nordberg saw his expression and held his hand high in the air, then close to Andreas' face. "Look at this, my friend. Ven vinter comes, you remember. Your gloves vill vear thin, and it gets mighty cold in the yard. So, be quick ven you drop the pin into the coupling."

A momentary hush settled over the table in spite of the noise surrounding them. Tired faces nodded in solemn agreement. Andreas caught Nordberg's meaning without having to respond. He'd only been on this job for a month, but his reflexes were sharp. And, so far he had been lucky.

He drained his beer mug. The sooner he could break away from here and see Ingrid, the better.

On the second day of threshing, Ingrid and Marta, the hired girl, loaded the wagon with lunch to take to the crew. At midday, the sun beat down unmercifully and, by the time they had traveled from the house to the field, rivulets of perspiration trickled down the sides of Ingrid's face beneath her straw hat. The bodice of her dress stuck to her like a second skin.

They entered the golden field. The sweet smell of freshly cut grain filled her nostrils. Ahead, several of the men had removed their shirts in the searing heat. They looked up expectantly when she pulled the team to a stop beside them.

Daxe, standing next to the threshing rig, hailed Marta. She climbed off the wagon and brought a water jug over to him.

Ingrid thought him especially unattractive in this state of undress. His sun-reddened, barrel chest was covered with coarse, straw-white hair that matched the straggly mop on his head.

Marta didn't seem to mind Daxe. In fact, when the women passed around the lunch baskets to the men, she leaned toward him and he said something to her in a low voice, causing her to blush and look away.

Ingrid joined her father and Jens at the edge of the field to share their meal under some shady trees. After lunch, Hans sent around a small brown jug.

"Ah, that is good," confirmed one farmhand after taking a swig. Waiting their turn, the others laughed and joked.

Ingrid knew it was *traesker pons*, the threshing punch many farmers rewarded their crews with during harvest time. Her father was a godly man, but he believed in easing the load for his men when he could.

Deciding to take a walk in the coolness of the woods while the men rested, Ingrid set out into the thick grove. The prospect of enrolling with Nettie at St. Agnes Academy this fall stood before her like a great open door. Beyond the door was Andreas, as well.

If she were in Minneapolis, she could somehow see him. A month had passed and no letter had arrived as he had promised. She prayed that he hadn't forgotten her.

Yet Andreas must wait in her daydreams. How to approach her parents about the school was her immediate dilemma.

She walked and pondered, gazing down at the forest floor at wild mushrooms and fallen acorns. Fertile smells surrounded her.

The murmurs came faintly at first, on the periphery of nature's sounds. Human sounds. Like one who has run a long distance and is panting to catch his breath.

Ingrid stopped. She heard a woman moan. Her body went rigid, stone still, like a wood hare caught in its tracks. Only her eyes moved, her gaze searching for the source of the sounds.

She saw them. They lay on the forest floor, their bodies entwined—not more than twenty-five feet from where she stood.

Marta was naked. Except for her black stockings. The right one had fallen below her knee; the left dangled from her toes. Her dress and undergarments lay crushed beneath her. She was a wild sight, thrashing about under that heavy lummox Daxe!

His work pants hung below his exposed white buttocks as he rode her.

Ingrid watched in stunned fascination. She had witnessed horses and sheep do this in the farmyard, but never a man and a woman so erotically inclined. She had only wondered what this human act would be like.

Marta suddenly emitted a thin, high-pitched scream. Like a lightning rod, it sent vibrations down through Ingrid's chest to her knees. She stared at the undulating couple.

Daxe clamped a beefy hand over Marta's mouth. "Shush!"

Was he hurting Marta? The farm animals never cried out like this. Nor had she ever heard her mother make such a cry in the night.

The girl didn't act like she'd been harmed. No, just the opposite. She clung to Daxe all the more!

Ingrid silently turned and hurried back the way she'd ventured. Such a disgusting sight! As she ran, the images of it boldly flashed in front of her.

What to do now? Should she tell her mother? The question burned within her.

When Ingrid emerged from the darkness of the trees, the sun blinded her. Head down, she busied herself collecting lunch baskets and water jugs, and loading them into the back of the wagon. She avoided direct contact with anyone for fear they would see the secret in her eyes.

Minutes later, Marta appeared at the border of the woods, her cheeks a blazing red. Several yards away, Daxe slipped back to his work in the field.

Ingrid took little satisfaction in Marta's disheveled attire and sheepish expression as the girl approached the wagon. She waited on the driver's seat, her temper rising. "Get up here, you shameless girl!"

Marta had barely climbed aboard when Ingrid brought the

reins down sharply on the horses' rumps. They started at the sudden swat, leaping forward into a trot.

"I saw you and Daxe in the woods."

Marta's doe-brown eyes opened wide in fright. Then her face seemed to crumple.

Ingrid again snapped the reins above the horses' backs. They left the field and clattered onto the hard dirt road. "How could you behave like such a hussy? Daxe could get you pregnant!"

Marta, now in a panic, gripped the side of the seat. "You will not tell your parents, Ingrid? Please do not tell them."

They bounced up and down like a pair of flopping fish. Perspiration bathed Ingrid's face and neck. She saw Marta's contorted features and the tears streaming down her face. The girl might soon become hysterical.

Ingrid eased the horses into a nodding gait and caught her breath. "We must finish the threshing, Marta. But, be careful. I do not want to have to tell Mama."

In the weeks that followed, Marta stayed to her work, helping Ingrid with the cooking and cleaning, her eyes downcast. And Ingrid was aware of no more disappearances of the two wayward lovers into the woods.

When the harvesting was done, she stole away in the afternoon to study her brother's English schoolbooks, careful to hide them when she was finished. Her desire was great to fill in the education she'd missed since leaving school at thirteen to help at home.

One night, as soon as Ingrid had finished the dinner dishes, she chased Jens halfway out to the barn, catching him by his shirttails. "Teach me, teach me, teach me!"

He cringed and pulled away.

"Jens! I will do whatever chores you want, even clean out the stables." She clapped her hands together in desperation. "Only, please teach me."

He puffed out his cheeks in weary consent. "All right. You will clean out the stables?"

She nodded, resigned. When she glanced up, Jens wore a victorious grin.

In the following days, they snuck out to the barn loft whenever Hans was out of sight. Ingrid made such progress her brother had to admit his tutorial role suited him.

On an August morning, Ingrid picked chokecherries with her younger sisters in the south meadow. She saw her mother walking up the hill past the apple orchard, toward the family cemetery. She knew Sigrie wanted to be alone. But today, Ingrid needed to be with her. To win her support before summer's end.

"Mama, wait," she called. "I will walk with you."

She left her half-filled bucket with Marie Lisbet and ran to catch up. When she fell in beside her mother, Ingrid noticed she was carrying pink roses from the garden. Sigrie smiled and placed her hand on Ingrid's shoulder.

The women came to a short white picket fence bordering the small burial place. They entered through the gate, where patches of tansy and purple sweet William bloomed, and stood before two stone markers.

Grandpa Johansson's marker was set in the upper left corner of the plot. He had passed away three years before, thousands of miles from Smaaland, Sweden, his childhood home.

A larger marker was erected closer to the entrance of the little cemetery. Ingrid read the inscription silently as she had so many times before.

Lisbet Johansson * Liv Johansson
Beloved daughters of
Hans and Sigrie

Born April 8, 1866
Died July 18, 1867

"My twin angels," Sigrie whispered. "They flew back to heaven soon after their feet touched the earth."

She wiped her eyes, then knelt and placed the matching bouquets of pink roses side-by-side in front of the marker. Her shoulders trembled.

Tears stung Ingrid's eyelids as she watched. Her heart ached for her mother. Summer cholera had devastated the community that year. Although her memory of her baby twin sisters was dreamlike, she still felt a loss for them.

She never wanted to have children if she must lose them to such cruel diseases.

In silence, they left, closing the gate behind them.

Starting down the hill, Ingrid said, "Mama, I have to speak to you about something."

Her mother smiled knowingly. "It is about your studies, isn't it. I know how Jens has been helping you."

"*Ja,* but it is more than that." Ingrid's heart beat with expectancy. "I want to go to school with Nettie. At St. Agnes."

"In the city?" Her mother looked doubtfully out over the meadow. "Oh, Ingrid . . ."

"You know I want to become a teacher. If I go to St. Agnes, I will be able to receive a fine education."

Sigrie's expression brightened. "I am proud of you for wanting to be a teacher. If you could talk your fater into selling one of the cows . . ." She shook her head. "But I doubt it would be enough."

In frustration, Ingrid kicked at a stone. Looking at the possibilities through her mother's eyes, she could see the situation was nearly hopeless. Her chin dropped forward, almost touching her chest, as she plodded downhill toward the house.

CHAPTER FIVE

In the Sunday lesson, Pastor Thornberg spoke of thankfulness for the harvest, but his words drifted right over Ingrid's summer bonnet. One row ahead, and across the aisle, sat Andreas Eriksen, city-handsome in his dark blue suit and starched white shirt. The newlyweds Hilda and Lars, their shoulders pressed together, were seated to his left.

Yesterday, Andreas had come by the Johansson farm to see her. He had been able to leave his job up north for the weekend. A happy surprise for Ingrid, although she had been wary of asking her father's permission to go for a buggy ride, and asked Andreas to let her persuade her parents for some time with him today.

Now, Andreas swiveled and looked in Ingrid's direction. His gaze found hers, and he winked boldly. She was too surprised to do more than nod.

The wink did not get past Marie Lisbet, sitting next to Ingrid. She glanced knowingly at her and snickered.

How daring he was, this Norskie. She lowered her eyes and smiled down at the handkerchief in her hand. He would be taking her on a picnic today. She had baked a plum pie for her father, his favorite, and coaxed him to let her go, for only an hour. She would be alone with Andreas. Her toes curled inside her shoes.

After the service, Andreas caught up with Ingrid in the church yard. "I was thinking, Miss Johansson, it is a fine day for a picnic."

She angled away from her parents and smiled up at him, cocking her head in a flirting fashion. "I was thinking it, too, Mr. Eriksen."

As Andreas escorted her to her family's waiting team and wagon, Ingrid spied Marta with her widowed father. They were walking toward the Pederson clan, who gathered like autumn turkeys, on the other side of the church. Marta's father wore a stern expression. She hoped no trouble was brewing for Marta.

An hour later, from the front window, Ingrid watched the Lindstrom's gleaming black horse and buggy prance up the lake road to the farm. Andreas was coming for her. She couldn't help dancing from one foot to the other. He reined in the black, and pulled a blanket and a satchel from the buggy.

Coming up beside her, her father stroked his beard. "So, the railroad man comes courting."

She stared at the handsome figure striding through the front yard toward the house, his black bowler set at a jaunty angle. Her mouth went dry as prairie dust.

Ingrid held her breath, praying Papa wouldn't change his mind and forbid her to go. She was about to dash out the front door when he remarked to her mother, "Looks like the goose has taken a liking to the gander."

"Papa!" Ingrid reproached.

She grabbed her wicker basket and met Andreas, standing tall and well groomed at the front door.

He removed his bowler hat. The sun highlighted his fine dark hair. A smile, just right for the occasion, turned up the corners of his mouth. "Good afternoon," he said to Ingrid, her father, and mother, hovering behind them.

She attempted to compose herself, but her face felt as flushed as a steamed pudding.

"You bring her back in an hour, young man," her father's voice boomed.

"Yes, sir," Andreas replied with a serious nod.

Ingrid flew out the door before anyone could stop her.

Andreas' gaze was attentive as they moved across the front yard. She was glad she had changed into her new violet blue dress.

"The way you wear your hair makes you look like a queen," he said, admiring the two braided coronets behind her ears.

Ingrid laughed, aware that her cheeks must be glowing. "Then you will be king . . . and the apple orchard will be our domain."

They climbed the hill behind the house. She wished he would take her hand in his, but knew this would be frowned upon by her parents, who were no doubt watching from the small rear window.

As they followed the path, Ingrid said, "My eighteenth birthday was a week ago."

Andreas walked close behind her. "I'm sorry I missed it."

Ingrid stopped abruptly, nearly causing him to step on her heel. "Nettie wants me to enroll with her next month at St. Agnes." She turned round and glanced up at him. "Wouldn't it be amazing if I could earn a teaching certificate there!" Then her gaze fell and her voice became low. "But I do not think my parents can afford it."

Andreas wished he could offer her the money, even though he knew her people would be too proud to accept it. He tilted her chin up to look into her face. "As much as you want to go, I'm sure there will be a way."

Her eyes misted with a hint of hope and doubt. She led the way to the top of the hill.

The crab apple orchard lay before them in ripened splendor, trees laden with scarlet fruit. They walked farther into the grove.

Andreas spread the blanket in the shade beneath a tree. From her basket, Ingrid brought out ham sandwiches, potato salad, and two plump tomatoes. He took a large bite of his sandwich, gazed out over the sloping meadows and lake beyond.

The pleasant fragrance of Ingrid's lavender cologne filled his senses. He couldn't believe he was really here with her so close to him. Their bodies nearly touched.

"And, how is your family?" she asked.

A sudden pain filled his heart. "My father passed away just after I returned home."

"Oh, I am so sorry." She touched his arm.

"He was a man of great purpose. He encouraged me to help build the railroad."

"Tell me about your new job in Breckenridge," she asked.

She had to be unaware of the tremendous surge of emotions she caused simply by sitting next to him. He briefly explained his job as brakeman, and his long hours on the St. Paul & Pacific.

"Is it exciting to work in a train yard, to load the cars and see them go off to different places?"

Ingrid had no idea of the danger in his work, and he didn't intend to tell her. "The work is challenging," he answered simply.

When they had finished lunch, she began clearing up the plates. He reached over to assist her and his palm brushed her forearm. An alarmed expression crossed her delicate features.

"Andreas! What have you done to your hands?" She stared at his badly scabbed and blistered palm, then compared it with his other hand.

"It's is my work. All the men have beat-up hands," he said lamely.

As if on impulse, she lifted his battered hand to her cheek and gazed at him tenderly. "If only I could stop you . . ."

The flesh of her cheek against Andreas' hand was as soft as a butterfly wing. His heart skipped twice. "Stop me—from what?"

She averted her gaze. "From hurting yourself."

An uncomfortable silence hung between them.

"You will be going back to the railroad work, then," Ingrid said. "Do you like it as well as you thought you would?"

After a long moment, he answered. "It is hard labor, but I'm proud to be a part of it." Andreas reclined against the tree trunk. "We're laying more track along the Dakota border and up to Fisher's landing. The job should be finished by the end of next year."

Even though she knew she shouldn't allow such a reaction, Ingrid's spine went rigid. "The end of next year?"

Andreas' dark brows lifted. "That is what I've been told."

Ingrid rose from the blanket like a puff of smoke and moved over to the crest of the hill.

"What's wrong?" Andreas called, getting to his feet.

Despite Ingrid's better judgment, frustration overtook her. She remained standing with her back to him, her hands clenching at the sides of her skirt.

He came up behind her and rested one hand gently on her shoulder. "Tell me what you're thinking."

Ingrid spun around to face him, her cheeks and neck flaming with heat. "You will be up north working on the railroad—until the end of next year? That is a long time."

Andreas flinched. "I think I know why you are upset." He reached for her hands but she held them stiffly at her sides. "My job requires some time along the border while I apprentice. It is important. I promised my father I would do this. But, I will come to see you every free moment I have."

With tears brimming in her eyes, Ingrid looked away. He encircled her waist and brought her to him. "Oh, Ingrid. You are such a treasure," he whispered into the shell of her ear.

His hard-muscled body enveloped her. Conflicting emotions raced through her head. Through the branches of the apple trees the midday sun was blinding. Her mother had been right, a railroad man never stayed near home.

"Wait, I almost forgot . . ." Andreas broke away and rummaged in the bottom of his satchel. He lifted out a small book. "I wanted to give you this—until I see you again." He handed the leather-bound book to her.

Ingrid ran her fingers over its smooth cover. The title on the binding read: *The Poems of Robert Browning.* Browning. The name was foreign to her, but she sensed this book would be very special. She leafed through the fragile pages, her eyes delighting at the English words. Love words.

"Andreas, this is too fine a gift."

"It was one of my father's books. Keep it for me, and we can read some of the poems together when you come to the city."

Ingrid set the book in her hamper and began gathering up the luncheon wrappings. "I hope I will."

The doubtful tone of her voice, the lowering of her long silky lashes, sent a stab of longing through Andreas. In one urgent motion, he reached across the space between them and embraced her.

"You will, my sweet Ingrid. You will see me again," he whispered fiercely into her hair, his lips finding her tender eyelids, her nose, her mouth.

Ingrid moaned and her lips moved willingly beneath his. A rushing sound filled her ears as if she were standing beside a thundering waterfall. She clasped her hands around his neck, and they swayed together against the fragrant breeze rippling through the apple trees.

How warm his lips were, caressing hers. How strong his arms around her.

In just a heartbeat, the hour had passed. She hated that he was returning to Breckenridge to work in the train yard. An unfamiliar raw ache unfurled inside her rib cage as they started back down the hill.

The next day, Nettie's letter arrived. Hans and Jens had gone to Lake Park for supplies and returned with an envelope, post-marked Minneapolis, addressed to Ingrid.

She held the envelope in both hands, the anticipation of what was inside causing her to tremble.

Everyone stared at her.

"Are you not going to open it?" Jens asked impatiently.

Ingrid took a deep breath and slit the envelope open with her fingernail. Unfolded, the neatly written page danced before her eyes.

"Here, Jens. I am too excited. You read it." She handed the letter to her eager brother. He read it aloud.

Dear Ingrid,

I have taken the liberty of talking to Headmistress Dahl-quist at St. Agnes about your enrolling with me in mid-September. I told her how sincere you are, of your home studies with Jens, and your desire to become a teacher. She responded that the school would assign you to a prepara-tory course. Mama and Papa say they would be pleased for you to stay with us while you attend school. Papa says you could help clerk in his dry goods store after your classes to pay for tuition. I am so excited for you to come! Please let us know very soon of your decision.

Love,
Nettie

A hush fell over the room.

Jens set the letter on the kitchen table and looked at Ingrid. The warmth in his smile showed the support she knew was always there.

To Ingrid, it felt like Nettie had waved a fairy wand, and she was about to be transported to a magical world. The academy—and Andreas. Her mother clasped her hands together, her face full of hope. Her sisters squirmed in anticipation, their questioning eyes turning from Ingrid to their parents.

The only one in the room whose face did not radiate enthusiasm was her father's. When Ingrid looked over at him for a response, he glowered at her. "You studied the English books when I said you could not."

Ingrid cringed at his admonition.

Marie Lisbet broke the dreadful silence. "Papa, is Ingrid going to stay with kusin Nettie?"

He cleared his throat abruptly. "We will talk about it later. Come on, Jens, we have work to do before supper." He stamped out the door and Jens followed.

The subject was not discussed that evening, her father remaining mysteriously mute. Nor was he approachable the following day at breakfast, or at the noon meal.

Ingrid grew more uneasy with every passing hour. "Why does he not say something?" she pressed her mother after lunch.

"He is thinking about it," was Sigrie's short reply.

"You will talk to him . . ."

"Ingrid, you know how your fater is. You cannot push him."

That night, Ingrid soaked her pillow with tears. She tossed and turned and cursed the dark, and her stubborn father. Marie Lisbet, lying beside her, reached out and stroked her arm. Finally exhausted, Ingrid rolled over on the straw mattress and dozed fitfully.

The following morning, she straggled into the cooking area. Her mother lingered near the early light from the front window, reading from a piece of paper.

"I found this pushed under the door." Sigrie lifted her eyes. "Marta is pregnant. She has run off to marry Daxe."

Astonished, Ingrid blinked. "But where will they go?"

"She says he has a job near Glyndon."

Ingrid thought of Daxe, his rough hands, his sour breath. "Poor Marta," she murmured and thought, *This will not happen to me.* Another thought struck her, of the extra work load ahead, and Nettie's urgent letter. Her head began to throb.

At midday, Hans and Jens came in from shoeing the horses. The day was as miserably hot as any August day had been. Marie Lisbet swatted at an invading fly, the size of a man's thumbnail, with grim determination.

One glance at her father's expression told Ingrid he was in a foul mood. She busied herself carrying food to the table.

"Marta is gone," he stated loudly, as if no one had heard the news. He bolted down the food from his plate in seconds. "You see how much more work your mater has to do now," he addressed Ingrid. "We have the fall harvesting ahead, collecting the maple syrup, making the soap and candles . . ."

"I know, Papa." A shroud of despair fell over her shoulders. "But could we not get one of the Pederson girls to help Mama?"

Ignoring her question, Hans got up from the table and shoved his chair aside. "Daxe is gone too. The randy lout!"

Jens attempted to placate. "We will all carry our share of the load."

"No. No." Her father was adamant. "We cannot spare Ingrid now."

Her mother approached him, a pleading in her voice. "Oh, Hans."

He looked sternly over his shoulder at Ingrid on his way out the door. "No fancy school for you, girl. Your place is here at home."

Ingrid's strangled cry chased her father out into the yard. "Papa—please!" Choking sobs caught in her throat. "Everything is ruined!"

61

"No. Everything is not ruined." Sigrie removed her apron and hung it on a wall peg, her shaking hands the only sign of her inner turmoil.

"Where are you going?"

"To talk to your fater."

Ingrid brushed away the tears from her cheeks and followed her mother. "I am coming, too."

With determined steps, Sigrie pushed open the front door and entered the yard. The two women walked past Briget playing blissfully with a new litter of kittens. Her mother's eyes focused on the barn, her lips set in a straight, unyielding line.

At the barn's entrance, Sigrie said firmly, "Wait here."

Ingrid sighed with resignation. Her mother knew how to handle her father better than she.

Inside the darkness of the barn, the air hung thick with dust. The strong smell of horse manure and fresh-cut hay filled Ingrid's nostrils. She watched her mother move toward the rear stalls where her father and Jens worked.

"Hans," Sigrie called in a strong voice, "I must talk with you."

Ingrid snuck closer, wanting to hear what her mother would say.

The man and boy looked up from shoeing their bay mare.

"Jens, please leave us."

Obediently, Jens straightened. He turned and walked past Ingrid, standing in a shadowed corner.

Her father raised questioning eyes, sweat lining his brow.

"Hans, we must find a way to let Ingrid go to this school."

He lifted a large calloused hand as if to stop her in her plea, but she continued.

"Ingrid is hungry to learn—and then to teach what she has learned. We cannot keep her here with us forever. She is eighteen and knows her own mind."

He rose to his feet. "I have just told her we cannot spare her—the fall harvesting and—"

"That is not enough reason, Hans." Sigrie began to pace before him. "We can find help as we have before."

"Woman, you will not argue with me. We do not have the money for this—this city school."

Ingrid's pulse raced as she imagined the flare in her mother's eyes, and knew her mind was set. "We can sell one of the cows for a handsome price," Sigrie countered.

Hans snorted at the air like a frustrated bull. "I will not sell a cow just for Ingrid to go away and live with your rich sister!"

Sigrie pointed a finger at him. "That is not the reason, you stubborn man!"

Unable to hold her tongue a second longer, Ingrid burst from the shadows. "Keep your cow, then! I can always scrub floors to pay my own way." Her heart banging against her chest, Ingrid stared defiantly into her father's surprised face.

A long, dangerous pause hung on the thick air.

Then Hans slammed his fist against the side of the stall.

The sudden loud vibration sent the two horses into a whinnying frenzy. The black gelding switched his tail nervously in the stall next to Ingrid. Sweat ran down her sides beneath her dress. Her knees threatened to buckle. Her father's decision would affect the rest of her life.

Ingrid saw tears glisten in his eyes. But, was his emotion from deciding to let her go, or forcing her to stay? The suspense of it rent her like a knife. She spun around and ran from the barn and all the way up the hill behind the house.

"Why, Marta? Why?" Ingrid cursed the hired girl as she weaved upward through the tall grass toward the crab apple orchard. Hot, choking sobs caught in her throat. A steady stream of tears blurred her vision.

Everything is ruined. Everything is ruined!

The scalding tears ran down her face and from her nose onto her upper lip. She brushed them away with the back of her hand and continued her stumbling climb.

"Damn you, Daxe!" she bellowed to the blistering heat. *Why didn't I tell Papa when you fondled me in the barn? He would have fired you and this never would have happened.*

Her shoe caught on a clump of rocks and she tripped, pitching forward and falling in a heap, just inside the perimeter of the orchard. She lay sobbing, her skirts bunched up beneath her, the sun broiling her back through her dress and searing her exposed face and neck.

When her mother came upon her, Ingrid was sitting crumpled against a tree trunk bracing herself against the jarring hiccups.

"Come, girl. We must not have you going on like this." Sigrie knelt down and sat beside her. "You have nothing to cry about. Your fater said you could go."

Ingrid stared at her in disbelief. "Does he mean it? That I can go to school with Nettie?"

Her mother moved closer to Ingrid and wrapped her arms around her. She began rocking her as she had when she was a small child and had hurt herself at play. "Dear dotter," she crooned. "You know we love you even though sometimes we are harsh." She paused, caressing Ingrid's flushed, tear-streaked face. "*Ja.* I think your papa has changed his stubborn Swedish mind."

"What did you say to him?"

"I told him I did not want to lose you any more than he does. But, we must."

"You would never lose me, Mama. Why is Papa so stubborn?"

"You are his first child. It is hard for him to let you go."

Overcome with relief and gratitude, Ingrid embraced her mother for a long moment, laughing with joy.

Then she dabbed at her eyes with her handkerchief and sat up straighter. "I will do my best to make you both proud."

Her mother smiled. "You will have a better life as a teacher than if you stayed on the farm."

Looking into Sigrie's tired eyes, Ingrid clasped her work-worn hands. "Thank you, Mama."

She released a deep sigh. And prayed her father would not change his mind again. If he did, she knew she would do anything, even hitch a ride to the city.

Even walk there, if she had to.

CHAPTER SIX

Ingrid surveyed her family, clustered around her at the Lake Park depot. She wanted to remember them as they were right now, to take a mental picture to last in her memory over the long months ahead. Her mother's fine-featured face glowed with pride above her best black sateen dress and white crocheted collar. She held Briget's hand at her side. Next to her mother, Jens stood grinning like a cat who had licked the last of the cream from his bowl, his unruly adolescent hair slicked down with goose grease.

Briget hopped excitedly between Sigrie and the edge of the platform, where the locomotive's engine heaved and puffed volumes of smoke into the early morning September sky. Marie Lisbet, with the prim admonition of an older sister, yanked Briget's dress to keep her still.

Looking deeply into Ingrid's eyes her mother implored, "Write to us when you find a minute."

Ingrid fought back the sudden emotion catching in her throat. "I will, Mama."

Pursing her lips into a pink rosebud, Briget stood on tiptoe and placed a small, wet kiss on Ingrid's cheek when she bent to hug her.

Her father strode up the platform to where the family waited. "Your trunk is loaded," he said to Ingrid. He reached into his trouser pocket. "And, here is your ticket." When he handed the ticket to her, a lopsided smile pulled at the corners of his mouth.

Tears welled in her eyes. "Thank you, Papa," she said softly, "for selling one of the cows."

Her father stepped forward and enfolded her in an awkward embrace, his muslin shirt brushing her cheek. "She was a good cow, too."

Ingrid breathed in the clean smell of homemade soap and the aroma of pipe smoke. "I will do my best."

Her father patted her arm. "We know you will."

"God speed. Give everyone our love." Her mother's blessing strained against the din of the train.

"*B-o-a-r-d!*" the conductor shouted.

Excitement to go and yet a longing to stay played havoc with Ingrid's racing heart. She climbed aboard the train and turned to take one last look at the beaming faces of her loved ones a few yards away.

Her mother's face, filled with hope, unleashed a ripple of guilt within her. She could only pray that extra hands would lighten her workload. Her father's proud, stern expression stiffened Ingrid's spine.

She had made her decision. There would be no turning back. Whatever challenge awaited her in Minneapolis, she would meet.

Quickly, Ingrid entered the coach car and found a window seat. As the train's whistle blew and the train lunged forward, she wondered just how far these tracks would take her.

Before the train came to a full stop at the Minneapolis depot, Ingrid saw Nettie and Aunt Hilda waving from the platform. Grabbing up her hamper filled with homemade bread and a chokecherry pie, she made her way through the departing passengers, down the steps and into her cousin's welcoming hug.

Nettie, a tall, full-figured girl, was smartly dressed in high-collared gray frock and stylishly hatted. "Ingrid," she cried. "You are finally here!"

Aunt Hilda, a slightly older and heavier version of Ingrid's mother, wearing a heather bonnet and matching dress, gave her a hearty squeeze. Her round face spread into a broad smile. "Uncle Nels has gone off to find your baggage."

"It is Grandpa Johansson's trunk that he brought all the way from Sweden," Ingrid announced. "So, you know it is old." The women laughed.

"I can't believe you are really here," Nettie kept saying as they jostled through the milling travelers and out to the Nelson's buggy.

Nettie's gray costume was complemented by a smart straw bonnet that dipped down in the front and curved up on the sides. The crown was draped in dove-gray satin, and sitting atop it was a small cluster of imitation buttercups. Ingrid hoped her own home-sewn dress didn't stand out conspicuously. She would never tell Nettie that the sale of a Johansson cow had paid her train ticket.

Uncle Nels and a porter loaded Ingrid's trunk into the waiting buggy. Her tall, wiry uncle then greeted her in a quiet manner, doffing his bowler hat to briefly expose his balding pate. After assisting the girls into the carriage, he helped her aunt up onto the driver's seat and climbed aboard himself. Nettie and Ingrid sat with their feet propped up on Ingrid's trunk.

A few blocks away, they turned the corner onto bustling Hennepin Avenue in the downtown business district. "These buildings are so tall," Ingrid exclaimed.

"The new Opera House is just a block behind us." Aunt Hilda pointed back toward the river. "You'll see it when you and Nettie come to work at the store."

Ingrid hardly remembered her last visit here eight years ago. Nettie and her aunt usually came to stay on the Johansson farm. She smiled, thinking how adventuresome living in the city was going to be for this country mouse.

Men and women walked along the boardwalks, the women holding colorful parasols to protect their faces from the sun, their bustled skirts switching with every step. The unfamiliar sights were captivating.

And Andreas' home was just across the river in St. Paul.

They turned off Tenth Street onto Elliott Avenue. Two-story houses sat back along the tree-lined avenue, each surrounded by small, neatly kept yards. At the end of the block, Nels reined in the horse. He smiled beneath his droopy mustache. "We are home."

Ingrid insisted on helping her uncle carry her heavy trunk into the white frame house. Nettie guided the two furniture movers up the porch steps through the open door, where a small sign read: *Valkommen.*

Once inside, Ingrid looked into the parlor. "Cabbage roses!" She glided over to the deep pink and lime green patterned wallpaper. "They remind me of the roses in Mama's garden."

Nettie took her hand with girlish enthusiasm. "Come upstairs. I will show you our room." The girls lifted their skirts and raced upstairs. Nettie's room was down a narrow hall, in the rear of the house.

A four-poster bed, covered with a delicate blue-and-white patterned quilt, monopolized the center of the room. A small writing desk and chair in the far corner gave her thoughts of writing letters home, and to Andreas. The ceiling sloped down toward a large window overlooking the tree-filled backyard.

Ingrid trailed her fingers over the white lacy curtains and said wistfully, "How lucky you are, Nettie, to have such a fine room."

Her cousin came over and stood next to her, a smile lifting her plump cheeks. "I am very lucky, now that you are here to share it with me, Ingrid."

"You are a dear girl for sharing. Thank you." She looked warmly upon Nettie as a sister. "And, when do we start school?"

"The first of the week."

"We should be studying. My English is not so good," Ingrid confessed.

Nettie's expression turned solemn. "I will help you to my best ability. I have heard Mistress Dahlquist expects her pupils to excel quickly."

A queasy knot of apprehension uncurled in Ingrid's diaphragm. Could she learn and fulfill what was expected of her? She must not fail. Too many had placed their hopes on her.

Dagmar Eriksen hovered over the black walnut hall table, focusing intently on the envelope. A letter addressed to "Mrs. Adolph Eriksen" lay on top of the stack of morning mail on a silver tray. With eager fingers, she picked it up. The letter was postmarked Breckenridge. The handwriting was bold, masculine. It was from Andreas.

A little thrill danced at the base of her stomach. Dagmar turned the letter over, a sudden desire to tear it open seizing her.

At that moment, the housekeeper scuttled down the hall from the kitchen. Dagmar half-turned toward the front door and slipped the letter into a pocket of her dressing gown.

"Oh, dear," came the familiar voice with its broken English. "I almost forgot the morning mail."

Dagmar jerked her head as if startled. "Gertrude," she said irritably, "You shouldn't come up on people so suddenly."

Gertrude responded in a cheerful voice. "Sorry, miss. I yust vant to bring this tea up to your mater. She is not feeling so vell this morning. Vun of her headaches."

"Not again." Dagmar sighed with impatience. "Her headaches do get tiresome."

The housekeeper slanted Dagmar a critical look. Then, as if to acquiesce, she replied sweetly. "Vould you put the mail on the tray, miss, and I'll take it up to her now."

With a patronizing glance, Dagmar scooped up the remaining mail and placed it on the side of her mother's breakfast tray.

"Tank you, miss." Gertrude made a little bow and hustled up the carpeted stairway.

Dagmar watched the older woman climb the stairs. Gertrude was efficient and certainly devoted to her mother, but she'd better keep her place—and not pop up at the most inappropriate times.

As soon as Gertrude's skirts disappeared at the top of the landing, Dagmar hurried back down the hall to the kitchen. Just as she thought, the copper teakettle was still steaming on the stove. Snatching a silver butter knife from a kitchen drawer, Dagmar moved over to the large, black iron stove. She fished the letter out of her pocket and held it above the teapot, moving the intriguing slender envelope back and forth.

Slowly, the flap began to loosen. Dagmar slid the knife under it and carefully lifted the flap open.

After a nervous glance toward the kitchen door, she went to stand beneath the tall windows over the sink. In the morning light, she quickly removed the three pages and began to read, skimming Andreas' greeting to her mother and his apology for not communicating sooner.

He spent several paragraphs telling about his job as brakeman in the Breckenridge depot, working ten- to twelve-hour days. How tiring that would be—and how needless! Why didn't he just come home to St. Paul and find a respectable job in the St. Paul & Pacific office here?

She read farther into the second page looking for a mention of her name, perhaps a reference to their July Fourth celebration at the park. So long ago. She found none. A tendril of hair fell across her forehead, and she gave it an irritated swipe.

How long will you keep me waiting, Andreas?

Scanning the third page, Dagmar sucked in her breath. Andreas had visited his Lindstrom cousins again in that God-forsaken little farming town—and he'd "especially enjoyed meeting the daughter of the Johanssons, an upstanding family in the community."

Drat! Dagmar stamped her slippered foot and whirled to stare out the window. How dare he flirt with some ignorant farm girl!

Barely able to finish the letter, Dagmar did find a ray of hope in the last sentence. "I will try to get back to St. Paul early next month for a long weekend. My love to you and Dagmar."

She sighed, letting some of the anger drain away. Andreas would be coming home within a month, and she could use her most persuasive wiles to make him stay.

She tossed her head. To the devil with this farm girl. She allowed herself an inward laugh. The farmer's daughter was probably as big as a cow and as attractive as a mule.

Dagmar carefully folded the letter and tucked it back into its envelope. She would reseal it with glue and return it to the silver tray tomorrow morning, without anyone knowing the difference.

CHAPTER SEVEN

Ingrid gazed up at the imposing, three-story red brick structure and was overwhelmed. St. Agnes Women's Academy. She was finally here—entering this institution of higher learning. In small groups around the front lawn, other young women gathered, many with awed expressions in their eyes.

She nudged Nettie, standing next to her. "Are you as excited as I am? My stomach is doing flip-flops!"

Her eyes shining, her curls bobbing against her shoulders, Nettie nodded.

A buxom, red-haired woman appeared in the wide doorway to the academy. She jingled a small silver bell to get everyone's attention. "Come, young ladies. Headmistress Dahlquist would like you to join her in the reception hall."

Inside the darkened interior, Ingrid inhaled the aroma of leather-bound books wafting through the hall. The red-haired woman guided them down an entryway to a large reception room where coffee was served.

Along the opposite wall of the room, sparkling windows reached nearly to the ceiling. A pedestal near the doorway supported a bronze bust of a young woman reading an open book. Photographs of St. Agnes graduates lined the wall behind the bronze statue.

Quivering with anticipation, Ingrid studied the accomplished faces of the graduates. This was the place where she would attain the same goal and fulfill her dreams.

Double doors to the side opened and a tall, broad-shouldered woman of about fifty entered. An aura of authority surrounded her. The woman wore a dark gray dress with pearl buttons descending from the high-collared neck to the waist. Her thinning, steel-colored hair was skimmed upward into a tight topknot.

Without acknowledging anyone, the matronly woman moved purposefully to the front of the room. From somewhere on the crowded perimeter, a bell again tinkled. The red-haired woman reappeared and introduced "our Headmistress Dahlquist."

A respectful silence followed, and all eyes focused on the woman in gray.

"Young ladies," the headmistress began, "I would like to welcome you to St. Agnes Academy. You will find that more than good manners will be taught here. Our pupils and graduates aspire to the highest goals of their calling . . ."

Without warning, Ingrid's nose twitched unbearably.

". . . to acquire knowledge, to teach others, to serve."

Ingrid's sharp sneeze punctuated the headmistress's address. Embarrassed, she stepped backward, her elbow jarring the pedestal behind her. It tilted, sending the bronze statue clattering to the polished wood floor. *Oh, no!* How could she have done this?

Everyone turned in unison to gawk at her, standing horrified at the back of the room. Aides rushed to retrieve the unharmed statue and replace it on the pedestal.

"Please forgive me, madam," she croaked and gingerly patted her nose with her handkerchief. Thank heaven, the statue remained intact. But still, she desperately wanted to become invisible at this very moment!

Madam Dahlquist's eyes, two wide black orbs, stared at Ingrid, seeming to penetrate right through her skull. The headmistress cleared her throat and continued. "Our courses of study include an array of fine academic choices and excellent instructors who will expect your complete attention and best efforts." She paused to survey the attentive new student body.

Ingrid fantasized a great matronly owl sizing up her brood.

The great owl concluded her address with a thin-lipped smile. "You may now proceed across the hall to enroll in your curriculum."

Resuming their chatter, the young women dispersed. As if walking on eggshells, Ingrid blended with the group.

Two hours later, she excitedly showed her class schedule to Nettie. She'd been assigned four preparatory courses for the fall semester: English grammar and penmanship, beginning English literature, mathematics (her least favorite subject), and botany. "All of my classes meet in the morning, so I can work afternoons at the dry goods store with you."

Nettie hovered over her class assignments. "Next year, I want to study French with Monsieur Blanc."

"Oh?" Ingrid observed. "And will your professor invite you after class to study the verbs? Jens told me Frenchmen are very romantic."

Nettie rolled her eyes. "Don't let the headmistress hear you talk like that. She's half German, I hear, and they say she has a mean streak."

Ingrid recalled the recent mortification of her clumsy actions. "The headmistress has probably put me on the top of her bungler's list." She glanced down the hall to be sure it was clear and whispered, "The old stiff neck. I will just have to stay out of her way."

"Hurry, Nettie! We can make it," Ingrid called over her shoulder three weeks later as they raced up the shade-dappled street to catch the horse car. Behind her, Nettie clamped onto her straw hat with one hand and her schoolbooks with the other. Her stout legs pumped to keep up with Ingrid. As they rounded the corner onto Hennepin Avenue, Ingrid flagged down the driver.

Catching up with the horse car, they climbed aboard. After paying the nickel fare, she and Nettie stepped inside the small car and found a seat.

"Whew!" Nettie exclaimed breathlessly and plopped down next to her.

Ingrid laughed. "We should run more often. I used to chase after Jens all the time on the farm." The thought struck her that she'd been away from home for a month.

"Do you still have the homesickness?"

Ingrid cocked her head. "Sometimes." She'd written home and to Andreas when she first arrived in the city. Jens had responded. No reply had yet arrived from Andreas.

Her letter to Andreas had been just a page, written in English with Nettie's help. She still felt somewhat shy toward him. Even filled with awe at what he had already accomplished in his life, and the difference in their family backgrounds. As she wrote, she had remembered Andreas kissing her in the orchard, his arms around her.

Nettie interrupted Ingrid's reverie. "If only we didn't have to work every afternoon. I would rather go shopping."

"I don't mind. I am always learning something new at the store. Your fater was so good to give me this opportunity." She squeezed Nettie's arm.

The horse car trundled along past hotels and theaters. "It would be grand to go to the theater," Ingrid mused.

"And wear one of those elegant gowns we saw in *Godey's* fashion magazine." Nettie sighed. "First, we have to find some handsome escorts."

Ingrid gazed out the window, her thoughts lingering on the Norskie working up north on the railroad.

That evening, when Ingrid returned to the Nelson's, a letter was waiting for her from Andreas.

He was coming! At the end of the week!

By Thursday, Ingrid was so excited she could hardly eat a thing. When a messenger delivered a sealed note early that evening, she could barely conceal her anticipation and raced upstairs to the bedroom.

Knowing Nettie would follow on her heels, she hurriedly read the note.

My dear Ingrid,

I am at last home for a short visit. Please let me see you tomorrow. I shall plan to meet you at St. Agnes, Friday at twelve-thirty. We can hopefully make plans for this week-end.

Are you enjoying the Browning book? There is a poem in it I would like to share with you.

Until tomorrow,

Andreas

The book. Yes, many times since that day in the apple orchard, she had read through the poems. There were several verses she would share with him.

Ingrid pressed the note to her pounding heart. Tomorrow she would see Andreas.

At precisely twelve-fifteen on Friday, Ingrid positioned herself inside the front entrance of her school. Her classmates were scattered during their lunch hour on this crisp autumn day. Ingrid's thoughts were miles away from food.

She wore Nettie's bonnet, trimmed with a side cluster of silk roses, that matched her sapphire-blue sateen dress. Aunt Hilda had updated the princess-style dress by adding a three-tiered underskirt that rustled when she walked. Ingrid's hair, fashioned by Nettie, was pulled back beneath the bonnet into a small chignon; a cascade of curls fell from it to the middle of her back.

In her perspiring palms, Ingrid gripped Robert Browning's book of poetry. She shifted her stance, her gaze fixed on the street. Anxious thoughts flew around in her head. Would Andreas be able to find the school? Wasn't he late? What time was it now? She desperately wanted to run down the hall and look again at the casement clock as she had a dozen times already this morning.

Finally, there he was . . . a handsome driver reining in his carriage alongside the front walk. Why did she suddenly have difficulty breathing? He descended from the carriage and tied the horse's reins to a hitching post. His broad back, turned briefly away from her, accented his powerful yet graceful physique.

He lifted a bright floral nosegay from the buggy seat. In the next second, he was striding up the walk. He appeared taller than she had remembered in his dark brown suit, matching waistcoat, white shirt, and dark cravat. He cut a dashing figure in his brown bowler. But what was most noticeable about him was the mustache and beard he'd grown since they had last met.

Ingrid took a very deep breath. She felt giddy. Her head was suddenly a wobbly balloon.

He came up the stairs two at a time. Ingrid wiped her clammy right palm on her skirt. With a silent prayer that she looked her best, she opened one of the doors and stepped outside to greet him.

Andreas took her small, sturdy hand in his, gazing down into her expectant face. My God, she was beautiful! Her eyes, the color of sapphires, held him from beneath a sweep of amber-fringed lashes. The fragrance of lavender surrounded her.

"Ingrid," he said and lifted her hand gently to his lips.

"Hello, Andreas."

He presented her with the lace-bordered nosegay of deep purple violets, and she accepted it with a delightful smile.

"I see you've brought along Mr. Browning."

"Yes." She glanced up just in time to catch his wink and blushed.

"Is there a place nearby where we can have something to eat and talk?" Andreas asked, taking hold of her elbow as they started down the walk.

"Oh, a wonderful place—Loring Park—just two blocks from here."

Andreas guided her toward the buggy. There was something regal about this country girl. Her long graceful neck. The uplifted tilt of her chin. She carried her fair head like a lily on a stem.

He assisted Ingrid up onto the upholstered seat, where she adjusted her skirts.

His attentiveness and the aroma of his pine-scented cologne exhilarated her. When he sat down next to her on the driver's side, she smiled up into his tanned face. "I think I like your new beard, Mr. Eriksen."

"I know I like everything about you," he returned, a boyish grin lifting the corners of his mouth beneath his new mustache.

His compliment and the warmth of his long, muscular thigh aside Ingrid's sent waves of excitement through her.

They entered the park from Harmon Place and left his carriage tied in the shade of a willow tree. Ingrid reached up on tiptoes and tucked her violet nosegay in the horse's bridle, behind his ear. "For safekeeping," she said to Andreas.

Strolling along one of the paths, they passed well-dressed mothers pushing baby prams and children playing tag. Glowing, healthy children. If only fate would let them stay healthy until they were grown, she thought. At a refreshment stand, Andreas bought them both a lemonade and a paper-wrapped sandwich.

The trees were alive with autumn color. Leaves rustled and fell in a medley of garnet, copper, and gold.

Warm sunlight cloaked Ingrid's shoulders. They sipped their lemonades. Finding a bench set back in the shade of an elm, they finished their sandwiches.

"Have you found a poem that pleasures you?" Andreas asked, his face very near her ear.

"*Ja* . . . Yes." Ingrid's fingers found the marked page in the book. " 'Two in the Campagna.' I have been practicing my English. Would you like me to read you a verse?"

"Please do." He smiled, completely at attention.

The nearness of him was disconcerting, causing her heart to quicken. She moved a few inches away on the bench and cleared her throat. Attempting to concentrate on her pronunciation, she began to read the first lines.

> I wonder do you feel to-day
> As I have felt since, hand in hand,
> We sat down on the grass, to stray
> In spirit better through the land,
> This morn of Rome and May?
> For me, I touched a thought, I know,
> Has tantalized me many times . . .

Ingrid stopped. She glanced from the page up into Andreas' blue eyes. "What does 'tantalize' mean?"

He leaned closer, caressing her upturned chin with warm fingertips. "It means to tease or torment, the way you do me."

His lips gently brushed her cheek, then her lips. His touch a warm temptation. Her limbs went weak. "I do not tempt you . . . do I?"

She turned slightly, the question going unanswered as the kiss she had dreamed of came true now in his arms.

The sensations of the moment seduced her: the firmness of his embrace, the softness of his beard, the fluttering leaves drifting around them. His lips warm on hers provoked a sweet urgency, and a sudden longing ache formed deep inside her.

Suddenly she was aware of passersby and a female voice. "Look at her . . . Isn't that Ingrid?"

Confused, she pulled a few inches away from Andreas and recognized two of her classmates strolling along a nearby path, gawking at her and her amorous escort. The taller one peered at them with intense eagle eyes above a narrow, beaky nose.

Ingrid stiffened and adjusted her hat, which had tilted to the side of her head.

Flustered to be seen in such a compromising position, she whispered to Andreas, "My classmates."

He also sat up a little straighter but left his arm around her, half resting on the back of the bench. "Don't let them bother you." He lifted the Browning book from where it had fallen on her lap. "Now it is my turn to read you a poem . . . my favorite."

But Ingrid found her thoughts torn from the page of poetry. Her glance strayed to the path and the disappearing figures of her two classmates, a chill of foreboding raising goose bumps along her arms.

CHAPTER EIGHT

Andreas removed his hat and set it on the far end of the bench. He opened the book to a page familiar to him and glanced at Ingrid. Although she had seemed distracted, now she brushed a blonde tendril from her face and leaned toward him expectantly.

"The poem is called 'Porphyria's Lover,' " he said.

She looked into his eyes and smiled. Above them, rays of sunlight filtered through the elm leaves as he began to read.

> The rain set early in to-night
> The sullen wind was soon awake,
> It tore the elm-tops down for spite,
> And did its worst to vex the lake:
> I listened with heart fit to break.
> When glided in Porphyria; straight
> She shut the cold out and the storm,
> Withdrew the dripping cloak and shawl,
> She put my arm about her waist,
> And made her smooth white shoulder bare,
> And all her yellow hair displaced,
> And, stooping, made my cheek lie there,
> And spread, o'er all, her yellow hair,
> Murmuring how she loved me—she
> Too weak, for all her heart's endeavor,

To set its struggling passion free
From pride, and vainer ties dissever,
And give herself to me forever.

Andreas paused to stretch his long legs into a more comfortable position in front of him. He observed Ingrid quietly. How would she interpret the last line he had just read?

Her shy gaze focused on her hands folded in her lap. Only the two bright spots of color blooming on her cheeks gave hint to her inner feelings.

He read on.

Be sure I looked up at her eyes
Happy and proud; at last I knew
Porphyria worshipped me; surprise
Made my heart swell, and still it grew
While it debated what to do.
That moment she was mine, mine, fair,
Perfectly pure and good: I found
A thing to do, and all her hair
In one long yellow string I wound
Three times her little throat around,
And strangled her. No pain felt she;
I am quite sure she felt no pain.

"Oh!" Ingrid exclaimed.

Before Andreas could finish the last verse, Ingrid had gathered up her skirts and hopped to her feet. Her face came close to his, a spark of fire in her eyes. "And would you strangle me, sir? Your little Porphyria?"

Surprise washed over Andreas. His mouth dropped open.

Without waiting for an answer, Ingrid spun around and

headed for the path, her golden curls swinging loosely down her back.

"Ingrid, wait!" he called. "Where are you going?" He grabbed his bowler, jammed it onto his head, and chased after her.

Ingrid skipped along the path leading to the lake, thoughts of the poem still in her head. She had loved the poem until the part where Porphyria's lover had strangled the poor girl—with her own hair! Ingrid felt contrary enough to let Andreas know she didn't approve of Mr. Browning's idea of courting.

Andreas easily caught up with her, matching her quick, small steps with his long ones. "Why are you running away?" he asked. "Didn't you like the poem?"

Slightly winded, Ingrid cocked her head to look up at him. "Yes and no," she answered. "I'm afraid Mr. Browning and I do not agree on what manner of courting a lady would prefer."

"I see," Andreas said, a serious tone in his voice. "And what type of courting would a lady prefer?"

Wrinkling her forehead in concentration, Ingrid thought for a moment. Ahead, she saw the boathouse and noticed that the number of lunch hour strollers had dwindled.

"Race me to the boathouse! The winner will decide." Ingrid laughed aloud at her own daring. "But you must give me a head start."

"All right, I'll give you a five-second start," Andreas offered. He gave a mock yawn.

Without giving him an extra second, Ingrid lifted her skirts and leaped forward like a deer. In sheer abandonment, she dashed ahead toward the boathouse, thinking she just might have a chance to beat him.

Gratefully, no one approached on the path to impede her progress. She reached an open space and left the path, coming up on the side of the boarded-up building. Her heart hammered in her chest, and she could hear her own panting breath in her ears.

Then Andreas streaked past her, taking long easy strides. His laughter followed him as he disappeared behind the building.

When she rounded the corner, he caught her and playfully pushed her backwards toward the boathouse.

"No fair," she cried, gasping for air. "You have much longer legs!"

He responded by coaxing her back against the wall of the boathouse. Andreas stood so close now that Ingrid's breasts pressed against his suit jacket. She saw the glimmer in his azure eyes and a tiny shiver ran down her body.

"You know," he said huskily, reaching behind Ingrid's shoulder and gathering a handful of her hair, "that Porphyria's lover wound her locks around her neck in an overture to love." He lifted her curls to his lips and kissed them invitingly, then wrapped them round her neck above the ruffle of her bodice.

His gesture was like a caress. Hypnotic, Andreas' gaze held hers and would not let go. She slid her hands up the smooth fabric of his jacket to his broad shoulders. "You tease me," she said.

For Andreas, it was the easiest thing in the world to lower his mouth to Ingrid's. He drew her closer and delighted in the slight tremble he felt in her lithe form. He kissed her gently several times, his pulse quickening. Then he left her sweet mouth to trail his lips across her velvet cheek to her earlobe and downward over the creamy slope of her neck. Her fine-textured hair brushed softly against his face.

God, he wanted her—had dreamed of her these many long nights in his lonely bed after an exhausting day's labor. He knew his thoughts were carnal, yet could not stop the desire to disrobe her, carry her naked inside the boathouse and make love right there on the floor.

He buried his face in the warmth of her neck and heard raw desire in his own muffled voice. "Ingrid—how I want you."

Ingrid moaned from somewhere deep in her throat, unable to quell the great longing for him to kiss her again. And he did. This time, more intensely, more passionately. His lips were knowing, his beard coarse, yet smooth against her chin. His hand came up behind her head and cradled it as his tongue gently parted her lips and entered her mouth. She let her tongue touch his, tentatively, thrilling to the foreign pleasure it gave her. He tasted of lemons, tangy-sweet. Her entire body was turning to jelly and she feared she would slide right down to the ground in a quivering mass.

His other hand raised up to caress her breast, his fingers stroking the fullness of it. She sighed with forbidden ecstasy.

And then her strict Lutheran upbringing and the reality of the hour struck her. Her pulse pounding, Ingrid straightened and forced herself to pull away from him. "I must know the time. I am afraid I will be late for work."

Andreas pulled a gold watch fob from his waistcoat pocket. "It's ten after one."

She saw the disappointment in his eyes and her heart fell. Why did minutes pass like seconds whenever they were together? "I have missed you so, and now our time together is cut short . . ." Raising up on tiptoe, she gave him a tender parting kiss. "Please forgive me."

Adjusting his coat, Andreas attempted a quick recovery from his strong arousal. He fetched his hat nearby, saying, "I understand. You are a working girl."

Ingrid smiled up at Andreas as they resumed walking along the path. "I really loved the poetry."

"Keep the book—as a memento of today."

She gave his arm an intimate little squeeze. "I will. Thank you."

"I will deliver you to your uncle's store," Andreas offered.

After he retrieved the nosegay from behind the horse's ear and assisted her into his buggy, he asked, "I know it's late notice, but would you attend the theater with me tomorrow evening?"

A combination of emotions clouded Ingrid's expression. "Well, yes . . . I would love to." Nervously, her gaze left his and fell to the violet nosegay in her lap.

What in thunder was wrong? he wondered. She had just broken away from him behind the boathouse, using her job as an excuse. Her uncle would have allowed a few tardy minutes. Now, the girl received his theater invitation like a field rabbit confronting a hunter's rifle. It was all he could do to tamp down his temper and display a controlled response.

Andreas snapped the reins over the horse's flanks. The animal jerked its head smartly and started off at a fast clip. "I will pick you up tomorrow evening then," he said evenly. "At eight."

"Can't you make those curls tighter?" Dagmar admonished Gertrude as the woman struggled with the heated curling iron. Holding a silver hand mirror, Dagmar scrutinized the thick, limp clumps of hair in the back of her head reflected in the dressing table mirror.

"I am trying, Miss Dagmar, but your hair is so tick." Gertrude, her round face turning rosy with the prolonged effort to create a coiffure, twisted the iron closer to Dagmar's nape.

"Ouch!" Dagmar sprung forward in pain. "You burned me!" Her head snapped back as Gertrude unwound the iron with a jerk.

"I'm sorry, miss. This yust isn't vurking."

Dagmar waved the woman away. "Oh, go back to the kitchen. I'll do it myself."

"*Ja*, miss." Gertrude set the curling iron on its metal stand and scurried out of the room.

Dagmar glared at the housekeeper's departing form in disgust. *The stupid woman.* She should never have asked for her help. In Chicago, Dagmar would have gone to the salon and had her unruly mane expertly coiffed by Jacques, but where did one go in St. Paul? Tonight, she must look her best.

Andreas was home. And, about time. He had only arrived this morning and before she could get downstairs to greet him, he'd taken the buggy somewhere and returned only a short time ago. If she'd been the least bit suspicious, she might have thought he was calling on a new woman, but who was there to court in this one-horse town?

Forgetting her uncooperative hair momentarily, Dagmar rose from the tufted stool and crossed the bedroom to a tall armoire. She reached inside and lifted out her dinner toilette, an elegant gown of faille and satin, and carefully laid it across her bed. The gown's vertical stripes of cream and purple would emphasize her jewelry, an amethyst pendant on a gold chain and matching drop earrings.

Dagmar smiled, imagining how seductive she would appear to Andreas tonight, with the gown's low, square-cut bodice such a temptation for his wondrous blue eyes. Hastily, she padded her corset to lift and display her fine breasts. Small they might be, but he would assume otherwise. When the time came for their revelation, which she hoped would be soon, she would make sure the room was dark.

The old casement clock on the landing chimed six times. Dinner would be served at seven. She must hurry. She rushed back to the dressing table and stared into the mirror. She would have to tidy up the chignon and try to do something with the rest of this mess. But now the curling iron was cold. Drat!

Cursing under her breath, she went over and yanked the bell pull next to the door. She needed Gertrude to help her get into her gown, and she needed her now!

At ten minutes to seven, Dagmar descended the stairs. She recognized the timbre of a male voice drifting down the hall from the parlor. Andreas. She hoped she'd kept him waiting, anticipating her entrance. From the kitchen wafted the succulent aroma of roast pork, Gertrude's specialty. Her stomach rumbled.

Even though she was starving, the way Gertrude had trussed her into this gown left little room for a full meal. She paused at the foot of the stairs to reposition her bosom pads and pinch her cheeks to heighten their color. Then, satisfied that she looked ravishing, Dagmar swayed confidently over the Scandinavian carpet toward the parlor.

Andreas was speaking to her mother when Dagmar entered the room. A bright fire crackled in the fireplace near his wing-backed chair, enhancing the healthy glow of his complexion. He came to his feet when she entered, his manners, as always, impressive. His new beard made him appear rather bohemian.

"Dagmar, how lovely you look." Andreas motioned to the chair he'd been sitting in. "Won't you sit here by the fire?"

His smooth voice ignited a flame that traveled through her like wildfire. No, she didn't need to sit by any fire to ward off autumn's early chill.

"Thank you, Andreas," she replied sweetly. "You are so thoughtful, but I'll sit here on the sofa next to mother."

Dagmar sat down next to Emma and adjusted her full satin skirts around her. Her mother appeared wan, but was making a visible effort to perk up for her stepson. She imagined Emma had been nipping at her flask again, hiding out in her bedroom, as she did more frequently.

Later, at the dinner table, Dagmar had to admit the evening was progressing nicely. The roast tasted divine, as did its culinary accompaniments: a duck consomme, whipped potatoes, and glazed carrots. While sipping on a ruby claret wine, she nibbled only small portions of everything; her gown would not allow her to do otherwise. Across the table sat the object of her affection. What could she say to catch his attention?

"Do you like the claret, Andreas?" She leaned toward him, allowing his eyes full advantage of her low décolletage.

"Yes," he answered, "an excellent choice." His gaze darted from her bosom to her face.

The wine spread a tingle all over her body, the candles glowed in their polished brass holders, and she felt assured that Andreas must be sharing thoughts of their mutual attraction.

Andreas finished the wine in his goblet and gazed down into its shimmering crystal. The dinner had been excellent and the conversation good. He'd brought the family up to date on the St. Paul & Pacific and his work in the yard, without revealing its sometimes dangerous details.

The only annoyance of the evening was his stepsister. Why was she acting so provocatively? Every time she had offered a comment during dinner, she'd dipped toward him at a most awkward angle, exposing more naked flesh than he'd seen of a woman since his one brief liaison at the university. The upper halves of her breasts thrust in his face like bulging billiard balls. At one point, Dagmar had narrowly missed dunking one of them in the consomme!

Emma patted her lips with her napkin then set it next to her plate. "Do you have a busy schedule for tomorrow?" she asked Andreas.

"Not during the day, but tomorrow evening I'm going to the theater in Minneapolis."

His stepmother awakened from her subdued demeanor with sudden interest. "With anyone we know?"

"No, not yet. She's the Swedish girl I met at the Lindstrom

wedding last June. Ingrid Johansson."

Dagmar fairly lunged toward him, her dark eyes glinting in the candlelight. "But how can she be here?"

"She is attending a women's academy in Minneapolis," Andreas answered, her pointed question testing his patience.

"Well, good for you, dear," Emma said. "You must get on with your life." Then, with a faraway look, she added, "We all must."

Andreas nodded, avoiding Dagmar's glare, as Gertrude entered the dining room carrying a tray with coffee and dessert.

Dagmar could hardly get the hot coffee past her lips, so angered was she at Andreas' announcement. The dinner, which had tasted divine such a short time ago, now rose like gall in her throat.

Andreas, how dare you?

Through the remainder of the meal, she stared at him in disbelief. She would squash his newfound dalliance like a bug under her shoe. She couldn't wait to get back to her room and tear off her suffocating gown.

Then she would think of something to wrest his attention away from the farm wench.

"And did Andreas look like a fine gentleman when he came for you this afternoon?" Aunt Hilda asked Ingrid.

The women were in the kitchen, doing the dinner dishes, all clucking at once about Ingrid's rendezvous earlier in the day.

"Oh, he looked very handsome," Ingrid blurted. Then, more shyly, "He has grown a new beard."

"Has he?" Hilda tossed a wink at Nettie.

Ingrid stared down at the table, a heated blush rising to the roots of her hair.

"And he read poetry to you?" Nettie barged in.

"Well, *ja*, he did." Ingrid glanced through the door to the parlor where Uncle Nels rocked in his chair, reading the evening paper, and saw the faintest hint of a smile hover at the corners of his handlebar mustache. He was no doubt listening to them and only pretending to read.

"Violets are my favorite flower," Nettie cooed enviously over Ingrid's pert nosegay anchored in a vase on the kitchen table. She produced one of her flower language books, *Flora's Interpreter.* "The violet's unspoken message is, 'You occupy my thoughts.' "

Ingrid glanced down at the nosegay's deep purple petals, a rich inner glow warming her. She could not, however, reveal the extent of Andreas' ardor on the park bench and behind the boathouse. Some things were better left to one's discretion.

"And, he has invited you to the theater tomorrow evening," her aunt gushed.

Ingrid bit her lip in frustration. "But what shall I wear? I have been nervous about it ever since he asked me."

Aunt Hilda wiped her hands on the dishtowel and looked at Ingrid conspiratorially. "Let's go upstairs and look in Nettie's closet." She glanced at Nettie, who nodded in agreement, brushed a wisp of auburn hair from her cheek, and headed for the stairs.

The girls followed her, single file, up to the second floor.

Ingrid tried not to get her hopes up. "But Nettie is taller and more amply endowed than I am," she said. "If nothing else, I have the blue sateen that I wore today." Brushed and aired on the line, it would have to do.

"We shall see, we shall see." Aunt Hilda went straight to Nettie's closet and began to dig. In seconds, four gowns were laid out across the bed. She picked out a yellow dress, held it up, glanced at Ingrid, shook her head, and deposited the dress next to the others. Finally she spied something that pleased her. "*Ja,*" she exclaimed.

Hilda emerged from the closet with the last gown. A deep rose color, it was made of a rich lustrous fabric her aunt called damask. The overskirt was three-tiered and trimmed with lace and silk roses. Ingrid caught her breath. "The gown is lovely, but will it fit?"

Nettie grinned. "Mama will make it fit."

Ingrid quickly wriggled out of her everyday dress.

"Put your arms up," Aunt Hilda directed.

Ingrid raised her arms and felt the satiny gown slip over her head.

"I made this for Nettie last year," Hilda explained. "But she outgrew it." Aunt Hilda laughed good-naturedly while Nettie screwed up her nose in mock indignation.

Ingrid looked down to her bosom. "Oh, no," she uttered. "The gown is too big." Its bodice, daintily edged in lace at the V-neck, pouched out in front and gaped on the sides. Her heart and hopes fell.

Hilda waved her finger in the air. "That can be fixed. Come to my room and we will see what can be done."

With bated breath, Ingrid followed her into the front room, where she stood before a full-length cheval mirror. In minutes, with measuring tape and pins, and a dressmaker's expertise, her aunt molded the gown to Ingrid's figure, emphasizing her small waist.

"Will it be ready in time?"

"Of course, young lady." Hilda patted Ingrid's cheek. "The dress will be finished for tomorrow evening."

Ingrid sighed in relief. "I will wear my new shawl." Deeply grateful, she looked from one woman to the other. "I love you for doing this, both of you."

On Saturday afternoon, a messenger delivered a mysterious beribboned box addressed to her. Eagerly opening it, she discovered an elegant bouquet inside made up of rings of flowers surrounding a central pink rose. Her heart fluttered as she lifted the bouquet from its packaging of damp moss.

"A tussie-mussie!" Nettie exclaimed. "And an extra fine one—it must have cost him at least five dollars!"

Ingrid beamed. "Five dollars? That is a king's ransom!" She was embarrassed that Andreas would spend so much on her, yet thrilled at the same time.

"Even when Nels courted me, he never sent one so extravagant as this," Aunt Hilda enthused. "He used to say the flowers were free at home in Hitterdal."

Nettie translated the bouquet's intent from her many flower books: the white azalea, "first love"; the blue bugle, "most lovable"; the central, thornless pink rose, "grace and beauty"; and the baby's breath, "a pure heart."

Ingrid danced around the parlor, holding the tussie-mussie close to her breast. Its mingled perfumes were intoxicating.

Andreas came for her that evening, dressed in a black evening suit and top hat. When she met him at the front door, her knees nearly buckled. He had never looked so handsome. Standing behind her in the entryway, Nettie sighed.

Ingrid carried her tussie-mussie in its gilt posy holder. Andreas helped her with her shawl, a glow of admiration in his eyes.

"You look like a princess," he said as they strolled to his waiting carriage.

Her heart leaped. "I feel like one."

The rose satin gown rustled magically as he assisted her up onto the seat. Andreas took the reins and gazed down into her uplifted face, sending her a jaunty wink. Ingrid smiled happily. Life couldn't get much better than this.

But when the carriage pulled away into the star-spangled night, she wondered if this was really happening to her. And how long could such joy last?

CHAPTER NINE

Monday morning, Ingrid stared out the second-story school window from her botany class. Her last evening with Andreas played vividly in front of her eyes. Bittersweet memories: the vibrant theatrical performance, a champagne toast at the Nicollet Hotel, their farewell kiss on the front porch. By now, he was on his way back to the northern border.

Mrs. Thornsey's sharp voice pricked her reverie. "Ingrid Johansson, would you please see Headmistress Dahlquist in her office immediately."

At the sound of her name, Ingrid's mouth fell open. She hopped to her feet as if yanked by invisible strings. "Now?"

"Yes, miss." The instructor sent her a reproving look before continuing with her lecture.

Feeling all eyes riveted upon her, Ingrid gathered up her textbooks and moved to the side door. Why would headmistress call her out of class? Had bad news arrived of any member of her family? Had she committed some terrible crime?

She hurried down the dark hallway to the stairs, her heart beating faster and her mouth growing dryer with each step.

On the first floor, Ingrid found the headmistress' office. She entered an outer room, where the red-haired director of admissions was seated at a mahogany desk. Ingrid remembered the smiling woman at the academy's reception that first day of the semester. Today, the woman was not smiling.

She glanced up from her work as Ingrid entered. "Headmistress is expecting you," she said flatly.

Fear of the unknown twisted Ingrid's stomach into a pretzel. She stepped to the closed door behind the director and knocked.

An icy voice answered. "Come in."

Ingrid turned the brass doorknob. The door creaked open. She forced herself to step inside. The room was dim, the only light meekly entering through one high window along the far wall. The room was airless. Her throat constricted. If she could only run to that window and throw it open. Now.

Behind a large foreboding desk sat Headmistress Dahlquist, her gray wispy hair skewered into a small knot atop her head. The woman's black, owl-like eyes pierced Ingrid's.

"You—you wished to see me, ma'am?" she croaked.

The headmistress inclined her head toward the only chair in the room, a few feet in front of her desk. "Sit down, please." The intimidating eyes continued their penetrating stare.

Ingrid seated herself. Unable to meet the woman's glare, she dropped her gaze to a stack of papers on the desk. An acrid smell, like camphor, assaulted her nostrils. Nervous perspiration dampened Ingrid's dress under her arms and trickled down her sides.

"You don't know why I have summoned you, Miss Johansson?"

Ingrid sighed miserably. "No, ma'am."

"Indeed." With one swift movement, the headmistress pushed her chair back and rose to her feet. "Then I shall come directly to the point." The woman stood ramrod-straight. "It has been brought to my attention that you engaged in unacceptable behavior with a man in the park, during school hours last Friday. Do you have an explanation for this behavior, Miss Johansson?"

An immediate memory flashed through Ingrid's mind of her classmates gawking at her and Andreas as they kissed on the park bench. Mortified and struck nearly speechless, she mumbled, "I can explain—"

Headmistress' thin lips tightened into a taut, unyielding line. "There can be no excuses for such conduct, young lady. Nor explanations. This academy expects only the highest quality of deportment from its pupils."

The headmistress bent over and picked up a wooden ruler on top of the desk. Standing before Ingrid, she raised the ruler to eye level.

Ingrid watched in horrified fascination.

"Place your hands on the desk."

Trembling, Ingrid did as commanded. Agonizing seconds passed. Fear knotting her stomach, Ingrid shut her eyes tightly.

The ruler whooshed through the air, slamming down across her fingers with a loud *smack!* Once. Twice.

Her eyes flew open. Gasping in pain, she jolted backward in her chair.

Headmistress Dahlquist stood like an ice statue before her, holding the ruler at her side. "If you intend to remain at this academy, Miss Johansson, you will adhere, from this moment on, to the upstanding, ladylike conduct that is expected from each of your classmates. Or you will be expelled.

"Am I understood, Miss Johansson?"

Her eyes watering, Ingrid answered in a quavering voice, "Yes, ma'am."

"Then we are in agreement."

"Yes, ma'am."

With a forced smile, Headmistress carefully laid the ruler down on the desk. "That is all, Miss Johansson."

Aware of the flaming heat burning her face, Ingrid got to her feet and found her way to the door.

Once out of the headmistress' office, all she wanted was to flee. At the end of the hall, she passed two classmates whispering and gawking her way. The very ones who had run to tattle on her last Friday. She didn't bother looking at them now, so anxious was she to be free of the terrible shroud of suffocating humiliation.

An unforgiving October wind whipped at her skirts as she ran from the school out into the street. Tears of anger sprang from her eyes, blurring her vision. Furiously she wiped them away.

She hated the headmistress for her cruel admonishment, and her petty classmates.

Ingrid ran a block before she realized she was going in the direction of the park. The park. It beckoned to her. A refuge. Only today was not last Friday. The sun did not shine gloriously down on her burdened shoulders, nor were there casual strollers and baby carriages. A northern cold front blew into the city, causing pedestrians to lean against it, holding onto their hats. When she reached the entrance to the park, she saw the trees swaying, their leaves plucked away and scattered to the clouded sky.

Without a shawl, she shivered against the wind. Her bruised hands were chilled and her nose was starting to drip. She stumbled beneath an undulating willow, pulled her handkerchief from her pocket and blew her nose. *Oh, Andreas. Where are you now when I need your arms around me?*

Ingrid sagged against the tree trunk, tears flooding her eyes once again. She dabbed at them and drew a long breath. Had her behavior really been so bad? What Marta and Daxe did in the woods that day last summer was wrong, but the affection she and Andreas had shared was still beautiful and innocent in her memory.

She blew her nose again and composed herself. She would return to the school and face her accusers, proudly. They could not take away her dignity. Her dreams and goals were not soiled; she would still become a teacher.

With renewed determination, Ingrid moved out from under the skeleton umbrella of the willow. Breaking into a brisk walk, she left the park and headed toward the school. Yet as she strode against the stinging wind, a niggling fear clawed at her. Her status at the academy had changed. The headmistress now focused on her like a targeted rabbit.

Her only choice was not ever to invite Andreas anywhere near the school. No one must see them together again.

Shoving her aching fingers into her skirt pockets, she made another vow. She would not allow her dream of teaching to escalate into a nightmare at St. Agnes.

Andreas reached for the next handhold of the ladder to the roof of the caboose. Below him the rumbling of the wheels over iron tracks filled his ears. For one slow second, the train's motion lulled him. His hands stiffened in the chill of a northern front blowing down across the Canadian border. He cursed himself for losing his only pair of gloves.

Turning the brake wheels to slow the train would be more than difficult now.

His shift had started at six that morning in Breckenridge with a stopover in Glyndon at noon. He would be glad when the St. Paul & Pacific pulled into Grand Forks, and he could get out of the miserable cold and into a warm pub. Hell, he'd just as soon get off the train right now and find a welcoming hearth in a nearby farmhouse. Better yet, he wished he could lie down by a crackling fire with Ingrid, bury his face against her warm breasts and make love to her.

The train lurched to the right. His foot slipped off the narrow metal bar. In the next second, his fingers tore away from the handhold and he skidded downward, almost dropping the brake club he held in his left hand. Clumsily he caught hold of a lower bar. He glanced down and saw the ground flying by beneath him. His body broke out in a clammy sweat.

Lightheaded, he struggled to regain his balance. Would his knees buckle, causing him to fall beneath the roaring wheels?

Get hold of yourself!

Cautiously, Andreas climbed back up the side of the car to the roof. Gaining a last foothold, he hoisted himself up over the top. A driving sleet struck his face, the north wind threatening to knock him off balance. Hunkering forward on all fours, he slipped then steadied himself with his brake club. His heart thudded against his ribs.

His right palm bled where he'd scraped it on the metal hand-hold. "Shit!" He wiped his hand on his grimy pants and crawled forward.

Through the wet gray fog, he could barely make out Nord-berg's stooped silhouette six cars ahead. Clambering to keep his footing, the stout brakeman moved slowly toward him along the clerestory rooftop.

In the distance, the engineer gave the signal. One sharp whistle blast. They were approaching Grand Forks.

Andreas reached the end of the car, inserted the club, and started to spin the brake wheel to slow the train. Another jolt rocked the car beneath his feet. It felt like the earth had been pulled out from under him. A shock raced up his legs and he stumbled, then steadied himself.

The conversation he'd overheard the day before between McPhergus and a Breckenridge yardman flashed through his mind. "Hell, there's thirteen different patterns o' rail laid in two miles o' track just before ye get to Grand Forks," McPhergus had cursed. "Man, it's no more 'n two streaks o' rust and a right o' way!"

The yardman had laughed coarsely, and Andreas had walked away wondering how a railway could be thrown together so haphazardly. Financial difficulties were no excuse for cheating on safety.

The train continued to jar over the multipatterned rails. Andreas spun the brake wheel and jumped to the next car. His hands ached bone-deep; his fingers had gone rigid as steel prongs.

Inching forward, he peered into the worsening storm. Icy pellets stung his cheeks and forehead. His fellow brakeman was only a hazy form in the distance. A sudden gust shoved Andreas to his knees. The brake club slipped from his hand, skittered across the roof, and was gone. "Oh God, no," he groaned.

Why had he made such an unbearable promise to his father?

Agonizing seconds passed before he regained his footing and resumed his forward painstaking journey.

Andreas squinted into the swirling sleet, looking for Nordberg. By now he should have been just a few cars up. But Nordberg had vanished. He prayed the brakeman had simply descended between the cars for momentary respite. With frozen hands, he spun the wheel.

The whistle blew again, a long shrill blast.

Thank God. The station. Shivering to the depths of his soul, Andreas moved back toward the caboose.

After the train pulled into the Grand Forks depot, Andreas joined some of the crew in the relative warmth of the station. He looked around for the stocky brakeman, but couldn't find him. "Have you seen Nordberg?" he asked one of the men.

Shaking his head, the worker cupped blue hands around his mouth and blew into them.

"Nope, ain't seen him."

Outside, Andreas pulled his coat collar high against his neck. Fear rising in his chest, he approached the yard foreman. "I haven't seen the other brakeman. I think he fell off the train just before we pulled in."

The foreman spit a dark stream of tobacco from his bulging cheek and stared out at the thick sleet in the distance. "What's he look like?"

Andreas hunched into his overcoat. "He's short, stout. A red-faced Norskie."

"We'll have a look 'round." The foreman moved his bulky frame in the direction of the cars. Andreas followed.

Men were getting off their shift, leaving the yard in a hurry to find the nearest tavern and something to warm their frigid bones. Andreas looked at every face he passed. None of them were Nordberg's. He began to panic.

The foreman stopped at the end of the yard. "You see him?"

A nasty knot worked its way up from the pit of Andreas' gut. "No, I don't see him. Goddamnit, we've got to go find him!"

The foreman spit. "In this weather?"

Andreas peered up at the swirling white blanket surrounding them and attempted to shake off his fatigue. "We've got to try."

The foreman shrugged his massive shoulders. "I'll get a lantern and my medical kit." He headed back to the station. What seemed like an eternity later, he returned driving a dilapidated horse and wagon.

Andreas recruited another man from the crew, and the three of them set off into the blinding sleet.

They followed alongside the tracks leading out of town. "This is a real bitch!" the foreman shouted into the wind. "A real bitch!"

Andreas tugged his collar farther up around his neck. He lifted the lantern in front of him, squinting ahead at the barren landscape.

By the time they had driven a hundred yards, Andreas couldn't see beyond the horse's bobbing head.

"Can't see nothin' out there," the other crewman hollered from the rear of the wagon.

The foreman grunted in agreement and reined the horse to a stop. The storm was worsening by the minute. Andreas knew the situation was hopeless.

"If the man don't turn up, we'll go out first thing in the morning," the foreman promised, a hoarse edge to his voice.

The men were silent as the stiff-gaited animal pulled the wagon back toward town. Up the street from the station, The Bully Dog was crowded with weary trainmen. Andreas elbowed his way inside and up to the bar. A slight hope existed that he still might find old Nordberg here, where he would naturally join his fellow workers. But scanning the tired faces lining the bar and not seeing the familiar jowly face among them, his hope ebbed away.

Unlike other nights, the crowd was subdued, beaten down. No raucous camaraderie here.

When the strong smell of sauerkraut filled his nostrils, he realized he was not only exhausted but hungry. He ordered a mug of ale, a plate of bratwurst and the kraut, and made his way to an empty chair on the other side of the room. Devouring his meal in seconds, he drained the ale as well, and ordered another from the bar. His soggy clothes clung to him. He wouldn't notice the dampness so much after he'd had several more drinks. His mood lightened as he returned to his seat. He told himself that Nordberg might have gone to the other bar at the end of town after his shift.

An hour later Andreas saw Cahill, a friend of his and Nordberg's, come through the front door. He made his way over to him. "Have you seen ol' Nordberg tonight?"

Cahill removed his wool cap and scratched his bald head. "I just come from the pub up the street and he wasn't there. Guess I ain't seen him since noon."

"I think he fell off the train on the way into town."

Cahill looked at him strangely. "No, yer jokin'. He'll show up."

In spite of Cahill's optimistic response, he saw fear creep into the man's eyes.

Andreas tried to shrug off his own trepidation. He gazed down at his hands, blistered and raw. Unlike Nordberg, he still had all of his fingers. And, unlike Nordberg, he was inside where it was warm. Only God knew where Nordberg was. Poor bastard.

He ordered a brandy. It had a cheap edge to it, not smooth like the brandy in his father's liquor cabinet. He didn't care. He gulped it down and ordered another. The room was taking on a fuzzy haze; voices around him blurred. He drained his glass.

A heaviness lay in the pit of his stomach and he sweated uncomfortably. He got up and weaved his way to the door.

Once out on the street, the freezing wind snapped at him like a wolf. The first wave of nausea hit as he moved unsteadily up the boardwalk. Then another. He managed to make it to the alley beside a mercantile store before he had to retch. Crumpling to his knees, he threw up his supper. The ale and the sauerkraut left a clinging bitter taste in his mouth.

Then he sagged against the building and retched until there was nothing left inside him but misery.

CHAPTER TEN

Early the following morning, Andreas set out with a search party to look for Nordberg. They had traveled less than a mile from the station when he spotted the brakeman. Limbs splayed wide, he lay face down twenty feet from the track.

"I see him—straight ahead!" Before the foreman could pull the horse to a stop, Andreas leaped from the wagon. He ran to the still form and fell to his knees. Nordberg's thick neck was twisted at an unnatural angle, his eyes in death stared blindly toward the rails. When Andreas touched the man's frozen flesh, a horrified shiver rippled through him. If not for the luck of the draw, he could have been lying here.

Cahill came up beside him. "Poor fella. Must'a broke his neck when he hit the ground." He removed his wool cap and held it to his chest.

In sorrow and respect, Andreas removed his own cap.

The foreman, whose name Andreas now knew as Pyles, spat a stream of tobacco. "Come on, men. Let's get him in the wagon."

All in a day's work, Andreas thought bitterly. Who was this hard-working man to Pyles? Only an expendable brakeman. He probably had some eager young roughneck waiting in the yard to take Nordberg's job on the next run out.

It took all three men to lift the Norwegian's remains into the wagon. Andreas had brought the worn blanket from his cot and wrapped the body in it.

A raw wind still blew down from the north, but the icy sleet of the previous day had passed farther on to the south. Andreas walked to the front of the wagon. His temples throbbed. Never again would he indulge in cheap brandy.

From under his breath Cahill muttered, "The railroad got him. He was too old for the job, but he couldn't find no other. And who else was going to feed his five kids?"

Andreas shuddered. Who would feed them now?

"We'll take up a collection for his family when we get back," Pyles told them.

Andreas climbed up on the wagon seat, reconsidering his hasty judgment of Pyles. Maybe he did care about his fellow railmen. The burly foreman snapped the reins over the horse's back and the mangy animal lurched forward. Andreas sat in silence, his mind unsettled. He decided the first thing he would do after Nordberg's funeral would be to wire his widow enough money to get on her feet.

His second move would be to request a transfer. He was serving no good purpose as a brakeman. The St. Paul & Pacific management was indifferent to bad working conditions and in desperate need of strong leadership. His goal was clear. In order to work toward a position where he could influence the future of the trainmen, he would have to return to St. Paul.

He must see Ingrid soon; the thought of her in his arms again warmed him.

Rounding a hall corner, in a hurry to meet Nettie for lunch, Ingrid crossed squarely in front of Mistress Dahlquist.

"Watch where you're going, Miss Johansson." The eyes and the tone of the woman's voice penetrated as cold as steel.

Caught in surprised agony, Ingrid croaked, "Excuse me, ma'am," and slinked away, clutching her books to her breast like a shield. "Clumsy, awkward, stupid," she muttered to herself. *Stay out of the woman's way.*

Up ahead, several classmates huddled around a bulletin board. "It looks like a challenging opportunity," a tall brunette observed.

Pausing for a moment, Ingrid read the posted information. A prestigious Chicago teachers' academy offered several grants to study their beginning English literature and continuing child psychology courses. A high grade achievement must be provided.

"Are you going to apply?" a demure student with pale green eyes asked her.

Taken aback, Ingrid mused, "It would be an advantage to study at such an institution. Chicago is a much bigger city than Minneapolis." She shrugged. "But what chance would I have?"

"As much as anyone else," the brunette suggested.

Ingrid considered the happy prospect of removing herself from the headmistress' constant harsh judgment. It would also take her away from Andreas and her family; although Andreas would be working up north for at least the next year. How often could he come to the city to see her? Probably only on holidays.

"Here, take one." The dark-haired student offered Ingrid an application form. Ingrid stared at the form. The cost of train fare to Chicago was included in the grant.

She slipped the paper into her satchel. Why not apply? And simply leave the rest to luck and fate.

With a singular purpose, Dagmar Eriksen strode into the newly built St. Paul train depot. She carried a hamper laden with luncheon fare: Gertrude's finest. The menu was sure to please Andreas. Dagmar had even tucked a bottle of her favorite Chablis in a corner of the hamper next to the apple strudel.

She couldn't wait to get him alone, then invite him to be her host at her upcoming twenty-first birthday party.

He had returned home the first of the week, having transferred to the St. Paul yard. A move that delighted her. She had longed for this for months. She planned to make herself indispensable to Andreas. Soon he would forget the farm girl ever existed.

Earlier this morning, her thoughts focused on her surprise rendezvous with Andreas, she had chosen a costume of burgundy faille that flattered her slender frame. Over the flounced walking skirt, her matching Roumanian cloak fell gracefully, its deep sleeves and hem edged in lustrous dark beaver.

Now angling her head in the reflection of a station window, Dagmar admired the curve of ostrich feather cascading from the crown of her dark red felt bonnet. Garnet drop earrings swayed winsomely at her neck, setting off her elaborate coiffure. She was becoming adept at fashioning her own hair.

Dagmar straightened her shoulders, her chin lifting a notch. She would make a fetching prize for Andreas. Their combined railroad shares would give them entree to St. Paul society.

Maneuvering among the groups of travelers, she sought out Andreas. She glanced into several of the cashiers' cages and up the platform. Several minutes passed and she began to feel foolish, having gone to all this trouble and not having an inkling as to where to look for him.

Ahead, a stocky young man eyed her from the side of the platform. She turned away. When he continued to stare, she lowered her lashes, bemused. He made her more aware of her fine attire and comely appearance. But she would not be sidetracked from her rendezvous.

Finally she spied her handsome stepbrother farther down the platform. He alighted from the engineer's cab behind a middle-aged gentleman who spoke to him in demonstrative gestures. The other man, dressed in a black suit, gave the appearance of one in authority.

Dagmar hesitated. As much as she wanted to rush up and surprise Andreas with her luncheon treasure, she did not want to disrupt his budding railroad career. They both had high stakes in that. She forced herself to be patient and wait for the opportune moment.

She stepped back next to a column and set the heavy hamper on the floor. When she glanced up, the young man had moved several feet closer on the platform and was openly appraising her. He wore no hat; his sandy-blond hair curled behind his ears to his collar. Were his eyes laughing at her?

The fellow was an outrageous flirt! She sent him a disapproving glance from beneath her long lashes and turned her back to him.

When she cocked her head to look once again for Andreas, he was walking straight toward her, still in conference with the middle-aged gentleman. His eyes settled upon her and he smiled in surprise.

"Dagmar, what are you doing here?"

Embarrassed at being caught off guard, Dagmar immediately took up the hamper. "I thought you would like some lunch," she explained, in a tone more businesslike than she had intended.

"How thoughtful. But let me introduce you to Mr. Delano, the superintendent of the St. Paul and Pacific." Andreas deferred to the gentleman at his side. "Mr. Delano, my stepsister, Miss Eriksen."

Delano gave an energetic nod to Dagmar, and she smiled respectfully at him. As she was about to offer some pleasantry to the superintendent, the fair-haired stranger moved up beside her. She was dumbfounded.

Andreas' gaze met the stranger's, and he smiled in recognition. "Thor! Sorry, I didn't see you there." Andreas extended his hand to the young man, then introduced him to Dagmar.

"This is my cousin, Thor Eriksen. He arrived last night from Detroit."

Thor gave a slight nod, his gaze hinting at amusement.

Dagmar blinked. "Your cousin?"

"Yes, my uncle Paul's son." Andreas patted Thor on his broad back. "I haven't seen Thor since we were boys and he taught me how to strip his neighbor's plum tree when he wasn't looking." The men laughed.

Thor shook Delano's hand, then faced Dagmar. His steady gaze lingered. Was he mocking her, or simply showing respect?

Dagmar observed that he stood two inches shorter than Andreas, with a muscular build and ruggedly handsome features. Hiding his thoughts, his hazel eyes were deep set and sly. His full lips curved up at the corners in a sensual way. Unlike Andreas, Thor did not possess immediate charm, but she would bet he had known many women in the biblical sense. She felt repulsed and drawn to him at the same time.

Andreas and Delano had fallen back into conversation as Dagmar made her observations. They started to walk toward the train yard. Remembering her objective, Dagmar moved to Andreas' side and slipped her gloved hand around his arm.

Raising up on tiptoe, she whispered into his ear, "You must taste the chicken. Gertrude basted it with her special herbs."

A mix of emotion crossed his features. "I wish I could, Dagmar. But Mr. Delano is training me to be his assistant. I'm afraid I can't break away."

At his rejection, Dagmar's temper flared. She balled her hands into fists at her hips. "Well—"

Seemingly indifferent to her wishes, Andreas led her over to a side office. His nervy cousin followed on their heels. "Why don't you and Thor enjoy Gertrude's culinary magic?"

His offered solution made Dagmar boil. She opened her mouth to respond negatively.

But Thor wagged his head up and down as if to assure Andreas his suggestion was indeed charitable.

Andreas ushered Dagmar and Thor into the semidark, miniscule office. "Looks like the ticket agent is out for lunch, so this should work fine for you."

"It's really too small," Dagmar fumed.

"Looks just right to me," Thor enthused.

Dagmar dropped the food hamper with a thud on a small desk in the middle of the room.

"This is the most difficult decision I've had to make all day," Andreas said, his gaze lingering on the hamper. "If you two aren't completely ravenous, maybe you'll leave me a drumstick." He leaned over and gave Dagmar a quick peck on her cheek, then backed out the door.

"Well, isn't that gratitude," Dagmar sputtered.

Thor went to stand beside the chair on the opposite side of the desk. He gestured for her to sit in the chair on her side. When she remained standing, fidgeting with the buttons on her cloak, he seated himself and casually observed her.

One tawny eyebrow quirked upward as he waited for her to make the next move. A cocky sort, he was! Waiting to pounce on the lunch she'd brought for Andreas. The idea rankled.

Dagmar started to remove her hat then decided not to. Her pulse beat strongly in her throat. She fumbled at the collar of her cloak.

Thor watched her, his eyes focused on her face. He made no offer to help her remove her cloak. Suddenly he stood and hung over the hamper toward Dagmar. "Won't you join me for lunch, Miss Eriksen?" His tone was mellow, inviting. "I would be honored."

Dagmar glared at him. The gall. He acted as if it was his lunch he was inviting her to share. "If you insist, Mr. Eriksen," she said, her voice sweet as arsenic.

She removed her cloak, draped it over the chair, and sat. For one long moment, silence filled the space between them. An herbal aroma escaped from the hamper, teasing Dagmar's nose and tempting her taste buds.

At last, she took off her gloves, laid them on the corner of the desk, and pried open the enticing hamper. Grudgingly she lifted out the plate of baked chicken wrapped inside a linen tablecloth. The remainder of the contents, Dagmar set on the unfolded cloth, including the wine. When she reached back inside the hamper for glasses, she found none. Damn! Gertrude would pay for this.

"The cook forgot to pack the wine glasses," Dagmar grumbled.

Thor took up a plump drumstick and tore off a large bite with his teeth. "We won't worry about the glasses," he said, chewing heartily. When he finished the drumstick and a roll, he popped the cork from the bottle and downed a generous swallow.

Afterward, he wiped the rim with his napkin and offered the bottle to Dagmar.

She shook her head. How uncouth he was. Expecting them to drink from the same bottle. Yet, what other choice was there? She finished her portion of chicken, savoring its succulent flavor, and delicately lifted the bottle to her lips. She felt his eyes study her as she covered the rim with her lips, tilted her head back, and let the tart-sweet liquid enter her mouth. But she misjudged her capacity, and some of the wine spilled over her chin and trickled down the front of her dress. Embarrassed, she dabbed at the sticky liquid with her napkin.

Thor's gaze remained fixed on her mouth, then slipped downward to her bodice. He licked his lips and stared at her as if she were the next morsel he would like to bite into.

In spite of herself, Dagmar felt a twinge at the base of her stomach and an unfamiliar ache between her legs. She was mesmerized by this strange new man. His eyes held hers and she could not look away. She felt the blood pumping through her veins and knew it was not from the Chablis.

After an uncomfortable moment, she managed to make light conversation. "Will you be staying in St. Paul, Mr. Eriksen?"

The deep-set hazel eyes continued to watch her, suggestively. "I hope to find a job on the railroad. It's what I've been doing for the last few years." He picked up another piece of chicken, a breast, and stroked it with his fingers. "And, please call me Thor." He smiled, his gaze caressing her.

Dagmar had trouble catching her breath. The office was stifling. "It's so stuffy in here." She rose and went to the half-open door. She took a deep breath, cursing her corset stays, and returned to her chair.

Thor had a voracious appetite. He made short work of the rest of the chicken, the rolls and asparagus, then ate half of the strudel as Dagmar munched on one piece. She wondered if this was the first meal he'd had in days. Nothing was left for Andreas but a small wedge of strudel.

Afterward, Thor walked with her to the buggy, carrying the near-empty hamper. Before he assisted her inside, he came close to her ear and said in a low voice, "You are an extremely beautiful woman, Dagmar. I take the liberty of calling you by your first name because I think we will be getting to know each other better in the near future." He stepped back, smiling confidently as she climbed into the buggy.

She was dismayed at his familiarity, yet flattered. No one had called her "beautiful" in recent days. She inclined her head toward him. "Thank you, Mr. Eriksen, for the compliment—but I believe your prediction is doubtful." She lifted her chin. "I choose my suitors."

Ignoring Dagmar's response, Thor leaned into the buggy and

took her gloved hand. As he dropped a kiss on her fingertips, he glanced up at her. "Then I hope you will choose me."

She withdrew her hand immediately to her lap.

Thor nodded to the driver, and the man snapped the reins over the horse's back.

When the buggy pulled away, Dagmar forced herself not to look back at the muscularly built young man standing in the train yard. She was surprised she didn't feel more disappointment in her missed rendezvous with Andreas. At the same time, she was glad she hadn't invited Thor to her birthday party next weekend. Only the sons of St. Paul society would be there. Thor might spoil everything. With his common manners and insatiable appetite, he would not be a proper guest.

CHAPTER ELEVEN

Dagmar couldn't believe her eyes. Alighting from the carriage in front of the house were Andreas and a young blonde woman, dressed in blue and carrying a white fur muff. Was this his farm girl? An uncontrollable anger erupted inside of her.

She stomped her foot on the hardwood floor. "How dare he bring her here to my birthday party!"

"Bring who, Miss Dagmar?" Gertrude, who had been buttoning Dagmar into her new velvet gown, craned her short neck to look out the second-story bedroom window.

Dagmar gasped in surprise at the third person she saw exiting the carriage. Thor! The cad—the interloper.

In a sudden rage, she whirled away from Gertrude. "This wasn't supposed to happen. This can't happen. I've planned my party so meticulously down to the very last detail. Now they're going to ruin it all—that farm cow and Andreas' shifty-eyed cousin!"

She rushed over to the bed and began pummeling the coverlet with her fists. " "No, no, no! All the available men on St. Paul's social register are invited. Even Papa Adolph's bank president is coming. This is a disaster!"

Gertrude only sent her a strange look, then stood at the window, watching the activity below. "It is only Master Andreas vit a young lady und gentleman."

Dagmar jerked upright, sputtering, "Gertrude—get away from the window. They'll see you!"

Shaking her head, Gertrude hustled over to her. "You should not get so upset yust before your party. Your face is all red. Let me finish helping vit your dress."

"No—no," Dagmar snapped. "I'll do it myself."

As Gertrude slipped out the door, Dagmar strutted to her dressing table and dabbed perfume on her wrist and between her breasts.

She fought to calm the hammering beat of her heart. She must focus on her future. The party intruders would not interfere with her plan to capture Andreas' attention and his love—to one day become his wife. And combine their inherited railroad shares. Nothing and no one would stop her.

Dagmar posed before the full-length cheval mirror, admiring her scarlet velvet gown. The shimmering fabric clung to every curve of her body, from the low-cut décolletage to the slope of her narrow hips. The diamond drop earrings and pendant, borrowed from her mother, glowed seductively in the gaslight from the chandelier.

At the threshold, Dagmar gave her bosom pads one last inspection, then entered the hall and glided toward the landing. On the surface, she appeared a lady—beneath her skin she felt like a wildcat.

Accepting Andreas' hand, Ingrid stepped down from the carriage and looked up at the grand house on Western Avenue. Three stories rose before her—an ivory mansion in a dream. Light beckoned from every room on the main floor and smoke spiraled from every chimney. Were there four?

She stared, completely awestruck. Nothing in her life had prepared her for this moment.

Andreas' cousin Thor came up beside her as the three started up the walk to the wide front porch. "Imagine you wouldn't mind being the mistress of this little abode, eh, missy?" he whispered into her ear.

Ingrid raised her eyebrows in surprise at Thor's remark, hoping Andreas had not heard. There was a coarse manner about him that she had sensed in only the time they had shared a carriage ride. Even his evening attire could not hide it.

Andreas smiled down at her as they approached the large, carved oak door, and he gave her arm a reassuring squeeze. The sparkle in his azure eyes made her knees go weak. But his warm countenance buoyed up her self-confidence. When the heavy front door swung open, Ingrid fairly floated into the house, her handsome escort at her side.

In the foyer, a uniformed gentleman accepted her wrap and rabbit fur muff, borrowed from Nettie, and also the men's coats and hats, then disappeared.

Music and gay voices drifted from the spacious parlor to her right. To her left was the dining room, where a long, lace-clothed table gleamed with china and crystal goblets. Across the foyer, a carpeted stairway climbed to the second floor, its banister adorned with lush green fir boughs tied with shimmering wide gold ribbons.

Descending the staircase was the most striking young woman Ingrid had ever seen. Tall and regal, the woman commanded one's attention; indeed, demanded it. Her brunette hair was swept up on top of her head; long side curls drifted to her naked shoulders. A diamond pendant accented the low neckline of her vibrant red gown. An aura of wealth, education, and self-pride surrounded her. She belonged to this house.

Her eyes stared straight into Ingrid's.

The young woman reached the bottom of the stairs and, dark eyes unwavering, strode directly up to Ingrid and Andreas.

Ingrid felt herself turn to jelly.

Andreas stepped forward and presented a package festooned with silver ribbons to the young woman. "Dagmar, you are enchanting. Happy birthday!" With natural charm, he bent over and kissed her extended hand, then cast a tender gaze at Ingrid.

At the touch of his lips, Dagmar's dark eyes glowed warmly. They fixed momentarily on his features as he looked away from her, then slid back to Ingrid. "And, who is this?" Dagmar asked in a cool voice before Andreas could make the introduction.

"This is Ingrid Johansson, the girl I've told you about from Eden Valley," Andreas said, his eyes shining. "Ingrid, this is my stepsister Dagmar."

Her face as stiff as a Halloween mask, Dagmar said, "Oh, the farm girl."

In that moment, Ingrid wished desperately she could have afforded a new gown for the occasion, that she had not worn the blue faille, the same dress she'd worn to the park with Andreas. When she had put it on, she'd felt very sentimental about the dress and its sweet memories. Now, face to face with this elegant creature, whose dark gaze bore into hers, she trembled with self-consciousness.

She managed a nervous "Happy birthday," while painfully aware that Andreas had said it wasn't necessary for her to bring a gift.

Dagmar smiled frigidly, appraising her as if she were a shabby country mouse.

A puzzled expression crossed Andreas' face when he looked from his stepsister to Ingrid, but he moved quickly over to Thor, who hung back watching the others. "Let's not leave Cousin Thor on the sidelines. He said he wouldn't miss your birthday, Dagmar."

Thor fished a package from inside his vest and handed it to Dagmar. "A small token," he offered. She accepted the gift, murmuring her thanks, and slipped it into the pocket of her overskirt.

Ingrid thought Thor observed Dagmar like an animal

contemplating fresh meat. He licked his lower lip. Would he begin to drool?

"Your age only adds to your beauty," Thor said, his lips forming a smile that resembled a smirk.

Dagmar regarded him with an expression as cool as a block of ice. "How very perceptive of you, Mr. Eriksen."

Ingrid had moved aside to let Thor greet the haughty hostess. The chilled reception provoked a queasy sensation in her stomach; she knew she must appear a foreign being in this world of comfort. Although she was falling in love with Andreas, she did not feel at ease with his people.

From the parlor, an older, sophisticated-looking woman approached. Her darkly expressive eyes bore such a resemblance to Dagmar's that Ingrid immediately assumed they were mother and daughter.

Andreas introduced her spontaneously, "Ingrid, I would like you to meet my stepmother, Emma Eriksen."

The older woman clasped Ingrid's hand and led her into the parlor. "Come join our guests, dear. And do tell me all about your family."

Dagmar wasted no time falling in beside Andreas and slipping her arm around his. She sashayed by his side, ignoring Thor following behind, his lips pulled in a taut line across his teeth.

In the parlor, decorated with greenery and glowing candelabrum, Dagmar planted herself in front of her stepbrother. "I've hardly managed to steal a minute of your time since you've been home, Andreas," she said, pouting. "Tell me all about your new position with the railroad."

He smiled politely at her. "Well, I'm the superintendent's assistant, which is a great challenge. But I thought you knew that already."

Dagmar moved a little closer to him. She hoped he would

comment on her gown, her seductive fragrance, or glance at the rise and fall of her tempting décolletage. Before she could press him further, she felt a hand on her arm and turned to see her mother at her side.

"Come and meet your guests, dear," she urged, "and let Andreas see to his guest."

Dagmar stepped back, feeling the muscles around her mouth twitch. Andreas excused himself. She watched him hurry over to the farm girl.

"What did you do that for, Mother?" she hissed into Emma's ear.

Her mother's eyes rounded. "Don't you want to cultivate those handsome young men you invited to your party?" She cocked her head in the direction of a far corner, where three single men stood stiffly, holding glasses of champagne and attempting conversation.

Dagmar jutted out her chin. "Oh, yes! Thank you for reminding me." She whirled away toward the young men, her curls bouncing on her shoulder. "You marvelous gentlemen," she trilled. "How grand that you've come to celebrate my birthday."

Dinner was served at nine o'clock in the dining room. It was none too soon as far as Ingrid was concerned. She'd been watching the clock for the last hour. When did these people eat? Her stomach growled so loudly she was afraid Andreas would hear it over their conversation.

At last, his uppity stepsister led everyone into the richly decorated dining room. At the table, Dagmar proceeded to seat everyone according to her whim, which brought an anxious frown to her mother's forehead. Ingrid was placed across the table and down from Andreas and Dagmar, between a young man with a terrible tic and a pigeon-breasted, gray-haired matron who chattered nonstop from the moment they were seated.

The first course was served, a seafood compote. Panic gripped Ingrid. Which fork should she use? Lord, she'd never seen so many eating utensils on one dinner table. She focused on the chatterbox's hands. When the woman picked up a tiny-pronged fork, so did Ingrid. If she could just make it through dinner without making a fool of herself.

To Ingrid's left, Dagmar monopolized her male guests with animated gestures, while leaning toward Andreas. Once, she actually pressed up against him. Several times, Ingrid caught Andreas' pained expression. That flirtatious stepsister of his. How could she be so self-serving? Birthday or no birthday.

Finally, a miniature woman in a black dress and starched white apron appeared at the threshold and cheerily announced, "Birtday cake and coffee vill be served in the parlor."

What a relief, Ingrid thought; now I can be with Andreas.

A lilting waltz greeted them as they entered the parlor. Ingrid's foot started to tap to the music. Sitting at the table for so long had made her eager to stretch her legs.

Andreas broke away from his stepsister and approached her. Her heart skipped a beat in anticipation of his touch and their first waltz.

"Andreas, wait!" Ingrid saw Dagmar move up behind him. "You must give me the first dance," she commanded, taking hold of his arm and swirling in front of him. "In honor of my birthday."

Glancing at Ingrid, he started to object. "But I—"

Dagmar thrust a sparkling goblet at Ingrid. "Here, have some champagne."

She fluttered her eyelashes sweetly at Andreas while reaching up on tiptoe to clamp her hand on his right shoulder.

Andreas sent Ingrid an apologetic smile.

Ingrid bristled. A long slow breath escaped between her teeth. As Andreas guided his stepsister across the polished hardwood floor, Ingrid clutched the goblet and stared at Dagmar's back. How annoying you are, she thought.

A masculine presence at her elbow made her jump. "Thor. You surprised me."

He also held a goblet of bubbly champagne and offered a toast. "To all worthy surprises."

Glad to get her mind and her eyes away from Dagmar and Andreas, she raised her glass and sipped. The champagne was pleasant to the taste.

Thor took a long drink from his glass. "Has the hostess stolen your dance partner?"

Ingrid forced a smile. "Only for the moment."

"They do make a handsome couple, don't they?"

Taken aback by his strange comment, Ingrid glanced questioningly at Thor. His brooding, deep-set eyes were unreadable. "Not if you consider them stepbrother and stepsister."

Thor arched one eyebrow. "They are that." His gaze focused on Dagmar, now being escorted back to where they stood.

"Cousin Thor," Andreas called. "Our birthday girl would love to take a turn around the floor with you, wouldn't you, Dagmar?" Before she could respond, Andreas steered her toward his cousin.

Thor looked down at Dagmar like a lynx ready to spring on a canary. He took her arm and swung her onto the parlor floor.

What plan of seduction hid behind those eyes? You are one sly fellow, Ingrid mused, finishing her champagne.

Andreas and Ingrid joined the other waltzing couples. He held her as close as good breeding would allow, his hand pressing warmly into her back. "I thought I would never get to hold you like this," Andreas murmured into her ear.

She tilted her head to look into the depths of his eyes. "I was beginning to wonder myself." She wished they could dance like this forever, floating away beyond the rooftops and up to the star-studded sky.

The music changed to a lively Scandinavian tune. Andreas whirled her about in a triple-time step. Her feet moved somewhere beneath her, but she couldn't tell what they were doing. Laughing, she threw her head back as the gaily lit room and guests swirled around her in a bright blur.

They danced faster and faster. She could hardly catch her breath. Then—one foot slipped out from under her and she wrenched away from Andreas. He held onto her arm, but it wasn't enough to stop her fall.

Something ripped, and Ingrid fell down on one knee, her skirts tangled around her. Someone cried out and the music stopped. Quickly Andreas helped her up. She attempted to straighten her dress. Her legs wobbled like a newborn calf.

Everyone was staring at her.

"Are you all right?" Andreas asked.

"I'm fine," she said, although her head swam as blood rushed to her face and her right ankle throbbed. Trying to focus, she looked down at the gaping shoulder seam. "But—my gown is torn."

Mrs. Eriksen rushed across the floor. "Oh dear, are you hurt? This terrible music is too loud and too fast for dancing."

Dagmar approached them. "What a shame, about your dress," she chirped, gazing at Ingrid's exposed shoulder.

"Come, dear. We'll have our housekeeper mend it." The older woman escorted Ingrid from the room as the musicians resumed their playing.

From the parlor, Dagmar watched Ingrid exit, the corners of her lips lifting in amusement. She became aware of another person standing behind her. "You put something in Miss Johansson's champagne, didn't you?" Thor accused in a low voice.

Her cheeks enflamed, she spun around to face him. "You are mistaken, Mr. Ericksen!" she retorted and stomped away.

Thor followed right behind her. Dagmar hurried across the front hall and entered the drawing room. She tried to close the door. But he held it open with one hand and moved his muscular frame inside the room. Then he swiftly shut the door and grabbed her bare shoulders, pinning her back against the wall.

She twisted within his grip, the bulk of his body allowing her no chance for escape. "Let me go, you beast!" she demanded through clenched teeth.

"If I am a beast, you are a bitch, my little Dagmar." Thor pressed himself closer still. Beneath his cologne she smelled his pungent body heat. He seemed to enjoy the way she writhed under him. His hands gripped her upper arms, his fingers bruising her flesh beneath her velvet sleeves. His eyes narrowed. "And I will tame you yet."

She flashed her eyes in anger at him. "No one will ever do that!"

Without further argument, Thor swept her to him and crushed her mouth beneath his. Dagmar struggled, trying to pull away. But when he continued kissing her, his hands rising to the sides of her breasts, she stopped. Although her mind fought against him, her body was overwhelmed with unfamiliar and maddening emotions.

As suddenly as Thor had captured Dagmar, he released her. He moved to the hearth before the crackling fireplace and turned to regard her. Dagmar's gaze followed him, her heart quaking in her breast.

"I think you want more from me, but you're afraid to admit it," he said, his hazel eyes staring into hers.

"There is nothing I want from you, Mr. Eriksen." With a

sharp glance, she opened the door and escaped from the room.

After the housekeeper mended her torn gown, Ingrid left the study in search of Andreas. He stood at the parlor threshold waiting for her.

His features brightened when he saw her. He took her hand as they met in the front hall. "Did Gertrude fix you up?"

"*Ja,*" she replied gratefully, still lightheaded from the champagne.

"Then let's have another dance." Andreas escorted her back into the warm light of the continuing party. "We'll take it easier this time," he added.

"A slow waltz," she suggested.

Soon after, Dagmar, appearing flushed, rushed into the room and began opening her gifts. She made appropriate expressions of surprise and delight. At last, Mrs. Eriksen announced that birthday cake would be served.

Dagmar elbowed her way through the guests, coming directly up to Ingrid and Andreas. "Andreas, come help me cut my cake," she coaxed, snaking her arm around his and smiling persuasively up at him.

Andreas sighed. With a brief expression of apology to Ingrid, he followed his stepsister toward the table.

Like a bull with a ring through its nose, Ingrid thought.

Somehow she swallowed a bite of the birthday cake, a sticky-sweet sponge creation with too much icing. When Dagmar and Thor danced by them, Dagmar grinning slyly over her shoulder at Andreas, Ingrid decided she'd had enough—of the self-centered hostess and the party.

When Andreas returned, she said, "I would like to leave now."

He nodded. "I'm ready. I'll get our coats."

After bidding goodnight to Mrs. Eriksen, they descended the front steps. Ingrid asked, "Where is Thor?"

"I don't know. He disappeared after we had the cake. And so did Dagmar."

"That sounds interesting." Now maybe her attentions would turn to Thor instead of Andreas.

Andreas helped her into the awaiting carriage and gave directions to the driver. "Guess Thor will have to find his own ride home," he said with a hint of humor and climbed in beside her.

Ingrid heard the driver call a command to the horse, a flick of the reins, and the crunch on gravel of the carriage wheels moving forward along the drive. She gazed out the side window, a cloak of melancholy folding in around her. Rather than glorying in the evening, the elegant dinner, the opportunity to meet Andreas' family, she felt a sense of doom. Beneath her light wool wrap, she shivered.

"You're cold," Andreas said, tucking the fur lap robe around her. "Does your ankle hurt?"

She shook her head. Her ankle had gone numb.

"I don't think you enjoyed the party."

Ingrid stiffened. "The party was beautiful. But, I don't think I made a very good impression."

"Of course you did. Emma said you were sweet and lovely."

"I am sure Dagmar does not feel that way. I think she is attracted to you."

He laughed. "That can't be. But, I know she is spirited and spoiled." His breath was warm on her face. "I wish it could have been our party with no one else invited."

"*Ja*," she said, slipping into her Swedish dialect. "I would like to be the hostess for your party." She smiled up at him.

His arms went around her, drawing her nearer. His lips brushed hers, his mustache soft and teasing. Nestled in his arms, Ingrid welcomed his kiss, parting her lips and letting the kiss deepen.

Too soon, the carriage delivered her across the river to the

Nelson's. Easily, she could have fallen asleep in the warmth and safety of Andreas' arms.

He sighed and released her. "I'm finding it more difficult to say goodnight to you each time we part."

She nodded and touched his cheek.

"If we were . . ." He sat up straighter. In the semidarkness of the carriage, she felt his gaze upon her. "If we were to marry—"

Her heart fluttered with an unwanted fear. "Andreas, I . . . cannot think of marriage. I am too young. To teach, I must finish school. My mater married very young and had babies too soon. She lost them . . ." She raised her gloved hand to her mouth in an effort to hold back the painful words.

Andreas took her hand in his. Its reassuring warmth penetrated her. "We don't need to talk about it now. I just wanted you to know how much you have come to mean to me."

She released a grateful sigh. Still, the catch in his voice bespoke regret. Leaning toward him, she pressed a tender kiss against his lips. "We are still young, Andreas. We have much time."

CHAPTER TWELVE

From behind the damask drapery in the parlor, Dagmar observed Andreas assist Ingrid into the awaiting carriage. Her blood roiled within her veins. Andreas and the clumsy farmer's daughter. How could he choose that simple peasant girl over her? It was incomprehensible.

"What an interesting turn of events." Thor's voice jarred her thoughts. "Looks like Andreas is leaving me afoot."

Dagmar whirled around to see Thor gazing over her shoulder, a bemused expression on his face.

"You don't seem very upset by his thoughtless behavior!" she snapped. "Why don't you run after them and tell them to wait?"

Thor raised his hands in a gesture of futility. "Sweet Dagmar. I'm afraid it's too late." His eyes laughed at her.

She half turned and glared out the window again at the shining black carriage that was gliding away into the night.

Thor moved closer to her, enclosing his large hand around her arm. The musky scent of him and the sudden strength of his touch made her go weak. "Maybe you need a man who can take your mind off your stepbrother."

Dagmar drew herself up to full measure, attempting an appearance of cool indifference. "What kind of man I need should not be of any consequence to you."

From the corner of her eye, she saw her mother across the room visiting with an aunt and uncle. Most of her guests had departed. "Where did that butler go with your coat?" She lifted the hem of her scarlet gown and swayed over the parlor threshold.

Thor followed her across the hall carpet. "Dagmar . . ."

She paused and swiveled back toward him. He stood regarding her, his gaze traveling from the flare of her gown over her hips, upward, to her padded bosom, to her face. She ignored his brazen eyes and kept her features guarded.

"What do you want from me?"

Thor moved his muscular frame toward her, pulling her into a darkened alcove. Despite her proper upbringing, this time she let him kiss her. One long sensuous kiss. A river of heat coursed all the way down to her toes. Then, fearing her mother might see them, she raised her hands to his chest and broke away. "I'd best be getting back to my guests."

Thor took hold of her upper arm. His touch and the kiss left her slightly breathless. "You will see me again," he said, his voice low timbered, confident.

Dagmar lifted her eyes to his and saw his desire, his strength, and his vulnerability. "Perhaps," she answered in a noncommittal tone.

Later, in her room, Dagmar found Thor's small gift in the pocket of her overskirt. She dismissed Gertrude with a brief thank you for her birthday dinner, saying she could prepare herself for bed.

The second the door closed behind the housekeeper, Dagmar carried the package over to the gas-lit lamp on her vanity. Tearing away the floral paper, she discovered a black lace glove. Only one glove? A tiny, folded note dropped from the paper.

She read Thor's masculine scrawl. *Come meet me, dearest Dagmar, and I will give you its mate. I will send a messenger later in the week. Thor.*

In the lamplight, Dagmar smiled to herself. For all his rough edges, Thor did pique her interest. And what better bait did she have to make Andreas jealous?

The heat Thor's kiss aroused within her lingered as she undressed and crawled between her silken sheets.

Dressed in a cranberry wool walking suit, Dagmar swished into the parlor.

Her mother glanced up from the *St. Paul Daily Globe.* "You look very fashionable, dear. That hat goes well with your suit."

"Thank you, Mother." Dagmar adjusted her feathered hat in front of a gilt-edged wall mirror. She had chosen her ensemble with care, assured that Andreas would admire it when she dropped in to visit him at the St. Paul rail yard.

"Come look at the nice article about your party in the social news," Emma invited.

Dagmar leaned over her shoulder, quickly scanning the article. "Too bad the hostess was abandoned before her party was over," she grumbled.

Her mother's forehead creased. "What do you mean 'abandoned'? There were several attractive gentlemen hovering around you, but they couldn't get past that forward cousin of Andreas'."

"At least Thor was concerned about my having a good time," Dagmar responded tartly.

"Where are you off to this afternoon?"

Dagmar glanced out the front window to the street. "As soon as Charles brings the carriage around, I'm going shopping. And then I might stop in at the train yard to see how Andreas is doing in his new position."

Emma rose to her slippered feet. "I have a wonderful idea. Why don't you come with me to my Ladies Altruistic Society meeting at two o'clock? It would do you good to become involved with a community charity . . . and it would take your mind off Andreas." The last bit of advice was given as she placed her hand on Dagmar's arm.

But Dagmar would have none of it. She shrugged away. "Why should I want to spend my time with a bunch of old hens?" She set a dark gaze on her mother. "And, why should I want to take my mind off Andreas? I think he fancies my attention."

Two spots of color flushed Emma's powdered cheeks. Her lower lip jutted out in firm resolution. "Dagmar, your—your infatuation with Andreas has gone on far too long. It simply has to stop."

Dagmar stood her ground, her hands straddling her hips. "You're being ridiculous, Mother."

Emma wagged her finger under Dagmar's nose. "He has a girlfriend now, a nice young lady—"

"A young lady indeed," Dagmar scoffed. "You mean a country cow!"

Emma retreated a step. "Why, she's a sweet girl. How can you be so contemptible?"

"Mother, you know as well as I that the girl he brought here was definitely not in our class. Andreas needs a woman of refinement, and I believe I am well suited for him."

Her mother's mouth dropped open. "You can't mean that, Dagmar. He is your stepbrother!"

"It doesn't bother me a whit. And very soon it won't bother Andreas either." Defiant, she strode to the front door, opened it, and dashed across the front porch.

"I'll make an adjustment to my will if you don't change your behavior!" Emma called after her.

Ignoring Emma's warning, Dagmar descended the steps to the awaiting carriage. Once she won over Andreas, her mother's desires wouldn't affect her.

A frigid gust of wind and newly falling snow whipped in around Emma as she watched the driver assist her daughter into the carriage. How had she managed to raise such a willful, self-serving young woman? A chill raced through her body like a lightning rod, prompting her to shut the heavy oak door.

Emma turned to see her plump housekeeper standing a ways down the hall.

"Vould you like a nice hot cup of tea, ma'am?" the woman asked cheerfully.

"No, thank you, Gertrude." She knew the housekeeper must have heard most of her unpleasant argument with Dagmar. She hoped the trusted servant would not spread the family's difficulties around the neighborhood. "I think I'll just go upstairs for a while."

The weight of Dagmar's words still unnerved Emma as she entered her room and closed the door. Although her daughter's judgment of the Johansson girl was cruel, Emma had to admit that she also was dubious about her background. How could a farm girl measure up to the social demands of Andreas' future wife? But then, she could never accept a marriage between Dagmar and her stepson.

Wouldn't local society call it "incest"? She quivered at the thought.

If only she could talk to Adolph about Dagmar's brash intent. He would have known how to handle her. How she missed his strength and stability.

She drew aside the lace curtain in front of the drafty window. Snow continued its steady downfall. The upcoming Thanksgiving weekend filled her with dread. How could she put on a cheerful face at the dinner table with the unsettled feelings between her and Dagmar?

She sighed miserably. She was not in the mood for a charity meeting today. What she needed was a nap.

Emma turned toward the bureau. What she needed first, though, was a little sip of the remedy.

CHAPTER THIRTEEN

Ingrid sat down on the feather bed and ripped open the letter addressed to her in Jens' familiar steady script. This was the first news she'd had from home in over a month. She ran her finger over the single sheet of paper before reading its contents. The handwriting blurred in front of her eyes, and she dabbed at them with her handkerchief.

Hungrily, she read Jens' letter.

Dear Ingrid,

The maple harvesting is finished now and we are well stocked for the winter. We all did our fair share, even Briget. She carried small buckets of the syrup and rode in the wagon, checking to see everything was done the way Papa told us. Always following on Marie Lisbet's apron strings.

Papa hired a new fellow from the Grinvold crew to help. It was not as much fun this year without you. Marie Lisbet gets too bossy.

Mama is busy making candles and knitting gifts for Christmas. She works into the night after we're in our beds, so she can keep them "a surprise." I worry sometimes; she works too long and gets too tired.

We miss you. Are you still liking your school?

Mama says she will make your favorite russin pudding for Christmas.

We will meet you at the Lake Park station next Friday.

Your brother,

Jens

Ingrid held the letter to her breast and sighed deeply. Through Jens' words she was transported back to the farm, memories flooding over her of autumn maple harvests, the rich smell of wet leaves under her shoes, the colors of the forest overhead—an umbrella of reds, golds, and umber. She could see the sticky brown sap flowing from a sugar maple trunk and taste its final amber sweetness on her tongue.

Nostalgia filled her and a sharp twinge of guilt twisted beneath her rib cage. She saw her mother's hands in the low light of the kerosene lamp making delicate stitches, knitting *jul* sweaters, hats, and mittens. Hands that worked from dawn to dusk.

I am sorry I have deserted you, Mama. I know I should be there to help. A tear slipped from behind Ingrid's lashes and trickled down her cheek.

Though her heart would miss sharing the holiday with Andreas, her place was with her family at Christmas. She brushed the tear away and folded the letter.

I am coming home for Christmas, Jens. I am coming home.

Andreas stood before the wall mirror in his upstairs bedroom fiddling with his best black silk necktie. He could never get the damn thing to sit just right. Through the tall window beside his carved mahogany bed, he could see swirls of falling snow. He glanced at his grandfather's clock, an Eriksen family heirloom, ticking somberly in the corner of the room. He took note of the time. Ten minutes of six.

Ingrid's train was due at the Minneapolis station in an hour. She had been gone for almost two weeks over Christmas, and it seemed more like two months. He'd thought of nothing and no one else since she left. The holidays had dragged miserably. Even holiday guests from the university and Gertrude's currant pudding, smothered in brandy sauce, had not appeased him.

He had sent Ingrid a dozen long-stemmed crimson roses just before she'd gone home to the Red River Valley. Every night in his cold bed, he had yearned to hold her close and explore her lovely body as he would a treasure map—kiss her plump, pink-tipped breasts, the slope of her small belly, and the moist, silken gold that he knew must lay below it.

Even now, when he thought about her, he had to steel himself from the arousal beginning beneath his trousers.

Tonight, after he picked her up at the station and whisked her away, they would dine by candlelight, where he would feast on her eyes as well as the gourmet fare. And wine—a special wine to celebrate her return.

Then he would invite her to the Upman's New Year's Eve soiree, a sumptuous dinner party this weekend hosted by his father's former employer, the president of the St. Paul First National Bank. Several of Adolph's railroad friends would be there.

The party would be an opportunity to introduce Ingrid to St. Paul society. The first of many parties. He imagined introducing her as "Mrs. Andreas Eriksen." The thought made color rise to his mirrored reflection, and he laughed to himself.

Wasn't it the male who was supposed to be skittish about matrimony? He welcomed the challenge of easing Ingrid's apprehension and changing her mind on an early wedding.

On New Year's Eve, he would propose to Ingrid.

"Andreas, you clumsy thing. Let me help you with your tie."

Andreas jolted out of his reverie. Beneath his nose, his stepsister had anchored herself, a mischievous glitter in her dark eyes as she raised fluttery hands to his throat.

"Dagmar," he complained, "don't you ever knock?" Her

entrance had been so silent, he hadn't even heard her step across the threshold.

Dagmar's eyes clouded beneath her black curling lashes, her thin fingers hanging in midair. "Well, your door was open."

He felt a momentary tug of remorse. The girl was only trying to be helpful. He shrugged and smiled down at her.

"And where are you off to tonight, looking so handsome and debonair?" Dagmar cooed as she retied his necktie. "Might you like some company?" She settled back on her heels, gazing up at him expectantly.

Enfolding her birdlike hands in his, Andreas answered in an apologetic tone. "I'm meeting Ingrid at the Minneapolis depot, and I'm late. But thank you for your assistance."

She withdrew her hands as if they had touched hot coals. A strange smile twisted her lips. "Oh, the farm girl." She cocked one eyebrow. "I must hurry now—I'm seeing Thor tonight."

Don't refer to Ingrid in that tone, he started to say, but Dagmar had already disappeared.

As he gave himself an appraising look in the wall mirror, Dagmar's door slammed shut down the hall. Picking up his evening gloves from the bureau, he muttered, "Moody little wench."

Andreas scanned the faces of holiday travelers along the platform, cursing himself for arriving only minutes before the train and having to search for a place to park his buggy in the crowded yard. It would be unforgivable if Ingrid had already gotten off the train and had to deal with her baggage alone. Pulling up the collar of his heavy wool coat, he braced against the frigid night air. What if she hadn't received his letter telling of his plan to meet her—and her aunt and uncle had met her instead? He frowned at the undulating crowd surrounding him.

Then he saw her. It felt as if someone had punched the air out of him.

She hurried toward him, her brimmed hat dipped to one side, setting off her upswept golden hair. A burgundy shawl, draped over her forest green frock, slid down over one shoulder as she walked. She carried two bags, no doubt filled with Christmas gifts from home. Her cheeks blushed a bright rose above her parted, heart-shaped lips.

He wanted to take her in his arms and lift her into the air—then cover her with kisses. To hell with this Victorian protocol. He strode quickly to her.

"Andreas!" she cried, smiling straight up into his face. Those sapphire eyes! For a moment, he was rendered speechless. She dropped her bags and let him take her gloved hands into his.

"Ingrid, what a lovely sight you are." Andreas breathed deeply, holding onto her small hands for one last moment. "Let's get the rest of your luggage," he said, stooping to retrieve her two bags, "and then I'll carry you away to the Nicollet and a fine dinner."

Her eyes sparkled in her merry face. "This is my luggage. I still have clothes at home, you know." She smiled. "Your invitation to dinner is gratefully accepted."

She hooked her arm through his as they stepped out into a world of careening snowflakes. She looked up at him. "I baked you a *plomme* cake. And, I cannot wait to tell you all about Christmas on the farm."

Plum cake and Ingrid. What more could he want?

As the carriage approached the multistoried English Tudor mansion, Ingrid glanced out the window and up at the lights glowing in every window. Anticipation of this grand New Year's Eve party mingled with her excitement and anxiety over her recent news.

Andreas nudged her gently. "You seem so quiet. Is something bothering you tonight?"

No way out; she had to tell him. "Two days ago, I received a letter." She could hardly contain her enthusiasm. "I have been awarded a grant to the Madison Women's Academy in Chicago."

"In Chicago?" he asked, his voice crestfallen.

"It was a total surprise, especially since I applied for it on a lark . . . A few months ago . . . after the headmistress threatened to expel me from St. Agnes."

Carriage wheels rolled over gravel, then came to a stop beneath the portico. "We can talk about it later," Andreas said. "First, let's enjoy the party."

She smiled up at him and squeezed his arm. "Oh, yes. I've been looking forward to this night with you."

A liveried coachman opened the carriage door, and Andreas stepped down and assisted her onto the expansive circular drive.

"You look beautiful," he whispered in her ear as they climbed the front steps.

"Thank you, so do you," she replied, admiring the jaunty angle of his silk top hat, the curve of his lower lip beneath his mustache. "I have the most handsome escort of the evening."

A magnificent wreath of blue spruce and miniature gold bells hung from the massive arched front door. In the middle of the door was a polished brass lion's head knocker, which Andreas lifted and banged loudly.

"Don't be nervous," he said, his blue eyes resuming their familiar twinkle.

"Tonight I feel like Cinderella going to the ball."

She wore the rose satin gown Aunt Hilda had redesigned for her. Nettie had swept Ingrid's hair up into a mass of curls on the top of her head, then fashioned cascading ringlets to her nape.

The front door swung open, and a butler took their wraps.

Andreas escorted her across a long, white-tiled foyer lined with potted palms toward a spacious parlor brimming with guests. Anticipation coursed through her. She so wanted to make a good impression on Andreas' friends and family.

Entering the parlor, Ingrid saw Mrs. Eriksen visiting with Dagmar and Thor. Her stomach tightened. What was it about Andreas' stepsister that made her feel like a mouse tiptoeing past a cat? Ever since Dagmar's birthday party, Ingrid had felt a wariness toward her.

Her unease did not dissipate when Andreas said, "Let's say hello to my family. I want them to see how wonderful you look."

Mrs. Eriksen exuded a heavy floral fragrance and gave Ingrid a sweet smile when they approached. Thor eyed her mysteriously from beneath his pronounced brows. Dagmar's lips parted, exposing small even teeth. "We thought you would still be home—milking cows on the farm."

Andreas sent Dagmar a critical glance. "Why should she milk cows when she can drink champagne?" He nodded to a servant carrying glasses of champagne on a silver tray.

Ingrid accepted one and toasted to a "Happy New Year" along with the rest. Andreas was a true gentleman, she thought, coming to her rescue by softening the sting of his stepsister's sharp tongue. She sipped the bubbly liquid, feeling more at ease and able to stand on her own.

Presently the Upmans joined them. After introductions, the host entreated, "Come, Andreas, there are some gentlemen you should meet."

Upman led him over to several men congregated by a blazing fireplace, leaving Ingrid to fend for herself.

She watched Andreas being introduced to the older men and knew a sense of pride. He merged into their circle with natural poise and assurance. He shook hands with a dynamic gentleman, tall and expressive, with receding dark hair, a full mustache and sideburns. Dressed impeccably, the man wore a tailored charcoal suit and a navy striped cravat at his starched collar.

"You look as if you'd like to have Andreas for dessert, Miss Johansson," Dagmar purred at her side.

Ingrid's face burned. "And why should that bother you . . . Miss Eriksen?"

Dagmar arched her condescending dark brows and strolled back to Thor's side.

For a stepsister, Ingrid thought Dagmar revealed an annoying obsession for Andreas. She avoided her cold penetrating gaze until a maid announced that dinner would be served.

At a table nearly the length of the dining room, and laden with ornate silver and translucent china, the guests were seated. Female voices surrounding Ingrid buzzed with observations on the latest eastern fashions.

Ingrid concentrated on her silverware. She remembered what procedure worked best at the Eriksen dinner—work from the outside inward to the plate. When in doubt observe your hostess, Andreas had suggested.

"The future of the Northwest hinges on the future of the St. Paul & Pacific," a voice suddenly boomed from the opposite side of the table. Over an elaborate centerpiece of holly and giant white chrysanthemums, Ingrid was again drawn to the striking man in the navy-striped cravat. The man's eyes glittered with enthusiasm, a magnetic aura radiating from him.

"Who is that fascinating gentleman?" Ingrid asked the quiet, brunette lady next to her.

The woman smiled, touching the pearls at her throat. "That's my husband, James Hill."

"Oh, yes," Ingrid responded, half to herself. Andreas had mentioned Mr. Hill often when he talked of the St. Paul & Pacific. "Isn't he the president of the St. Paul railroad?"

Mrs. Hill nodded. "It takes up a great deal of his time." A

faraway look came into her eyes, and Ingrid did not want to intrude by asking any further questions. She wondered, though, how long the railroad as well as her schooling would continue to separate her from Andreas.

To Ingrid's left, Mrs. Upman inquired, "Have you moved to the city recently, dear?"

"I am staying with my cousin in Minneapolis and attending St. Agnes Academy."

Mrs. Upman's winged gray brows pulled together in a tiny frown. "Is that a local school?"

All the ladies, including smug Dagmar Eriksen, stared at her.

"*Ja,* and it is a very good one." She heard her own voice quaver, her Swedish accent resounding in her ears. "I am studying the English and other subjects. I plan to be a schoolteacher."

Mrs. Upman smiled a patronizing smile. "I see. Well, we do need good teachers."

At the society woman's slight, heat climbed up Ingrid's neck. She lowered her gaze to her goblet. What did these women of wealth and privilege know about working outside their homes? Drawing herself up in her chair, she said, "We do need good teachers. I have just been awarded a grant to the Madison Academy in Chicago. I will feel honored to receive my certificate there."

The hostess's lips pursed, her brows inching higher. "Indeed."

But Dagmar's intent gaze, a mixture of surprise and satisfaction, gave Ingrid pause. Should she have kept her news just between Andreas and herself?

"Ingrid! There you are." Andreas exited the smoky den and strode down the hall toward her. There was a spring to his step and a mischievous glimmer in his eyes. "Where have you been?"

She gave a little shrug, not able to hide her irritation at his hasty departure after dinner to the camaraderie of cigars and brandy with his male companions. Left to fend for herself among the women, Ingrid had kept her composure and a smile on her face until her cheeks ached.

"I went to powder my nose." The acrid odor of cigar smoke clung to his suit. "I can smell where you've been."

Andreas laughed good-naturedly and took her arm. "Such a pretty nose you have, Miss Johansson."

He ushered her away from the busy parlor, along the hall and into a grand mahogany-paneled library. There in the low light, Andreas gathered her into his arms, drawing her flush against him. Through the satin of her gown, her breasts and belly molded into the length of his torso. He lowered his face to hers, the aroma of expensive brandy on his breath.

Ingrid gasped, his body heat sending her reeling. She raised her hands, feeling the taut muscles of his upper arms beneath his suit coat. "Someone might see us."

A chuckle started from low in his throat. "No one will see us, my darling Ingrid. And, after all, it is New Year's Eve."

She turned her face to glance through the partly open library door and was relieved to see no one in the hall. His closeness made her lightheaded, and the heat from his body stirred up forgotten embers deep within.

Andreas lifted her chin to gaze into her eyes. "You must know how much I care for you."

She looked into sparks of blue fire and her knees went weak. His hands slid down the back of her gown, sending chills up her spine. "You know you mean so much to me." She leaned against him, her face tilted up to his. His lips, warm and inviting, found hers.

When his tongue explored her lips, she moaned softly and opened her mouth as a budding flower opens to a bee. Their tongues met in longing. His hand ventured to her breast and began a circular caress. An intoxicating thrill radiated from his fingertips.

So loud was her own heartbeat in her ears, Ingrid failed to hear approaching footsteps on the tiled floor.

At the doorway, the female voice cut like a knife. "Andreas. Please excuse me."

Taken by surprise, Ingrid pulled away slightly from Andreas' embrace.

But he held onto her. "Dagmar . . . what is it?"

Color flamed across her high cheekbones as she strode into the room. Her glinting eyes focused on Andreas' face. "I don't know what to do. I must speak with you—now."

As if taking root in the thick Oriental carpet, Dagmar planted herself in front of them.

His features expressing annoyance, Andreas took Ingrid's hands in his. "I'm sorry . . . this should only take a moment. Please wait for me in the parlor."

He escorted her to the door, then left her standing alone in the cold empty hallway. She was stunned. What was so important that Dagmar had to rudely interrupt them? Why should she be dismissed like a child?

From the corner of her eye, Ingrid saw Andreas move across the Oriental carpet to his stepsister. The door was left ajar, providing her with a full view of the couple. She stepped back into the shadows, debating whether to retreat to the parlor or stay and observe. Curiosity won. She had to know what was behind Dagmar's untimely interruption.

"You know it's always been a problem . . ." Dagmar said, waving away Andreas' response. She moved deeper into the room near the faltering light from the fireplace.

Ingrid strained to hear their voices, but couldn't and dared not step closer to the doorway for fear of being seen.

Andreas said something, and Dagmar broke into tears. He

put his hand on her shoulder. She sagged against him, dabbing at her eyes with her handkerchief.

From the far end of the hall, Mr. Upman and another male guest emerged from the den, the host coughing loudly. Feeling like a peeping tom, Ingrid pressed herself against the wall, her heart sounding like a trip hammer. The two men swayed together into the parlor. She exhaled to her toes and looked back into the library.

Dagmar had not receded an inch. Andreas looked down at her and smiled. Before Ingrid could guess what was happening, Dagmar reached up on tiptoe, slipped her arms around Andreas' neck, and kissed him fully on the lips!

He stood stiffly. Then his hands moved to her shoulders.

Ingrid stared in disbelief. The little hussy! Shock waves surged through her. *Oh, Andreas. How could you?*

Having seen enough, she whirled and propelled herself down the hall toward the parlor, where voices lifted in lively accompaniment to a grand piano.

What seemed like an eternity later, Dagmar and Andreas crossed the parlor threshold to join the New Year's celebration. Andreas wore a stern expression, his face flushed. Dagmar glanced provocatively at Ingrid. Her smile was victorious.

Chapter Fourteen

In the carriage, en route home from the party, Andreas moved closer to Ingrid. His arm encircled her. She edged away and looked out the side window.

He inclined his head and touched his lips to her earlobe. She shrugged him off.

"Ingrid, something is bothering you and I—"

"*Some one* is bothering me. You know who it is."

His back straightened against the tufted seat cushions. "Yes, I know it's Dagmar." His arm remained encompassing her. "Her interruption this evening was rude, but it involved a family matter."

Ingrid gave a short, disbelieving laugh. She looked him in the eye, wrath rising in her throat. "Was it a family matter when she threw her arms around your neck and you kissed her?"

Andreas angled a few inches away. In the shadowed carriage, she could not make out his expression, but the impatience in his voice was clear. "I did not kiss her—she kissed me!" He moved still farther away. "You watched us?"

"Well, you left me standing just at the doorway . . . and, of course, I was curious about Dagmar's intentions."

Nodding in the affirmative, he said, "I can understand that."

Insistent, Ingrid prodded, "What was the 'family matter,' then?"

He exhaled deeply and raked his hand through his hair. "My stepsister is given to bouts of exaggeration. She would like me to believe that Emma is a hopeless alcoholic, unable to manage the railroad stocks she inherited from Dagmar's father's estate."

"Is that why she was crying?"

Andreas' reply surprised her. "Dagmar and Emma don't get along well. I think Dagmar is afraid she'll be cheated out of her full inheritance. Of course, there's nothing I can do about that."

Ingrid wasn't totally convinced. "So, you let her kiss you to make her feel better?"

"My darling Ingrid. I guess you didn't see me push her away as soon as I realized the game she was playing." He nuzzled her cheek. "You must believe me."

At the sincerity in his voice, Ingrid mellowed. Why shouldn't she believe him? He had never done anything to cause her mistrust. She touched gloved fingers to his face.

A street lamp reflected the light in Andreas' eyes. He moved closer, the length of his thigh grazing hers beneath the lap robe. "Let me remove your gloves and I'll warm your hands."

Obediently, she placed her hand in his. Andreas slid the glove down her fingers, carefully removing each fingered tip. He did the same to her other glove. A hush filled the interior of the carriage. Then he raised her right hand to his lips, tenderly kissing her palm, trailing his lips down each finger.

His lips were honey warm. A stirring started low in her belly. She licked her lips, her eyes following his movements. He lifted her left hand to his mouth, touching his tongue to the inside of her wrist.

The stirring within ignited and spread in fiery rivulets up her body. In the undulating shadows, his gaze lifted to hers. She saw a burning in the depths of his eyes.

Where this was leading, she could not be sure. It was a different kind of intimacy than what they had shared before.

"My beautiful Ingrid," he murmured, then drew his window curtain closed.

In a slow dance of desire, she let him remove her wrap. The lap robe tumbled to the carriage floor. She watched him remove his coat and necktie and unbutton his shirt collar, her breath quickening in her throat. His eyes never left her face.

Andreas took her in his arms, and she came eagerly. His lips softly met hers. With strokes from the tip of his tongue, he moistened her lips. He tasted like champagne. She returned his searching kisses with a seeking of her own. Her body melted into his.

"I love you so, Ingrid," he whispered into her hair. His lips caressed her neck. He raised his head a few inches. "I can feel your heartbeat in that tender vein beneath your ear."

In the gentle rocking of the carriage, she slid her arms around his shoulders and brought him closer. "My heart beats for you," she replied recklessly. Her fingers wandered through the curling hair at the nape of his neck.

His face nestled against her breast, his beard softly brushing her flesh. "I want you to be mine, always . . ."

Always? She could not make that commitment now. Her schooling came first. Her grant at the academy.

Urgently, Andreas began kissing the swell of her breasts above the ruffles of her gown. She moaned with pleasure, the grant suddenly all but forgotten. With deft fingers, he unbuttoned her bodice. His lips followed, pressing seductive kisses in their path.

The carriage rocked them in a sensual cradle. Ingrid closed her eyes, drifting into a near hypnotic euphoria.

Andreas slid the bodice of her dress down over her shoulders and untied the silken ribbon of her camisole. She sighed in eagerness. At last, her freed breasts welcomed his warm hands. He kissed them with growing passion, fondling one, then the other. When he took one nipple into his mouth, she heard herself purr like a kitten.

Raising one hand beneath her skirts, he caressed her buttocks through the thin silk of her drawers. When his fingers moved over her hip and glided onto her maiden's mound, a warm moistness came between her legs.

The hardness of his arousal through his trousers grew hot and enticing against her inner thigh. "Oh, Ingrid." His voice was husky with need. "Will you let me love you?"

A voice hovered somewhere beyond reasoning. What they were about to do could make babies. No. Not just this one time . . .

She trembled with longing. "I love you, Andreas. I want you."

In a dreamlike trance, Ingrid raised her hips. He eased her undergarment from her legs. Her breathing came in quick shallow breaths. His forehead glazed with perspiration, he lowered his face to hers.

"You will feel a slight pain, but it will be the best pain you've ever known," Andreas whispered and covered her mouth again with a long deep kiss.

Before she could respond that she would gladly take the pain to have him, that her trust in him was absolute, his fingers returned to that place of mystery between her legs. Her back arched beneath him. Nothing existed but the ecstasy of his touch. He lifted her to him, his cheek pressed hotly against hers. Willed by her body, her thighs parted and she felt the power of him enter her. She gasped in wonder then gave way to him.

He moved inside her, again and again, upward until she thought he could go no farther. She moaned on the steady, sweet tide of pain.

Rapidly, his breath came in short growls. When he began to withdraw his hardened member, her legs tightened around him. "Andreas . . . love me more," she begged.

He returned in rhythmic response, his thrusts igniting her like liquid fire. "Oh, God! Ingrid—" He lunged inside her in one last explosive spasm.

Her heart pounded so wildly in her breast she thought she too would explode. "Andreas!"

He gave a ragged sigh. "My love . . . you've just taken me to paradise."

Ingrid floated in a weightless euphoria.

Minutes later, as they lay together, sated, the lap robe retrieved and cocooning them, Andreas beseeched her, "Don't go to Chicago. Come share my life with me, now. If you wish, we can postpone having children. Marry me, Ingrid."

Suddenly she was too warm, his body upon hers too heavy. The sharp, steady beat of horses' hooves across the limestone Suspension Bridge jostled her to the moment.

"Andreas." She forced herself upright, pushed back the pain rising in her breast. "Please don't ask me to—to give up my dream. I must get my education first, before I marry. I will be more confident . . . and a better wife to you then."

"You can get your teaching certificate here at St. Agnes."

"No. A few months ago, after we were seen together in the park, the headmistress threatened to expel me. I know she will do it, given the least provocation. That is why I applied for the Chicago grant."

"You never told me you had applied."

The tone of his voice prompted a twinge of guilt. "I never thought I would get it. But now they have offered me the grant."

For a moment, an uncomfortable silence fell between them.

"There is so much I can give you," he insisted. "I could arrange for your admission to the university."

His offer caused an immediate resentment to well up in her. "I don't want you to arrange anything. My parents taught me to earn my own way. And, besides, the specialized classes are what I need."

"Ah, Ingrid." His voice fell. "Why must you be so . . .

independent?"

His disappointment was genuine, and she felt a deepening sense of regret that her good fortune would separate them. "It does not mean we won't be seeing each other again. You can visit me in Chicago."

She straightened her dress and attempted to smooth her coiffure back in place.

The pause before he answered seemed to last a lifetime. "Yes. I could do that."

Ingrid heard the jingle of harness as the carriage pulled up alongside the Nelson's front yard. Fear crept into her throat. "Well . . . are you not happy for me?"

Andreas shrugged into his coat, combed his fingers through mussed hair. "I'm happy that you are getting what you want, Ingrid."

She was stunned by his cool response, his obvious change of attitude from only moments ago. "I want you, too. But, I cannot have you and get my education at the same time."

As though he had not heard her, Andreas replied, "I'll see you in." He extended his hand and assisted her from the coach.

The winter night wind moaned; the naked limbs of an oak tree in the yard quivered in the pale moonlight. A shiver raced through her.

At the front door, Andreas bade her goodnight without a kiss.

"Nettie is accompanying me to our great aunt's house near the city," she remarked with growing anxiety. "We will take the evening train next Friday. If you would like to see me off—"

"The superintendent will be sending me up north soon to oversee more track extension," Andreas interrupted, his voice noncommittal. "I wish you well."

Her reaching out to touch his sleeve did not deter him from turning and striding down the walk.

Do not leave like this, Andreas. She stepped inside and closed the door. Pain reamed her heart. How had such strong desire brought them together, then abruptly torn them apart? She trailed her fingers across her belly.

For all she knew, their intimacy may have created a baby. She shuttered her fear. No, that fate would not, could not, come to her.

Fellow travelers hustled past Ingrid, bumping her elbow, knocking her shoulder, in their hurry to board the train leaving for Chicago.

Could one of them be Andreas? Surely he had received her letter with the train departure time. By now, wouldn't he have forgiven her for leaving? If he came to see her off, she would forgive him his cold indifference at their last parting. Then again, maybe he had already gone up north to work on the railroad.

"You have got Aunt Genna's address?" her aunt asked Nettie for the third time.

Nettie fluttered about next to Ingrid, picking at the lint on her shawl. "Yes, Mama, I have it right here in my bag."

Hilda's gaze shifted to Ingrid. "You have your money from Nels?"

"Yes, Aunt Hilda." Ingrid squeezed her aunt's plump arm. "Thank you both for paying me so generously, and for my room and board." She fished her handkerchief from her pocket and patted her misting eyes. These dear people had gone beyond their family obligation to her. She didn't know how she would ever repay them.

"You are welcome." Her aunt pushed them toward the train. "Aunt Genna will be pleased to see you girls. She's been after me for months to come stay with her after her heart attack. I will write to your parents, Ingrid," she shouted over the huffing of the engine.

"Thank you, Aunt Hilda. I will not forget your kindness. Uncle Nels, thank you, too," she called to her uncle who stood behind her aunt.

She scanned oncoming passengers, her chest tightening with anxiety. Might Andreas still come racing down the platform?

Nettie kissed Hilda and Nels and climbed aboard. "Don't worry, Mama, we will be fine," she said. "I will be back next week."

Ingrid lingered on the platform.

Other passengers filed behind them, pushing to board the train. The conductor walked past shouting, "Boarrrd!"

Her vision clouded with tears, Ingrid caught hold of the handrail, then hurried into the car.

Nettie motioned from midway up the aisle. She had found a vacant seat for two and was saving the window space for Ingrid.

"You are so thoughtful, Nettie." She slid across the upholstered cushion and glanced morosely out to the platform. The whistle gave its shrill blast. They waved to Hilda and Nels, disappearing from view as the train eased away down the tracks.

"I cannot believe Andreas didn't come to see you off," Nettie complained.

Ingrid dabbed at her eyes with her handkerchief. "I cannot either."

Nettie patted her hand. "Maybe he . . . maybe his boss had him work late."

"It doesn't matter." If Andreas hadn't cared enough to come, it really didn't matter.

She leaned back against the seat. What lay ahead in Chicago? For Nettie it was only a visit. The stakes were high for Ingrid: she was leaving everything and everyone she loved behind. Deep inside, a hot little poker pricked her stomach. But her resolve was strong. She would earn her teaching certificate and return to Minneapolis.

A few minutes later, Nettie pulled a package from the hamper beneath her seat. "Mama couldn't let us go hungry," she said, handing Ingrid a paper-wrapped scone.

Ingrid had little appetite. Her mind drifted far away. What were Andreas' thoughts when he'd read her farewell note? Had he decided he never wanted to see her again? Was he sharing a hearty meal with Dagmar at this hour? Perhaps a glass of wine? An achy lump formed in her throat. She folded the wrapping around the scone and stuck it in her bag.

Deciding to stretch their legs, they ventured two cars down to the dining car. Ingrid ordered hot tea; Nettie asked for coffee with cream.

"Wish we could have ordered an entree from the menu," Nettie mused, clearly spellbound by the fancy dinner menu on the table. "Oysters on the half shell . . . lamb cutlets, *à la Soubise*. Don't they sound exotic?" Then her expression wilted. "Even if the price is seventy-five cents."

Observing the well-dressed travelers at the next table, Ingrid shifted in her wicker chair. She set her jaw determinedly. "We will have that and all the champagne we want—some day."

Nettie's eyebrows flew up like a sparrow's wings. "Ummm, that will be a fine day."

Back in their seat, Ingrid attempted to settle in for the night. She wished she could get to the few books packed in her trunk. The smell of cigar smoke irritated her sinuses and her stomach; the woman behind her had a rasping cough. Next to Ingrid, her head cushioned against a pillow made of one of her shawls, Nettie's eyelids closed.

Ingrid gazed into the blackness outside. She wondered what Chicago would be like. It was definitely larger than Minneapolis. How many students would attend the new academy? And, how difficult would her classes be?

Had she made the right decision?

She fought her longing for Andreas. His strong arms. His lips, tender on hers. The soft brush of his mustache. A tear trickled down her cheek. She swiped it away with the back of her hand.

She remembered New Year's Eve and their intimacy on the way home. The enticing smell of brandy on Andreas' breath. The fragrant leather upholstery beneath them. "Ingrid," he had implored, "Will you let me love you?"

She had trembled with longing. "I want you, Andreas."

"Be mine, always," he had whispered.

It all seemed a dream. Had it really happened?

Might she already be carrying his child? Her monthly wasn't due for several weeks. A wave of fear shuddered through her. Her knowledge of intimacy was so limited. She chastised herself for not learning more of these things before she made love with Andreas. Having a baby now would only jeopardize her future and Andreas'. She must force herself not to think of him.

Nettie mumbled something in her sleep.

Ingrid coaxed her cape up around her neck and attempted to get comfortable. If only someone would stoke the fire in the potbellied stove at the front of the car. She rubbed her hands together for warmth, then slid them beneath her cape.

Banishing all fearful thoughts, she squeezed her eyes shut. Let her new life in Chicago come quickly.

Andreas returned home late Friday afternoon in a frustrated mood. Just as he'd dreaded, the superintendent had given him an immediate assignment. Overseeing repair work on the tracks outside of St. Cloud. He did not look forward to going. In these freezing January days, the job would be difficult, the crew overworked and peevish.

And, to add to his doldrums, Ingrid was leaving for Chicago tonight.

In the foyer, he hung his coat on the hall stand. His glance slid to the silver tray on the side table. It was empty. Damn! He had half-hoped for a letter or message from Ingrid by now, including her forwarding address. Perhaps adding a brief expression of regret . . .

But then, why should he expect any word from her? He had made a horse's ass of himself when she'd revealed her grant. Although disgusted with himself, he would just have to live with his stubbornness. There still might be a sliver of a chance that she would forego the grant and stay here where she belonged.

He hated to see her go yet was powerless to stop her.

The hall clock revealed the quarter hour. Just enough time for a bath before the family's six o'clock supper.

"Gertrude," he called from the stairs, "Would you please draw water for a bath," then hurried upstairs. A good hot bath should dull the anxiety that had become an unwelcome companion.

In the steaming tub, he envisioned Ingrid, her tawny hair tumbling like a golden waterfall around her naked white shoulders. And felt an instant yearning for her. Already he missed her voice, her touch, the country-fresh aura of her.

"She won't like Chicago," he said out loud. "It's too big and windy, and dirty. She'll be back."

Later as he descended the stairs, he saw his stepsister seeming to hover over the hall table. She wore a bottle-green dress, its tightly fitted sleeves giving her the appearance of a spider.

He cleared his throat, not really desiring to engage her in conversation. She had avoided speaking to him the last several nights, since he'd approached her about Emma and her drinking problem—the "urgent matter" they had discussed in the Upman's library on New Year's Eve. A condition he believed

155

was largely fabricated. Dagmar had offered no real proof of her accusation.

Now she glanced up, a haughty glimmer in her dark eyes. "Andreas . . . it appears you have a letter."

"Oh?" he answered, surprised. "There wasn't any mail when I got home this afternoon."

Without responding, she lowered her long lashes and glided into the parlor, where he heard Emma's bright greeting.

He strode to the table where the letter lay on the silver tray and recognized Ingrid's handwriting. Why hadn't he seen it when he arrived home? The letter was postmarked Tuesday.

Tuesday. It should have arrived by yesterday. He tore open the seal and scanned the first sentence. Blood pounded at his temples.

I will be taking the early evening train for Chicago, departing at seven o'clock. I so look forward to seeing you, holding you, if only once more before I leave.

The hall clock chimed the hour. Six o'clock. If he hurried, he could ready a carriage and just make the rail station before seven.

Dagmar stood at the parlor threshold. "Andreas, are you joining us for dinner?"

He jerked his head in her direction. "I'm afraid not. Did Ingrid's letter arrive earlier?"

Her devilish dark eyes widened. "Ingrid's letter? I wouldn't know."

He sensed she was lying. But there was no time, no time to grab her and shake her bony shoulders until she revealed the truth. "We'll talk about this later," he vowed before shrugging into his coat and rushing out the front door.

The clop-clop, clop-clop of the horse's hooves on the icy street resounded in his ears. Andreas snapped the reins over the animal's back, urging him to a full gallop down the hill. The night wind stung his cheeks and the frigid air chilled his lungs.

Was she already gone? If she was there, would she even speak to him for arriving so late? His heart thumped faster, his thoughts tumbling ahead of one another.

Had Dagmar held back the letter until it was nearly too late for him to see Ingrid off on the train? Was she that mean-spirited? He had never given her the least reason to encourage such deceit.

His stomach tightening like a twisted rope, he neared the St. Paul station. Lord, let her be there.

Pulling in the horse a short way from the depot, he tied the reins and jumped from the rig. In several long strides, he reached the front entrance. The hands on the station clock read three minutes past seven.

Maybe it wasn't too late. He might still have time. He sprinted toward the departure platform. If only he could reach her, take her in his arms, touch her silken hair once more.

Ahead, the train whistle blared.

His vision blurred; his breath rasped in his dry throat.

He came to a skidding halt on the platform. And swallowed hard. Only the acrid smell of engine smoke and scattered pedestrians lingered as the train eased out of the station.

She was gone.

How could he have been such a fool to think he could have arrived on time? His shoulders sagging with regret, Andreas returned to his carriage. He must write Ingrid a letter of apology. Try to make things right again.

But would she even open it? Most likely she'd tear it up.

The night air shrouded him in its black, icy grip as he turned the horse back toward home.

CHAPTER FIFTEEN

Ingrid stepped down from the train Saturday morning, her body aching from having to lie in a cramped position, her eyes gritty with sleep. The Chicago, Milwaukee & St. Paul depot bustled with activity as she followed Nettie to the baggage area. They had managed to get a cup of bitter coffee from the dining car earlier and eaten one of Aunt Hilda's cinnamon buns, but her stomach longed for something more.

Outside on the street, the sky was overcast and a brisk wind blew an unpleasant smell from the Chicago River. Their porter found them a hack pulled by a pair of old plugs whose days were numbered. She was relieved to climb inside the well-worn carriage. Just get us to where we're going, she prayed.

When they were at last on their way, Ingrid looked out the window to the east and gaped in amazement. Rising in the distance beyond the river, buildings of unimaginable heights stretched for miles.

"That is Chicago?" She sucked in a huge breath. "It must be five times the size of Minneapolis!"

Nettie chuckled. "Bigger and windier—and much more exciting!"

Ingrid blinked in awe. This city was a giant, waiting to swallow her in one gulp.

As if reading her thoughts, Nettie squeezed her arm. "It won't be so big once you learn your way around."

The carriage rocked along the wide streets, heading farther

away from downtown. "What is Aunt Genna like?" Ingrid asked presently.

Nettie frowned. "I haven't seen her in a few years, but I do remember she likes to visit. She is short and bent over and she walks with a cane. Her husband died when I was little. They had no children, so I imagine she must be lonely."

Lonely. Ingrid gazed at the passing street activity from the window. She had never had a chance to be lonely. But in the days ahead, without her family and Andreas nearby, loneliness might be a new companion.

A few blocks later, the horses rounded a corner and the elderly driver announced, "This here's Crystal Street." He brought the team to a jerky stop in front of a small frame house, similar to its neighbors.

The once-white paint had faded to a dreary gray. The curtains were drawn tight in the front window. "It looks kind of forlorn," Ingrid said, observing the drooping eaves. With resignation, she trailed Nettie across some flagstones to the front door.

Lifting a weathered brass knocker, Nettie tapped three times and stood back. Promptly, the narrow door opened; a small pale woman with strained eyes appeared on the threshold. "Are you the nieces from up north?"

"Yes." Nettie introduced herself and Ingrid. "We're here to visit our great-aunt Genna."

The woman drew back into the depths of the house. "Come in, then." She glanced beyond them at the carriage driver staggering under the weight of Ingrid's trunk as he weaved toward them. Shaking her head distractedly, she beckoned him to enter and pointed to a corner of the front room where he set the trunk.

Nettie paid the man, and he wheezed his way out the door.

A feeling of discomfort pervaded the still house. It smelled of dust and stale air, of windows too long latched against the outside, of medications, of sickness.

The woman did not offer an introduction nor an explanation of Aunt Genna's whereabouts. She observed Ingrid and Nettie with melancholy eyes for a moment, then gestured behind them to the parlor. "I think you both should sit down."

Ingrid's stomach gave an odd twist as she and her cousin walked over creaking floorboards and sat themselves in horsehair-covered chairs. The woman positioned herself between them, her hands fumbling nervously in her pocket for her handkerchief.

"It's my sad duty to inform you that your great-aunt passed away in her sleep last night."

Nettie gasped and stared in disbelief at the pale featured woman. Ingrid gripped the arms of the chair, her throat constricting.

"Poor thing. She'd been ill for some time, but she was so excited to have you both come to stay with her." The woman made an attempt to smile. "I'm sorry, I should introduce m'self—I'm Mrs. Hogan. I live next door. Your auntie and I was both widows." Mrs. Hogan wiped her narrow nose and continued. "I found her early this mornin'. She always fetched in her milk bottle to feed her cat. But the bottle was still sittin' on her stoop around eight o'clock. When I knocked and went in, I found her—already cold in her bed."

Tears spilled from Nettie's eyes. "I wish we'd arrived sooner."

Mrs. Hogan's nod was sympathetic. "The doctor just left with the . . . with her remains. He said her heart gave out." She fixed her strained eyes on them. "Guess you girls will want to make plans for her funeral, now that you're here."

With a grief-stricken expression, Nettie turned and looked at Ingrid. Stunned, Ingrid closed her eyes, fighting the sinking feeling in the pit of her stomach. Without a roof over her head, she soon would be forced out on the streets—alone in this foreign city.

Wednesday morning, the day after Aunt Genna's funeral, Ingrid waited for Nettie outside the telegraph office on Washington Street.

They had taken a horse car downtown, Nettie fretting all the way. "Here it is, the middle of the week—and we're just sending Mama and Papa the news about poor Aunt Genna." Her gloved hands had worriedly played with the frog closings on her brown cape.

"We haven't had the time, or the opportunity." Ingrid had sighed. "Everything happened so fast—the funeral arrangements, Uncle Eric's arrival." Their aunt's younger brother, a balding gentleman with chronic catarrh, had wasted no time taking inventory of the estate.

Now Ingrid paced the boardwalk, her two main priorities prodding her. She had to find a place to stay near the downtown area where the academy was located, and she had to find a job to pay for her rent.

Nettie finally emerged from the telegraph office, and they continued up Washington to State Street. Ingrid's mouth fell open in amazement as they rounded the corner. "These buildings are over six stories high!"

"The city's been entirely rebuilt since the Great Fire, six years ago," Nettie said.

Craning her neck to look upward at the towering structures, Ingrid almost fell off the boardwalk.

Nettie caught her by the arm just in time to save her from falling into the path of an oncoming horse car. "Watch where you're going, girl."

They walked amidst the throng of teeming humanity and gazed wishfully into shop windows. In front of one dress shop,

Nettie pulled Ingrid aside. "I'll go in with you while you apply for a position. When the manager asks, tell him you've had a year's experience in sales."

Ingrid rolled her eyes upward in jest. Before she had a chance to straighten her hat, Nettie pushed her in the front door.

In a few minutes, they were back on the street. Ingrid fumed. "That was humiliating! I hope they are not all so snobbish."

Nettie patted her shoulder. "Don't let yourself get discouraged." She glanced toward the end of the block. "Let's go have a bite of lunch."

On the way, Ingrid stopped to purchase a copy of the *Tribune* from a newsboy. They found a busy tearoom and waited to be seated. "A 'bite' is probably all we can afford in this city," Ingrid commented as a young, red-haired waitress showed them to a small table near the window.

She wore a white frilled cap that barely confined snippets of curls around her face. "And what would you ladies be havin' today?" the girl asked in a lilting brogue. They ordered sandwiches and coffee. The waitress smiled and scurried off, her flame-fettered mane bouncing halfway down her back.

Ingrid gazed out the window at a couple strolling by. Her stomach lurched. Andreas! She focused on the young man's face: blue eyes, strong nose, short beard. But it was not Andreas' face. Pain stabbed at her heart. She already missed him more than she wanted to admit. Pulling herself away from her fantasies, she concentrated on the "rooms to let" section in the back pages of the paper.

"I am so anxious to see the Madison Academy," Ingrid enthused after their light lunch. She grabbed Nettie's arm. "Let's find it first."

Farther down State Street, they rounded the corner and there it was—a stately, brick five-story building. Young women climbed the front stairs. A sense of expectancy filled her. "They are hurrying to get to their afternoon classes."

Nettie smiled, tucking a stray curl inside her plumed hat. "One of them will be you, very soon."

Then they set out in search of a room for Ingrid. Leaving State Street, they headed east toward the river. The first two hotels advertised were close to the downtown area. One was fully occupied and the other far too expensive.

"Ten dollars a week?" Ingrid exclaimed incredulously. "That is a fortune!"

Nettie agreed. "The boardinghouses farther away from the business district will be less."

Four blocks later, on Quincy Avenue, Ingrid noticed a prim, four-story boardinghouse with a vacancy sign posted on the wrought-iron fence in front.

Ingrid knocked at the door of the first-floor apartment and waited expectantly. The smell of frying fish drifted from under the door. Presently a round-faced woman, wiping her hands on her long apron, answered the door. When she saw the two of them, she said, "I've only got a single room available. If you want a double . . ."

"It would be for me," Ingrid said.

"Well, I'll be right with you, soon as I take off my apron."

The available single room was small but neat. Located on the second floor, it overlooked the street. Its furnishings consisted of a narrow bed, a chair, a potbellied stove, and a writing desk in the corner. Although sparse, Ingrid liked the room; it fit her state of mind. Solitary and of a single purpose.

The landlady made a sweeping gesture with her plump hand. "Just five dollars a week—paid in advance. No pets and no guests."

Ingrid frowned. The twenty dollars pinned to her bodice would not go far. Could she afford it, without first finding employment?

The woman pushed a stringy lock of hair back into its bun. "Well?"

Ingrid looked at Nettie doubtfully, then back to the landlady. "Sorry to take up your time. I think I will have to wait."

"At least you can stay at Aunt Genna's for the time being," Nettie consoled as they strolled back to State Street. At the corner of Monroe and State, the Palmer House rose majestically before them. "My, that is a grand hotel," Nettie sighed. "I would think only presidents and kings stay there."

Bursting with curiosity, Ingrid said, "Let us go look inside."

Nettie stiffened. "We are not properly dressed . . ."

Ingrid took her by the arm and escorted her into the hotel. Once inside, they gawked up at the gargantuan two-story rotunda, a shimmering chandelier hanging from its center.

"Look at those naked women!" Ingrid exclaimed.

Nettie's face turned crimson. "Where?"

"Up there. Next to the columns." Ingrid stared in fascination.

"Those are statues," Nettie sputtered indignantly. "I thought you meant, well, real women."

Ingrid laughed heartily at her own mischievous deception. "Let's look down this grand hall." Before Nettie could stop her, off she went.

Two men in elegant black evening suits and top hats walked from a great room ahead. As they approached, they tipped their hats. Ingrid smiled and blushed. After the men passed, the fragrance of their costly colognes floated on the air.

Ingrid poked her head around the corner, and her eyes grew wide. Before her stretched an immense salon, a gilded fountain rising from its center. Along each wall as far as she could see were floor-to-ceiling mirrors lit by sparkling gaslights. Gentlemen hovered over white-caped patrons reclining in lounge chairs, cutting their hair and shaving their beards. Masculine voices combined with the precise sounds of a hundred pair of scissors snipping.

Ingrid gave a low whistle. "This is no ordinary barber shop."

Nettie stared downward beyond her feet. "The floor is inlaid with silver dollars!"

"This is probably where Andreas would have his hair cut—if he came to Chicago," Ingrid remarked.

One of the barbers glanced over at them and winked. "Hello, ladies. Are you new in town?" asked the gentleman whose hair he was trimming, and the two men chortled.

Ingrid and Nettie looked at each other, chagrined. They quickly backed out into the carpeted hall and scurried out a side door.

On the next block, they found a lively German restaurant and ordered dinner. The jovial proprietor poured them each a glass of ale "on the house." They dined on franks and hot potato salad. And toasted to their futures: to Nettie's return to St. Agnes and to Ingrid's success at Madison Academy and finding a well-paying job.

After their toast, Ingrid grew somber. When she lifted her gaze from her plate, she saw Nettie's eyes glisten with tears. Ingrid choked back a sudden sadness. "This is the last dinner we will have together for some time."

"I wish you were coming back home with me tomorrow," Nettie said in a low voice.

Ingrid's throat constricted. "You will see," she said hopefully, "it won't be long before you will be visiting me—and we'll go shopping and buy expensive new hats—covered with ostrich feathers!"

That night, lying in Aunt Genna's small bed next to Nettie, Ingrid drifted in and out of restless dreams. Some time later, Nettie's light snoring awakened her. She opened her eyes to see a narrow shaft of moonlight slanting through a crack in the pulled curtains.

She shivered in the dark. This was to be her new city, far away from the ones she loved. Back in Minneapolis on a Friday night, she used to nestle in Andreas' arms, returning home in his carriage.

Even now, she could feel his lips warm against her brow, hear his voice: "Ingrid, you are so beautiful to me . . ."

Would she ever see him again?

On the windy railway platform, Ingrid watched Nettie attempt to straighten her bonnet. An errant dove-gray plume defied her efforts, flipping forward into her line of vision. She drew her cape closer over her full bosom and focused concerned eyes on Ingrid.

"You will take good care of yourself," she said, lapsing into her familiar Scandinavian accent.

Ingrid nodded bravely, thinking of Nettie as an older doting sister, not her cousin of the same age. "I will," she said. "Don't worry. I will be starting classes next week. And a good job should come along soon."

The engine gave a jolting huff, its stack shooting bursts of gray steam upward into a clouded sky.

Ingrid took a breath and almost choked on the cinder-filled air. "Tell Aunt Hilda I will write when I can . . ." Her voice faltered as tears pricked the back of her eyelids.

She reached out for Nettie's gloved hands, holding them tightly, and could not find more words.

"I know you will do well in school," Nettie said. "But come home if things do not work out here." She wrapped herself around Ingrid in a tight bear hug.

Ingrid smelled Nettie's rosewater cologne, felt the warmth of her familiar plump arms beneath the wooly cape, and feared her heart would break. Hot tears trickled over her cheeks down onto Nettie's shoulder.

The train whistle gave its last warning blast. A conductor approached, his features sympathetic but firm. "Time to board, ladies." He touched his cap and continued down the platform.

Nettie withdrew slowly from the hug. She made an effort to smile at Ingrid and hiccupped. "Goodbye, for now." She picked up her large bag, turned and boarded the train.

Ingrid watched her with misty eyes. In that moment, she wanted to run after Nettie, to return to her former life, Andreas, and the academy. But it was too late.

She had made her decision, and she must abide by it.

Nettie waved soberly from a window seat.

"Goodbye, dear cousin," Ingrid whispered.

With a mighty hiss, the giant wheels lunged forward. The Chicago, Milwaukee & St. Paul rumbled away down the tracks. Ingrid's gaze followed the train from the front of its wide cowcatcher, back along the many passenger cars. Colors and faces blended together in one swiftly-moving blur.

Alone on the platform, Ingrid stood watching until the caboose was a mere smudge in the distance.

Chapter Sixteen

Entering through the rear of the house, Andreas strode up the carpeted hallway. From the dining room, he heard Emma and Dagmar's voices over the soft clink of silverware on china.

Still agitated after missing Ingrid at the station, he removed his hat and coat and hung them on the hall tree. Dagmar's meaningless chatter set his jaw on edge. He suspected her deceit, and he wanted some answers.

Emma appeared on the dining room threshold. "Andreas, we didn't expect you back. Dagmar said you were going to the station."

"I did, but I missed the train."

Dagmar appeared at her mother's side. "What a shame," she said, her mouth turning downward into a pout.

Emma shook her head. "You've missed your dinner."

Andreas shrugged. "I'll find something in the kitchen."

As Dagmar stepped into the hallway, he clasped her arm. "I think we need to have a talk," he said, aware of the sharp edge to his voice. "If you will excuse us please, Emma."

His stepmother's brows lifted slightly. "Of course. I was just retiring to my room to read. Goodnight." She swished away toward the staircase.

Dagmar flapped her long dark lashes coquettishly. "Andreas, I always enjoy a private moment with you."

Andreas observed her affected mannerism, the way she cocked her head in his direction. How inane she was, and unpredictable. How really unlike her mother except in physical resemblance. Where Emma evoked a certain breeding and vulnerability, Dagmar projected willfulness and a defiance of all that was gentle in a woman. He realized how much he disliked her.

"Shall we go into the study?"

The corners of her thin lips lifted upward. "I have something to do first. I'll meet you there shortly." With a mock bow, she turned and ascended the stairs.

Andreas entered the study. Fighting an edgy anticipation of his confrontation with Dagmar, he went to the liquor cabinet and poured a whiskey. And slugged back half the glass. The liquor burned all the way down his throat to his belly.

Although he did not relish accusing his stepsister of a deceitful act, he wanted some answers.

Fifteen minutes later, Dagmar had not yet appeared. He'd finished his drink. What was keeping her? Frustrated, he went upstairs to look for her.

Her door was closed. He knocked on it and heard her soft reply. "Yes . . . come in."

Andreas paused. He'd never entered his stepsister's bedroom before, and the idea of it went against propriety. After a moment, he turned the brass knob and opened the door. The room was dimly lit by gaslights above Dagmar's bed. He couldn't see her.

"Dagmar?" he called.

To the side of the room, he heard a whispering sound like the fluttering of a bird wing. He stuck his head a short way over the threshold and looked to the left.

Dagmar sat at her dressing table in front of an oval, gilt-framed mirror. She was brushing her hair, which fell in dark waves halfway down her back. She had changed from her woolen frock into a shimmery Oriental wrapper.

169

He was instantly taken aback and irritated.

Seeing his reflection in the mirror, her eyes grew brighter and her hand stopped brushing in mid-stroke. "Andreas. Come in." She made no effort to turn and face him.

Disgruntled, he stepped a few feet into the room. "I want to speak with you," he said tersely.

Dagmar swiveled on her tufted chair, her wrapper falling loosely open above her breasts. "Oh, yes," she replied coyly, as if she'd forgotten. "Well, I was going to take a bath, but you may talk to me now."

Indecision gripped him. His first impulse was to tell her she could damn well take her bath and slam the door behind him. But he wanted to question her about Ingrid's letter. So, he stayed rooted on the spot and swallowed his indignation.

He straightened his shoulders. "I wanted to ask if you had seen Ingrid's letter before this evening?"

Dagmar, so nonchalant a moment before, shot up from the chair to her slippered feet and came across the room to him. Her dark eyes flared. "What do you mean—before this evening?"

"Did you see or come in contact with her letter earlier?"

"What a silly question." She exhaled impatiently. "Why would I care about her letter?"

His eyes narrowed in disbelief. "The letter was postmarked Tuesday. It should have arrived yesterday."

"What difference does it make?"

"Because the letter arrived so late, I missed her train departure," he ground out.

Dagmar smirked. "Forget her, Andreas. If she cared about you, she wouldn't go off to Chicago. You might as well accept it."

Andreas clamped his jaw, attempting to shield himself from what truth might lie behind her needle-sharp words.

In that vulnerable moment Dagmar moved closer to him, slipping her thin hands up over his shirt front.

Looking down at her, he saw the silk wrapper draped over the small pointed mounds of her breasts, smelled her strong tangy perfume. She was naked beneath the thin fabric—a wily ploy to weaken his resolve to know the truth. He jerked her hands away.

But she reached clammy fingers up to his face and pulled it downward to hers. Dark and smoldering, her eyes beckoned him from beneath ebony lashes. "You and I are so drawn together, Andreas," she entreated. "Why don't you give in?" Her tongue, a sharp little serpent's tongue, darted from between her lips and glided around their circumference.

Andreas grasped her by her narrow shoulders and shook her. "Come to your senses, Dagmar. You're behaving like a common street whore!" Disgusted, he pushed her away. "What if Emma should hear you?"

Dagmar threw back her head, exposing pebble-size teeth, and let out a derisive laugh. "Mother's tucked away for the night with her little flask. She can't hear a thing." She flung herself at him, snarling, "Now, get out of my room. I won't let you call me names that are only fit for that farm cow!"

Andreas caught her by the arm. "You little witch! You wouldn't know a lady if you saw one." Roughly he tossed her back across the bed. "Never refer to Ingrid that way again!"

Her thick hair flying out wildly around her head, Dagmar's features twisted into a sneer as she fell. "To hell with you!"

Without a backward glance, Andreas strode to the door and yanked it shut behind him with such force the sound echoed down the hall. He didn't care if it woke the dead.

Blood pounding at his temples, he reached the landing and thundered down the stairs. God, he'd come within a hair's breadth of strangling the deceitful little bitch! His nerves were stretched to the limit. And he was damned if he knew more now than he did before entering her room.

If he hadn't made that last promise to his father to take care of Emma and Dagmar, he would move out of the house tonight. A stiff drink and male camaraderie was what he needed. He would find both downtown at McNally's Pub.

Andreas grabbed his hat and coat from the hall stand and escaped out the front door.

After seeing Nettie off, Ingrid left the train station and walked toward the Madison Street Bridge. Across the Chicago River loomed the downtown skyline. It was time to focus her energy on finding part-time employment.

But on the street the temperature had dropped, and a brisk wind from the river cut sharply through Ingrid's cape. Large wet snowflakes slapped at her cheeks as she stood indecisively in the middle of the boardwalk, holding onto her billowing skirts.

A barrage of snow pellets, like a snarling wolf, hurled around corners of buildings, chasing pedestrians in all directions. "Job hunting will have to wait," she muttered into the wind.

She hopped aboard a horse car and headed to the outskirts of the city and Aunt Genna's house.

Once back in the cold empty house, she quickly shed her hat and cape and began pitching coal from the corner scuttle into the potbellied stove. She lit the stove and waited for the fire inside to create some heat, then set a cup and saucer on a hot plate. She found a tin of tea from home on a cupboard shelf.

On the shelf, she also found three of Aunt Hilda's two-day-old buns wrapped in a napkin. Chewing on one, Ingrid stared out the window onto the snowy deserted street and sipped her lukewarm tea.

A chill of loneliness washed over her, the new feeling foreign and frightening. How had she decided to actually come here? At least at the Nelson's she'd been surrounded by family— people who loved her. Now she was a stranger in another world, dependent entirely on herself to survive.

Well, if she had accepted the grant too hastily, she must learn to live with her decision.

Seeing her trunk in the corner gave her momentary comfort. Drawn to it like a magnet, she dropped to her knees on the rag rug, reached out, and lifted its lid. The faint aroma of cedar escaped. Grandpa Johansson had made this trunk when he was a young married man and had brought it and his two sons to America after his wife died.

Ingrid leaned over the trunk, surveying its contents. *The Godey's Lady's Book* that she and Nettie used to dream over while brushing each other's hair at bedtime lay on the top. She leafed through the first few pages, smiling at the memories. The book flopped open at the middle and a dried bouquet fell to the floor. Ingrid's heart leaped.

The tussie-mussie!

She picked up the stiff arrangement still held in a lacy paper doily. Enfolded by baby's breath, white azalea blended with the central pink rose. Holding the bouquet to her nose, she caught barely a hint of its original scent.

She closed her eyes, remembering that special night. Andreas, so tall and groomed in his black satin evening suit and top hat; she, a princess, wearing Nettie's rose damask gown to attend the theater. He had kissed her tenderly in his carriage and told her how beautiful she was.

Releasing a deep sigh, Ingrid pressed the faded tussie-mussie to her breast. Tears slipped from beneath her lashes and dripped onto the bouquet. "Oh, Andreas," she whispered. "What has happened to our love?"

★ ★ ★ ★ ★

Monday morning, Ingrid made her way down State Street to Madison Avenue. Despite a difficult weekend, fraught with nostalgia and longing for Andreas, she had awakened with renewed resolve. Her anticipation was high, if not as girlishly expectant as it had been when she had entered St. Agnes. Today, she would register for the new semester at Madison Academy.

The new day held promise, scattered clouds giving way to a glimpse of sun after a weekend of intermittent snow. Icicles clung to gables and frost rimmed windows in opaque crystal frames. Her teeth chattered in spite of the two pair of woolen stockings she wore beneath her petticoats.

Friendly faces greeted her at the registrar's desk. She was pleased to find a wider range of classes offered here, such as the psychology of child development, which she added to her curriculum. Classes would begin the following Monday.

A search for employment came next. As she approached downtown Chicago, the buildings grew taller. She felt giddy just gazing up at them. The opportunities for young women in this city must be unlimited.

She came to a fine hotel where a smartly uniformed doorman stood at attention. Venturing inside, she was impressed at the doorman's quick move to hold the door open for her. A reputable hotel would be an intriguing place to work, with guests arriving each day from places all over the country.

Ingrid caught sight of herself in a lobby mirror and paused to straighten her hat and smooth her skirt. Approaching the registration desk, she observed three men working behind it. All men. Her stomach did a nervous flip-flop.

"Could I assist you, miss?" one of the men asked.

"Yes. I would like to apply for employment," she said, her mouth dry.

"There might be an opening for a maid. You'll have to inquire

174

in the manager's office."

"A maid?" She pictured herself changing dirty linens and mopping floors for a pittance. No, that did not fit her plan, as vague as her plan was at the moment.

The man looked at her impatiently. "Well, miss?"

Ingrid replied, "Thank you, no." She turned abruptly and swished out the front door.

On the next block, green letters on a store window advertised "Chicago Dry Goods." Now this was more to her liking. She took a confident breath and entered.

The interior was narrow, stretching back to a second-story loft, and smelled of stale air. She moved around customers in the crowded aisle, past barrels of merchandise. Clerks behind the counters appeared frazzled and unkempt. The well-designed floor plan and sense of professionalism in her uncle Nels' store was not evident here.

She was directed to the back, where a balding man hunched over a desk piled with boxes and papers. A cigar stub protruded from the side of his mouth. Absorbed in his work, the man ignored her until she cleared her throat.

He scowled, peering up at her through thick-lensed glasses. His black eyes, twice magnified behind the lenses, penetrated Ingrid's thin coat of self-confidence. Spitting into a cuspidor, he asked gruffly, "What d'you want?"

Quivering beneath her skirts, her throat irritated by the smoke of his cigar, she opened her mouth to answer.

"Sir, we're out of those horse-hair bustles," a harried female clerk interjected at Ingrid's elbow.

The store manager sprung up from his stool and began flailing his arms. "Check the order! Check the order!" he shouted. "That's your job, you half-wit. Don't bother me."

"Yes, sir," the woman replied in a high reedy voice. She cowered away like a whipped animal.

Ingrid shuddered. She could never work for a man who treated his employees like beasts. Before those hostile black eyes could penetrate her again, she backed down the aisle. The sound of the bullying store manager's harangue followed her halfway to the front door.

Tying her bonnet more securely under her chin, Ingrid bowed her head into the wind. An icy gust blew under her skirts. She gathered her cape tightly around her and hurried along.

Up ahead was the café where she and Nettie had taken lunch the past week. Fantasizing about a hot cup of tea and fresh scones, Ingrid entered the cozy establishment and waited to be seated.

"Afternoon, miss," a young waitress greeted her in a melodious brogue. "Come with me."

Recognizing the flame-haired waitress from her past visit, Ingrid followed her to a small table. "And what will be pleasin' ye, miss?" The girl's eyes sparkled a mischievous green above the smattering of freckles across her cheeks and nose.

Ingrid smiled, warming to her friendly face, and croaked out her order, her throat raw from breathing in the morning's chill air.

The waitress frowned. "Hmm. Have ye got a wee bit of a cold?" She cocked her head thoughtfully. "Not to worry. I'll bring ye some herb tea that will take care of that." She spun away with a flip of her long red mane cascading from her white frilly cap.

Ingrid's order arrived shortly: warm cinnamon rolls and a fragrant pot of tea. She finished everything down to the last crumb. When the waitress brought her bill to the table, she gathered her courage. "You've been so helpful, miss. Could I ask you one more favor?"

The girl leaned toward her curiously. "Yes, miss?"

"I've just moved here from Minneapolis and I need an

afternoon job. I clerked in my uncle's dry goods store, so I have some experience." Ingrid licked her lower lip and looked up expectantly.

The girl cocked her head to one side and placed a hand to her slim hip. After a moment, a light came into her eyes. "Of course—Madame Larousse! She has a fine hat shop just up the block—she makes beautiful hats. I always send me fancy customers there."

Ingrid's demeanor brightened. "She might need a saleslady?"

"Aye, she might." The waitress's green eyes shone with encouragement. "Best ye go up there right away. And tell her Megan Killeen sent ye."

CHAPTER SEVENTEEN

Ingrid hurried up State Street until she came to Madame Larousse's Millinery Boutique. She entered and found herself in an intimate front room vibrating with female chatter. Several patrons of obvious wealth, dressed in fine frocks and draped in fur-trimmed capes, milled about trying on a variety of hats.

Hats for all occasions lined shelves along the side walls in the small but inviting interior. Ingrid imagined a European parlor. A powder-blue sofa and cream-colored side chairs were arranged in a comfortable seating area. A small table stood before the sofa, a pastel floral carpet beneath its curved legs. Atop the table sat a silver tea service and a silver tray filled with the tiniest iced cakes Ingrid had ever seen. Her mouth watered.

A vibrant, dark-haired woman with an undulating voice that fluctuated up and down like musical notes fluttered among the women. Madame Larousse, she suspected.

Preceded by her vivacious perfume, the woman approached. Observing bouncy side curls, a black mole above painted crimson lips, and discerning dark eyes, Ingrid was aware of her own country girl appearance.

With courage, she introduced herself. "I am seeking half-time employment." Then added, "Megan Killeen suggested you might have a position open."

The arched eyebrows raised an inch. "Ah, *c'est possible.*"

She lifted a finger to the side of her rouged cheek, just above the bold black mole. "Do you have the sales experience, mademoiselle?"

"Oh, yes, Madame. I have done sales work in my uncle's dry goods store in Minneapolis."

"But *chapeaux*—the hats. Do you sell the hats?"

Ingrid smiled at Madame's strange English, then answered, "No, but I could learn."

Madame waved her arms, her bejeweled fingers sparkling in the air. "You will come to the back room and we will talk."

Ingrid followed her to the rear of the shop and was offered a chair at a small table.

"I do need a smart shop girl," Madame said. She poured a strong, aromatic liquid from a china coffee pot into two cups and sat down across from Ingrid. "The other mademoiselle desert me. She run off to marry a sailor—and leave me with all of the patrons screaming for *les chapeaux, les chapeaux!*" The woman sighed wearily. "I have only two hands—I work so fast."

"I could help you sew, Madame," Ingrid offered. "At least I could do some of the trimmings, ribbons and such. My mater . . . my mother taught me how to make my own clothes."

Madame's dark eyebrows arched. *"Oui?"* She rose from her chair, her saucy curls bouncing above her lace collar. "Come show me, *cheri.*"

With nimble fingers, Ingrid sewed ribbon trim on two hats while Madame Larousse waited on a client in the front room. When Madame returned, she eyed Ingrid's work critically. Ingrid folded her hands in her lap, waiting for Madame's response and wishing her palms would stop perspiring.

Madame Larousse set the last hat on a shelf next to several others. *"Tres bon.* You will work for me, Mademoiselle Johansson?"

Ingrid fairly leaped to her feet. "Oh, yes, Madame. When do I start?"

"Immediatement! But we will never tell the patrons that you

do some of the sewing." She winked in conspiracy. "They must think it is only my creation."

Ingrid worked until six o'clock when the shop closed, then caught a horse car back to Aunt Genna's house. By the time she arrived there, she was famished and exhausted. But she had a job! Madame Larousse would pay her three dollars for working six half days a week. Now she could set aside money for a room, even if it meant getting by on only one meal a day.

The small mailbox held several advertisements . . . and a letter from Andreas! Her heart jumped for joy. She tore it open. The familiar masculine script read:

My dear Ingrid,

I must apologize for not seeing you off at the train station the night of your departure. I didn't receive your letter in time. I should have been in touch with you long before, but my stubborn nature interfered with better judgment. I hated to let you go, although I realize now how important furthering your education is to you.

Can you forgive me? Please say you will.

I will write again, informing you when I can break away from my railroad obligations. My strongest wish is to be with you.

As ever,
Andreas

Ingrid held the letter to her breast, overwhelming feelings of love and longing flooding through her. *Come soon, Andreas.*

While seated at a writing desk the next morning, responding to Andreas' letter, an ache tugged at her from deep inside her belly. Her monthly had arrived. There would be no baby.

She sighed in relief. Yet why did the answer to her prayer leave her with such an empty feeling?

The following Friday, after her first week of classes, Ingrid stopped by the tearoom on her way to work. "Megan, you were right. Madame Larousse hired me as her new assistant."

"Ah, me girl, that's cheery news!" Megan exclaimed. "I'm so glad to hear it."

"But, Megan," she implored, steering her friend to a side pantry. "I need to find a room immediately! The bank notified me that Aunt Genna's house has been sold. The buyers are from upstate, and they are anxious to move in."

Megan's green eyes went wide for a moment, then twinkled with enthusiasm. "I've got an idea. Why don't ye come out with me and me brother Paddy, after work tonight? We're goin' to a neighborhood pub. Maybe we can find ye a place to stay."

"Besides, it'll be lots of fun—and a pretty girl like you should have some."

"I . . . don't know." Ingrid hesitated. "A pub? I have never been to one."

Megan pushed back her errant red curls. "We'll pick ye up. Paddy's drivin' his friend's wagon tonight." She stood with her freckled hands placed staunchly on her hips. "Ye'll like it, I know ye will. And, we can celebrate yer new job!"

At quarter-past six, Ingrid heard voices out on the street. She peeked through the millinery's front window and saw Megan Killeen and a stocky-built young man sitting in a delivery wagon. "Come join us, Ingrid Johansson. We're on our way to a party!" the young man called in a husky voice.

It was hardly proper, but Ingrid wasted no time in throwing on her wrap and skipping out the door.

O'Riley's Pub reverberated with the sounds of lively banter, melodic notes from a corner piano, scraping chairs and clinking mugs. The tables were full and the lights low. Smells of dust and ale and close bodies reached Ingrid's nose as she followed

Megan and Paddy Killeen inside.

They found several vacant chairs at a side table and squeezed in among the group seated there. Megan seemed to know everyone and introduced Ingrid as her new "Swedish friend," which drew smiles and handshakes all around.

Ingrid blushed and nodded a greeting to the sea of faces.

"Paddy's getting us a round of drinks," Megan announced.

When her dusky-haired brother returned, he set three large, foaming mugs of dark ale in front of the girls. "Drink up!" he said, raising his mug to his wide-lipped mouth and taking a mighty gulp.

Ingrid raised her mug and tried to imitate Paddy. The dark ale flowed over her tongue, the taste of it strong and somewhat bitter. What ale missed her mouth dribbled down her chin and onto the front of her dress.

Megan hooted with glee. "Take it slow at first—yer not supposed to keep up with the men."

Acutely embarrassed, Ingrid dabbed at her dress with her handkerchief. Through the crowd she saw a lanky, dark-haired young man climb onto a small stage next to the piano. He began to sing a lilting folk song that captured all ears.

"What a beautiful voice," Ingrid whispered to Megan in pleasant surprise.

"Aye. 'Tis Sean Slattery." Megan smiled. "Handsome he is and a cocky fellow. Paddy knows him."

Then a grizzly, bearded little man pulled a stool up next to the piano and lit into his fiddle with a vengeance.

"An Irish jig it is!" Megan winked brashly at the fellow seated next to her. Off they went to kick up their heels in the center of the room, along with several other bawdy couples.

Ingrid watched in fascination. The memory of her first dance at the Lindstrom wedding party flashed before her. Andreas had taught her the steps to the polka, and then she'd trounced on his toes. Looking up into those eyes as clear a blue as the morning lake, she'd known she was in trouble. How bittersweet to remember it now.

She grew increasingly more uncomfortable, alone at the long table except for Paddy seated at the far end. He seemed content in a solitary way to drain his mug and stare out at the undulating crowd with guarded eyes.

"Good evenin' to ye, lovely lady. Would ye like to be dancin'?"

At the sound of a friendly male voice, Ingrid glanced upward. Her gaze swept over a dark forest velvet vest that accented a pair of flirtatious emerald eyes beneath wavy black hair. It was the pub singer. Handsome as a fox. Flushing with self-conscious heat, she smiled, but declined. She knew nothing of this strange jig they were doing.

The dark-haired singer returned to the small stage, and the mood of his wistful Irish ballad filled the smoky pub.

> I'll take you home again, Kathleen,
> across the ocean wild and wide,
> where your heart has ever been,
> Since first you were my bonny bride.
> Your voice is sad when-e'er you speak,
> And tears be-dim your loving eyes.

Later, when Megan flounced back to the table, flushed and rosy as a school girl and mopping the perspiration from her brow, Ingrid had slumped forward, her chin cupped in her hands. "What is this? Ain't ye been dancin', girl?"

Ingrid shook her head miserably. "Guess I am just homesick. The song made me think of someone . . . a young man from St. Paul."

"Come now. Forget the bloke. We're here to be havin' some

fun tonight."

Megan took a hearty swig from her mug, sashayed up to the piano player, and drew the singer to her side. They spoke for a moment, then he nodded. The singer glanced back to the table and flashed a bright smile toward Ingrid.

"Sean's going to sing some Irish tunes and we're all goin' to sing along!" Megan announced excitedly, brushing her fiery mane away from her face.

On stage, the black-haired crooner spread his arms and sent forth the first line of another Irish ballad, "My Wild Irish Rose." Before long all the revelers in the pub joined in, raising their voices in camaraderie, clasping each other arm in arm around the scattered tables. Ingrid swayed in time to the winsome melody, her heart a little less lonesome.

Warmed by ale and companionship, Ingrid leaned over and spoke into Megan's ear. "I want to thank you for inviting me tonight, Megan. You and Paddy have taken the lonely hours away."

"Ah, 'tis nothin', me girl—and will ye stop callin' me Megan?" She leaned back against Ingrid's shoulder, a slight slur to her speech. "Me friends call me Meg."

Ingrid laughed. "Meg it is."

"And while we're on the subject o' friends." Meg pondered a moment. "Why don't ye move in with Paddy and me? We'd have a bloody good time. And you'd only have to pay a third o' the rent."

Ingrid was stunned. "Oh, Meg. I don't know . . . would it be proper?"

"Proper, me eye!" Meg scoffed. " 'Tis proper as can be. We've got plenty o' room—if ye don't mind sharin' me bed. Paddy sleeps in the front room."

Ingrid blinked. Share the rent? She might even save a few dollars to buy textbooks.

Meg observed Ingrid's thoughtful expression. "Then it meets with yer approval?" She jumped up and grabbed her nearby brother by the sleeve. "Come, Paddy. We've got a fine proposition to make."

Before Ingrid could interrupt, Meg blurted out her plan. "Wouldn't it be a great idea to have Ingrid stay with us? She could share me room and we could split the rent three ways instead of two."

Paddy's gaze, red-rimmed from drink above his pug nose, slid from girl to girl. He half-grinned. "Yer always bringin' home stray puppies."

Ingrid winced. "I don't think of myself as a 'stray puppy.' "

Paddy's eyes softened. "Might not be such a bad idea." He looked at Ingrid and smiled. " 'Tis okay by me."

"Well, Ingrid." Meg lifted her near empty mug. "Will ye seal it with a toast?"

Ingrid's tired mind whirled with thoughts. The Killeens had taken her under their wings when she had no one else. They offered her a chance to support herself. There was no need to find a solitary room. And, Meg and Paddy were fun. "Let's seal it with a toast," she said, lifting her mug.

Dagmar entered the Northridge Hotel in lower St. Paul and breezed across the small lobby toward the main floor café. Her head held high, she looked neither right nor left, her eyes focused directly ahead. Her thoughts spun about like bees whose hive has been disturbed: agitated, angered, and ready to sting.

Andreas was the object of her wrath. He must pay for the way he had treated her over the farm cow's stupid letter. And, his nasty rejection of her affections.

Through the black net veil of her hat, she saw Thor sitting at a corner table. Sandy hair combed back in waves. Full mustache lifting in a suggestion of a smile. Familiar navy broadcloth suit fitting snuggly across muscular shoulders.

He stood when she approached the table.

"Thor," she said with a measured degree of coolness and extended her gloved hand. If he couldn't provide assistance, no one could.

"Dagmar." He reached out and lifted her hand to his lips, brushing them across her fingers. "It's been too long since you've graced my path."

"Spare me the gentleman act," she purred. "Just help me off with my cape."

With exaggerated courtesy, Thor eased the charcoal cape from Dagmar's shoulders and hung it on a nearby wall peg. He held her chair as she sat down, her back ramrod straight.

A waiter approached, and they ordered a light lunch and two glasses of red wine. Dagmar noticed with irritation the man's frayed coat sleeves and whisker stubble. Well, at least Thor's choice of meeting places was a discreet one. None of her acquaintances would ever stay here. She saw a food stain on the tablecloth and slid her napkin over to cover it.

She glanced up to see Thor's hazel eyes staring at her. An intense little thrill started at the base of her throat, traveled downward to the V of her bodice, and continued swiftly to her lower belly. She shuddered inwardly, awestruck at how this arrogant young man could arouse feelings in her like no other—not even Andreas.

Andreas. The mere reminder of him triggered the buzzing in her head again. "I have to talk to you about your horrid cousin," she said, still seething. "He has me so upset, I could spit!"

Thor gazed at her curiously. "I can see the fire in your eyes, dear Dagmar," he replied in a near-amused tone. "What has Andreas done now?"

"Don't make jest of this, Thor. I have every right to hate him!"

The waiter brought their wine, and Dagmar took a sip from her glass. "He barged into my room the other night and tried to force me to admit that I hid the letter from his little farm cow."

"And, did you?"

"Of course not." Dagmar averted her eyes to the threadbare tablecloth. "Why should I?" She eagerly swallowed more of her wine. "The simple girl has no doubt found someone else by now, anyway."

"Could be she has." Thor reached over and traced the tip of her earlobe. "Those are beautiful earbobs . . . garnets become you."

A tingle danced from Dagmar's ear down her neck. "You're not listening," she said, moving away slightly. "Because I wouldn't admit to anything, Andreas called me a witch, even a common street whore!"

Thor frowned in mock concern. "He doesn't sound like much of a gentleman."

"He's turned into a beast. You've got to help me. Andreas doesn't deserve an inheritance from Mother or Papa Adolph's estate. I want to see him rendered useless to the railroad."

Without answering, Thor observed her, which caused a discomforting tick in Dagmar's right eye.

Their lunch arrived, but she ignored it. Thor finished his wine, then leaned toward Dagmar, placing his hand just above her satin-covered knee. The pressure of it sent pleasant heat waves up her leg.

He edged closer, his lips inches from her ear. "Why don't we get a room upstairs and discuss this matter further?"

She started to pull away, then stopped. She fluttered her eyelashes, her fingers touching the pulsing heartbeat at her throat. Beneath the table, Thor's hand eased farther up her leg, coming to rest on her thigh.

"I'm certain I could provide a great deal of comfort, as well as cooperation," Thor coaxed, his voice silky smooth.

Dagmar dared raise her gaze to meet his. His eyes smoldered in answer to an aching desire deep inside her. She knew why she had met him here. She wouldn't lie to herself. A coconspirator against Andreas was not the only thing she needed.

Dagmar glanced around the room at the few diners seated with their backs to her. She swallowed and brought her gaze back to Thor, still so close, his hand still on her thigh. "I'll wait here while you see to the room," she said decisively. "Please remember to be discreet."

He winked at her and strode toward the lobby.

A few minutes later, Thor motioned from the doorway. Dagmar adjusted her net veil across her face. She met him on the threshold and, like a princess, let him escort her over the lobby's faded carpet to the stairs.

But upstairs, when she heard Thor close and lock the door behind her, Dagmar's knees trembled. So this was how she would lose her virginity on a Sunday afternoon. Not as she had imagined, in elegant surroundings with Andreas, but in this meagerly furnished hotel room with his not-too-polished cousin. What would her mother make of it, when she'd been affronted by the possibility of a liaison between Dagmar and her stepson? And Andreas? Her back stiffened, and a derisive smile lifted the corners of her mouth.

She had made her decision. To hell with the rest of them.

Lifting her hat's veil, she removed the anchored filigreed pin then set the hat on top of a chipped bureau.

Thor moved up behind her. "Your perfume makes me wild," he whispered, his warm breath teasing the nape of her neck. His steel-strong arms came around her, his hands moving boldly upward to cup the rise of her breasts. When his lips lightly caressed her neck, she moaned. Quickly he removed his coat and bow tie, dropping them to the floor by her feet. He turned her around and gazed down into her eyes. "You know you've been wanting this . . . for a long time."

Before she could answer, his mouth crushed hers, the force of his desire driving urgently against her belly through the fabric of her gown. She tasted the tart wine on his lips. What would the bared skin of his chest taste like?

His tongue glided along her lips. She tipped her head back, opening her mouth to receive him. His hands slid down to mold to her buttocks beneath her layers of petticoats.

Like a cat in heat, she flung her arms around his thick neck and leaped onto him, her legs twining around him. Thor carried her to the bed and laid her back across the coverlet. Bending over, he began kissing the upper globes of her breasts then nibbled on one exposed nipple. When she moaned in wanton anticipation, he reached up under her skirts, found the split in her silk drawers and titillated her.

Dagmar lay back amidst the folds of her satin gown, her heart knocking against her rib cage. She felt Thor's fingers sliding her stockings down her legs and the moisture coming between her thighs. His tongue, rough yet smooth, began licking her in the most delicate places. She gasped. "Oh, Thor."

Heat radiated out from her inner thighs. She arched her back and started tearing open the buttons of her bodice.

Suddenly he stood up over the bed, watching her with what seemed intense pleasure. "I should make you wait, my lusty Dagmar. Just as you've made me wait." He smiled, touching himself.

Panting, Dagmar raised herself up onto her elbows and half smirked at him. Her gaze dropped to the burgeoning area beneath his hand. "If you're man enough," she taunted, "you won't make me wait another second."

Thor deftly removed his clothing while her eyes grew wider with each body part revealed: matted chest, heavily muscled arms, narrow hips. Her gaze came to a halt at the tawny triangle surrounding Thor's arousal. Then he fell upon her, pulling her gown down over her hips and to the carpet. In an instant, he covered her nakedness with his own. His fingers found her moist and wanting.

Dagmar grasped his massive shoulders, enfolding him like a vise, her nails raking tiny trails across his flesh.

Thor introduced his pulsing manhood to her, the tip of it teasing her maidenhead until she could stand no more. When he finally took her, thrusting far up inside her, Dagmar screamed in pain and in pleasure.

Thor held his hand over her mouth and grinned, his eyes burning with a devilish fire.

Afterward, still breathless from their sensual coupling, he murmured, "I will help you, my little bitch . . . Just tell me what you want me to do."

CHAPTER EIGHTEEN

"Here we are," Meg announced, pushing open the door to the third-floor walkup apartment. "Our wee castle. Wait a minute now—I'll be lightin' the lamp."

Ingrid followed her through the door, slightly out of breath from climbing the steep stairs. "It is good not to have to take that long ride across the city to my aunt's house."

Meg set her shopping bag of groceries down on a table in the middle of the sparsely furnished front room. In no time, the lamps were lit and a stew pot bubbled on the stove.

"Paddy's workin' late tonight with his deliveries, so we'll have plenty o' time to visit," Meg said over her shoulder as she bustled merrily about the small kitchen.

"You've got more energy than I do after a half day's work," Ingrid said, helping her put away the groceries. "And, I still have to do my studies for tomorrow."

She sank back into the lumpy sofa, inhaling the stew's savory aroma, and imagined the three of them sharing the evening meal in nights to come. She was reminded of family suppers at home and felt a twinge of nostalgia. These people would be her substitute family.

Yet there could be no substitute for Andreas. She must write him and send her new address. Her heart ached for his voice, his company, his touch. She had reread his letter until the paper wore smooth beneath her fingers.

Ingrid wished he had closed his letter with "love" instead of "as ever." She hoped he still loved her.

At bedtime, she and Meg retired to the back room where they shared a thin mattress, which was large enough but couldn't compare with Nettie's soft feather bed. Sometime later, she heard Paddy clunking around in the front room before the sofa springs groaned. He was a mysterious one.

Troublesome dreams of Andreas and Dagmar haunted her. Could his stepsister have kept her letter from him, causing him to miss her departure? If she did it once, she could do it again. Even destroy her letters. She fought to keep her fears at bay.

Sleep did not come easily.

Andreas squinted into the icy northern March wind and gritted his teeth. Up ahead fifteen men, backs bent, shoveled in ragged rhythm attempting to clear the track into Grand Forks.

Fisting his hands in his stiff gloves, he said testily to the foreman, "Looks like we're in for another one of those Canadian witches."

"Yep. Gawd damnit!" Pyles rolled a tobacco wad from one side of his grizzly cheek to the other, then disgustedly spat a rust-colored arc into a snow pile. "Second one this week." He wiped his mouth with the edge of his frayed coat sleeve. "She's ridin' that broomstick somethin' fierce."

Andreas nodded, acknowledging the man's dark humor. "The damn snow's turned to ice." He pulled his heavy coat collar up around his neck, wincing at the shaft of pain between his shoulder blades. He had worked this shift himself, coming on at Breckenridge ten hours ago. A fatiguing misery burrowed into his bones, and he knew what each man felt with every heft and swing of his shovel. The long outdoor hours took their toll. He had seen age creep into young men's eyes.

"Yeah," the shorter man replied, starting toward the crew, "I'd like to call it quits for the day, but I've gotta go on Hill's orders. 'Specially when he's sittin' back there in his car."

"To hell with Hill," Andreas muttered into another arctic blast. The slave master had probably been sipping on a brandy ever since the train stopped less than fifty feet behind them an hour ago. He yanked his scratchy wool cap farther down over his ears and moved up to join the others.

A steady barrage of sleet stung his face as he slammed his shovel into the stubborn pockets of ice lining the track. He paused to wipe a few ice pellets from his eyelashes and remembered Nordberg. This time last year . . . heading into Grand Forks. Old Nordberg had taken his last fall. The ghastly image of the brakeman's frozen body—stock-still, eyes glazed, sprawled out beside the track—flashed before him.

Nothing had changed. Not the working conditions, not the hours.

This Hill, the Scots-Canadian, the former shipping magnate, was supposed to be devising a plan to take over the St. Paul & Pacific, upgrade it, and extend it to the Canadian border. Adolph had insisted the man could do it. Andreas shoveled another heavy chunk of ice from the track, his hands numb beyond aching. He hoped Hill could pull off his plan, but his hope was laced with doubt. He'd heard the men joke about this "two streaks of rust and a right of way" for too long.

"Shit!" a burly crewman cursed up the line. "This job ain't worth no two bucks a day." He slumped over his shovel, the sleet beating down on him.

"Can't feed my wife and babies on this measly pay," another worker echoed the first.

Andreas sighed miserably, glancing back toward the hulk of the engine. Through the gray mist, a tall, dark figure approached. Andreas blinked and stared. He recognized the assuredness of the man, the dark mustache and beard, the prominent nose. James Hill himself.

193

When Hill had come several feet from Andreas, he stopped, his eyes glinting from beneath his black beaver hat. "Who's in charge here?"

Stiffly, Andreas raised up and looked around for the foreman, but didn't see him. He answered, "Pyles and I, sir."

"And you are?"

Realizing the rail baron didn't remember him from their New Year's meeting, Andreas stepped forward. "Andreas Eriksen, sir, assistant superintendent."

"Oh, yes. I'm Jim Hill." His hand enclosed Andreas's in a bold grip. He pumped it vigorously, his body heat emanating through Andreas's thick glove.

"You men have put in a damn full day's work," he shouted to the crew. "Come back with me to my car. There's hot coffee and sandwiches for everyone."

He turned abruptly and, with long steps, strode off toward the train.

The men dropped their picks and shovels and hung back a short moment, gawking at each other in disbelief. Then one after another broke out in a howl of approval, and all shambled after the tall, dark figure moving toward his private car.

Once inside, after stomping the wet from their outer clothes, the men crowded near a blazing manteled fireplace. Andreas saw the weariness in their eyes begin to disappear when a stocky Chinese passed trays of steaming coffee mugs and hearty, stacked sandwiches. They ate standing up, elbowing each other and commenting on "the good feed."

Andreas removed his filthy, ice-soaked gloves and stuffed them in a coat pocket. In doing so, a vision of Ingrid tucking her smooth, tapered hands into her rabbit muff passed across his mind. How beautiful she'd been that winter night on the way home, when her muff had tumbled to the carriage floor. The night they had made love for the first and only time. Pain like an arrow pierced his chest, causing him to shudder and take a deep, needful breath. He closed his eyes for an instant, hoping she was safe and warm.

Hill moved among the men in the limited space of the car like a king consulting with his court.

But unlike a king, he said affably to one of the crew, "Call me, Jim." Then he turned to the rest of the men, his coal-dark eyes beaming with enthusiasm. "Stick with me, men, and together we'll build this little scrap of a railway into the biggest, most successful line between here and the Pacific West Coast."

When Hill's gaze fell upon him, Andreas was reminded of the man's artificial left eye. During a childhood game, Hill had lost the eye when struck by another boy's arrow. It was said that the flamboyant Hill saw as well with one eye as most men did with two; and Andreas, listening to his prescient words, believed it.

"Like some of you," Hill continued, "I've traveled this territory on horseback and on snowshoes. I've followed the rails in a handcar and a caboose.

"A group of my fellow Canadians and I are working on a takeover plan, and by the first of next year, I predict the St. Paul & Pacific will have a new name and a golden future." He paused for a moment, looking into the weary but expectant faces surrounding him, and then boomed in an emotion-filled voice, "I want you all to be a part of it."

A burst of applause greeted his entreaty, followed by handshakes all around.

The enthusiasm in the cramped train car was palpable. Hill had kindled every trainman's dreams to build a decent future for himself and his family. When the men dispersed, Andreas stayed back to give Hill his unqualified support. The Scotsman smiled appreciatively and clapped him on the back.

"Thank you, Eriksen. You know, I miss your father. He was always a strong supporter of the railroad."

"Yes, sir. He's the reason why I'm here."

Outside the car, he heard the foreman holler, "There's another hour of light. Let's give it that before we call it a day."

Groans emitted from the cluster of men walking in front of Andreas. One groused to the others, "Hill may have his grand ideas on how to get rich, but if he cuts my pay like they're talkin' about on the eastern lines—I'll strike with the rest of 'em!"

Curses shot out from the weary group. "You've got my word on that," another man chorused.

A sour taste rose at the back of Andreas' throat. The future of this railroad seemed to be as mercurial as the weather. Sleet at his back, he hunched down into his coat and grudgingly moved up the ice-choked rails.

It was difficult to stay focused on his future with the St. Paul & Pacific when rumors of a strike stalked the rail lines.

May 1877. Ingrid tilted the short brim of her new Tuscan straw bonnet, anchoring it at the back of her head with a pearl-tipped pin, before leaving the shop for the day. She admired the hat in the gilt-framed mirror. Its rose satin ribbon draped at the crown, and the matching ruche trimmed the inside of the upturned brim. Then, with an anxiousness she couldn't quite identify, she removed her shawl from a wall hanger and slipped it around her shoulders.

"Bon soir, cheri," Madame called as Ingrid moved toward the front door. "Your gentleman is waiting?"

"Bon soir, Madame," Ingrid replied, embarrassed. "My friend is waiting."

Sean Slattery stood outside under the awning, waiting to escort her home as he had on occasion over the past few weeks. She appreciated his company on the walk to her apartment. Her neighborhood, unfortunately, bordered on the rough side.

"Good evening, Sean," Ingrid greeted him companionably.

" 'Tis a beautiful evening, but not nearly as beautiful as you, m'dear Ingrid."

Sean beamed down at her with those flirting green eyes. They caused her discomfort. He always seemed to throw her just a bit off balance. His quick wit and silver tongue were qualities she was not used to in a man.

Meg had told her he'd kissed the Blarney stone. Andreas, charming as he was, never swept her along at this pace. And she thought Andreas a gentleman in every sense of the word.

Why hadn't he answered her last letter? It had been nearly two months since she'd written.

Sean took her elbow protectively and they started up the street, weaving among the Friday night throng. "I want this to be a special evenin', I'm taking you to a favorite place of mine." He winked as if to add, "this will be our secret."

"You make it sound so inviting." Although she did not want to lead him on, Ingrid replied, "How can I refuse?"

They continued down State Street, going beyond the route they usually traveled toward the river and her apartment.

At Van Buren, they turned east for a few blocks. The area was unfamiliar to Ingrid. Faces on the street seemed to harden. The women wore masks of heavy makeup; the men's eyes either stared at the boardwalk or sent Ingrid sly, sidelong glances.

Notes from a tinny piano rollicked out onto the street on the night air from a pub a few doors up. "Here 'tis," Sean said expectantly.

Guffaws and the clink of glasses greeted them at the door. Ingrid simply wanted to step inside, sit down at a table, and get off her feet.

The interior was dim; it was not a place where she would run into her fellow students from the academy.

"Aye, Sean!" one lobster-faced fellow called. "Who's yer new pigeon?"

Several heads at the bar swiveled their way. Ingrid cringed, unused to such brazen attention.

Sean squeezed her arm in his. "Don't mind 'em. They just like a long look at a pretty lassie."

They found a table along the wall. "This is me lovely girl, Ingrid," he announced to the waiter, puffing up his chest. "Be a good fella and bring us some of that fine punch ye have."

I'm not your "lovely girl," she thought. Soon after, the waiter set two brimming mugs before them.

Sean raised his and gave a toast. "To the fairest lass this side of the Emerald Isle." He clinked his mug to Ingrid's. "Drink up, luv."

Ingrid raised the mug to her lips. "What is this?" she asked, smelling the sweet alcoholic fragrance of the drink.

"A mix of herbs and other good things—I think the leprechauns made up the recipe." Sean winked, a lock of shiny black hair falling across his brow.

Ingrid took a sip and smiled, finding the drink pleasurably fruity with an undertaste of spirits. She studied Sean's adoring face and wondered what made him look as if he needed caring for. Maybe it was because he always looked slightly unkempt.

"Down the hatch!" Sean urged minutes later, when she had only taken a few sips.

Ingrid looked at him sideways. "Are you trying to get me tipsy?"

"Who me?" He looked wide-eyed at her.

Her stomach cramped uncomfortably. "And when are we going to have dinner?"

Sean grinned. "Soon, luv." His eyes, flecked with tiny gold stars, held hers captive for one long moment. He lifted her hand and gently kissed it.

Ingrid withdrew her hand and looked for a waiter.

The lobster-faced fellow returned, tugging at Sean's coat sleeve. "Sing for us, Sean. Sing a song for yer little blonde sweetheart."

Sean waved him away. But other voices chimed in. "Sean, Sean!" they called. He relented finally. "I won't be long," he said as someone ushered him to the piano.

"This is for a lovely lady here tonight," Sean announced. "A song I wrote m'self." Voices lowered and heads turned in his direction.

On cue the piano player began, and Sean's lilting tenor lifted over the crowd. Ingrid was no longer aware of the untuned piano, only the sweet melody of the song. A string of voices joined in the chorus.

Ingrid, my fair lassie,
I'm in love with you.

Sean's arms reached out toward Ingrid, seated against the wall.

Won't you tell me that you love me too? he crooned.

Don't sing those words to me, a voice inside her pleaded. Her heart could not love anyone but Andreas.

Sean returned to the table, flushed with the rapture of applause, and wiped beads of sweat from his forehead. He removed his coat and hung it over a chair.

"You should not sing of love to me, Sean," she reprimanded.

"Don't break me heart, lassie. Another round," he called to the waiter. "Drink up, sweet. Yer fallin' behind." He held her glass up to her lips, and she reluctantly took another swallow.

The music became lively again. Voices around the table blurred. Her head felt as light as cotton candy.

Sean suddenly burst into laughter. "Why, here's a leprechaun come to see you, Ingrid."

A little man, his head rising only about six inches above the table top, appeared in front of her. He was dressed in emerald green from his pointed hat to his slippered feet. "H'lo, miss. May I have this chair?"

Before she could speak, the little man hopped onto her lap. "Oh!" Ingrid gasped.

The surrounding merrymakers roared.

Wearing the silliest expression, the leprechaun cocked his childish face to and fro. The tassels of his hat tickled her nose, and she was forced to giggle.

"You like my hat?" he squeaked. She nodded. "I like yours!" Swiftly he yanked Ingrid's hat pin free and exchanged their hats.

She blinked, disbelieving her eyes. He wore her new rose straw bonnet pulled down around his pointy ears. She wore his green hat, one tassel drooping across her nose.

"My hat!" she cried, reaching for it. Too late. The little man dashed between the patron's legs. "Sean, help!" she screamed. Sean was doubled over, laughing too hard to be of any help.

"Here I am!"

Ingrid looked in the direction of the squeaky voice. There he was—doing a ridiculous jig on top of the bar—wearing funny green tights and her hat. "Somebody get him!"

Finally, a brawny patron wrestled the little demon to his knees and, holding him under one arm, returned Ingrid's hat. He set the squirming prankster on his slippered feet.

Ingrid fell back in her chair, her head spinning. No sooner had she landed when he stood directly before her again.

The little man pointed a short finger at her, his voice a high-pitched whine. "You're no fun, no fun. A hex on you."

Heat from her acute embarrassment spread outward in waves.

The nasty little toad then dived under the table and tried to bull his way up under her skirts! Ingrid leaped to her feet and whacked him soundly on the ear. He yelped and disappeared into the raucous throng.

Across from her at the table, Sean swayed, his eyes flooded with tears of laughter.

Feeling lightheaded, she steadied herself. "Why didn't you stop that monster!"

Sean reached out to stroke her arm. "Let's order ye a special drink. It'll make ye feel better," he cooed.

"No!" She shrugged him away. "I don't need another drink. Take me home, Sean."

Once outside, she took a deep breath and attempted to regain some of her lost dignity. Sean's simpering expression made him look like a court jester weaving beneath the street light. "Well, are you going to find me a ride or do I have to find one?"

He winked and trotted a short way up to the corner.

Some time later, bouncing along on the hard seat of a broken-down dray, between the Irish crooner and the toothless driver, Ingrid vowed she would never let Sean Slattery escort her home again.

Chapter Nineteen

Ingrid shook the last of the bedding and draped it over the sill. Leaning out the open window, she breathed in the June morning and let the breeze caress her face and shoulders.

The Chicago air was nowhere near as sweet as the summer smells at home on the farm. Fresh-mown hay, honeysuckle outside her bedroom window, her mother's baking bread. What were they all doing right now on a Sunday morning? Her mother was probably hurrying the children to get ready for church. Marie Lisbet was tying ribbons in Briget's long blonde hair. A pang of homesickness gripped her.

The bedsheets billowed out beneath her propped elbows. And what was Andreas doing this moment? Just waking up on a cot far from home, his dark hair tousled, his body warm from sleep?

She shook her head, attempting to shake away the longing her imaginings provoked, and unfolded herself from the sill.

"Meg! Ingrid!"

From the front room, she heard Paddy's impatient voice. He had slunk in late again last night after attending one of those secret workmen's meetings and drinking away the hours with his cronies. She knew he would be as friendly as a bear with a thorn in its rear, and she was slow to wash her face and brush her hair.

"Damn girls," he snarled through the bedroom door. "Where are ye when I want ye?"

Ingrid sighed and reluctantly opened the door. "Good morning, Paddy. Would you like some coffee?"

He grunted something under his breath that sounded like "aye." So she set about boiling the water in the coffeepot with her back to him, avoiding his state of semi-undress.

Approaching her in the small kitchen area, he demanded, "Where's Meg?"

"She went up on the roof to wash her hair."

"Did she now?" Paddy raised his dusky brows. He leaned against the washstand, his eyes red-rimmed.

He wore gray underdrawers and a rumpled nightshirt that hung loosely to his knees. Ingrid regarded him unfavorably in the crowded space. She wanted to say, *Why don't you wash and put on some decent clothes?* but didn't have the nerve to confront his guarded eyes.

"She knows I need somethin' to eat when I get up."

Ingrid poured coffee in a cup and set it on the table. She had eaten her breakfast earlier and didn't feel like joining him in his present ill mood. "I think I will go up to the roof and wash my hair."

"Don't leave so fast on my account." Paddy dropped his head heavily into his hands. "Oh, me poor head aches."

Ingrid observed Paddy's day-old whisker stubble and disheveled hair. Although she did not take to strong spirits, she felt a sudden pity for him. What devils urged him to drink himself into such a state?

"Paddy," she said, managing a lighter tone, "just sit down and have your coffee. I will send Meg to fix your breakfast."

He attempted a smile, but his eyes were humorless.

In the bedroom, she grabbed a clean towel from the cupboard. Before leaving the apartment, Ingrid went over and patted him on the shoulder. "I hope you feel better—and think twice before drinking so much next time."

Sprawled in a kitchen chair, Paddy smirked at her.

On the roof she found Meg, sitting on a stool, toweling her hair dry in the morning breeze. She had stripped down to her shift and petticoat, exposing her cinnamon-freckled face and arms to the sun.

"Thought I'd give my hair a wash, too," Ingrid called as she approached.

Meg nodded toward a tub of sudsy water. "You'll want to dump that. The fresh water's in that barrel over there."

Ingrid rolled up her sleeves then dragged the metal tub to the edge of the roof, hoisted it, and emptied its contents over the alley side. Returning, she set the tub down near the barrel and began ladling the collected rainwater from a small bucket into the tub.

"Paddy's growling for you to fix his breakfast," Ingrid said, unable to keep irritation from her voice. "He tied one on again last night."

Meg clucked her tongue. "Aye, well he can wait."

"I fixed him some coffee." Ingrid filled the tub half full and accepted Meg's offer of the stool. Sitting down on it, she dipped her head and poured a bucketful of the water over her hair, thankful the water was lukewarm from the sun's morning rays. She worked up a lilac-scented lather with the store-bought soap she'd fished from her dress pocket.

Meg brushed her Titian curls in the sunlight. "Don't be judgin' Paddy too hard," she said when Ingrid had rinsed off the soap and wrapped her hair in the towel. "He sometimes sees the ghost of our father, who died in that great evil fire."

"Your father died in the Great Fire?"

Meg nodded. "Just when the smoke and flames was burnin' the city nearly to the ground. Poor man was workin' late at the lumberyard, as usual, and he got trapped inside and couldn't get out. With our mother dead, we was left on our own."

"Oh, Meg." Ingrid shook her head sadly, commiserating.

"Men don't get over things as easy as women. So now he goes to those bloody workers' meetin's—and he drinks to forget."

Ingrid finished drying her hair and shook out her towel. "Well, if the meetings are of some comfort . . ."

"Some comfort, indeed." Meg made a face. "They're talkin' about strikin' along with the railroad workers."

Ingrid bit her lower lip. "That could be dangerous. Couldn't Paddy lose his job?"

"Aye. And that would be a fine kettle o' fish!" Meg swept up her stool and started for the stairs. "I've tried talkin' to him about it, but he won't tell me anythin'."

Ingrid looked after her with a pained smile. "At least you've tried."

After Meg left, Ingrid crossed over to the retaining wall and stared blindly toward the river. Church bells chimed a few blocks away, their usually uplifting sound sending goose bumps up and down her arms. A sense of foreboding consumed her.

She walked along the edge of the rooftop, worrying over Meg's words. Should Paddy strike and lose his job, they wouldn't be able to pay the rent. She knew little about strikes, only that she would not dare to strike against Madame Larousse for higher wages. The woman could turn right around and hire an eager new immigrant girl to take her place.

Ingrid closed her eyes, the errant breeze tossing her hair carelessly about her face. She willed herself back with the Nelsons in St. Paul, where she and Nettie had attended St. Agnes together, and she and Andreas were about to plan their future together. If only he were here with her now. She choked back sudden tears.

Could things ever be the same between them again?

Then, swiping away her salty tears, she took heart. Things always had a way of working out. The workmen would settle their differences. There would be no strike. She would continue at the academy and become a teacher. And, she would see Andreas again.

If only tomorrow's mail would bring a letter from him.

Andreas moved along the track in the St. Paul yard, taking inventory of the emptied cars, making a few notes before returning to his pigeonhole office to go over the schedule. Another big shipment of lumber was due from Crookston tomorrow.

A lazy June sun warmed his shoulders through his shirt. It was his first day back in the yard and one that made him want to find a hammock and a cold drink. He stopped to take out his pocket watch. Two o'clock—quitting time was hours away. He shrugged off his daydream. At least the working conditions here were far preferable to the last four months he'd spent up north, breaking his back supervising rail crews.

The elements had forced him to put Ingrid from his mind, if only during the days. But the nights had been filled with her.

He approached the end cars and heard voices.

"Bet he's got a friggin' ace up his sleeve!"

"Shut yer yap and make yer play."

The last voice sounded all too familiar. Andreas walked up to the next car, stepping lightly on the gravel beneath his shoes.

When he had a clear view inside the open door, he halted. He saw four yardmen hunkered down in Indian fashion, enjoying an afternoon game of cards. Two of the men he knew worked in the roundhouse. Kelly, the engine boy, who at nineteen looked sixteen, sat facing him, his shaggy head bent over his hand. To Andreas's right, his cousin Thor, sleeves rolled above his elbows, also hunched over his cards.

Thor was just starting to shuffle the deck when Andreas shot out, "Fine time for a little game of poker, right men?"

The two roundhouse workers dropped their cards and stared at him. Young Kelly's green eyes popped wide as a circus clown's. Thor angled his head toward Andreas, his only hint of surprise the lifting of one bushy brow.

Andreas caught hold of the doorframe and jumped inside the car.

Thor's smile was smug. "Well, cousin . . . thought we'd take a short break. Want to sit in?"

"Not on company time," Andreas growled.

Kelly giggled nervously. He made a clumsy attempt to slide a beer bottle behind his back.

Andreas felt his patience wearing thin. Beads of sweat broke out beneath his hairline. "You know you could all be fired for this." He focused his contempt on Thor. "I would have expected more from you, Eriksen."

The men clambered to their feet, fear invading their faces. Tightlipped, Thor gathered up his cards and slowly stood. He gave a slight mocking bow and stuffed the cards in his back pocket.

"I'll let it go this time," Andreas relented, "but don't let me catch you at this again." He pinned Thor with a furious look. "Is that clear?"

Thor tipped his cap. "Very clear." He brushed past Andreas and jumped to the ground.

The other three dived after him, scurrying away down the track.

Damn you, Thor, Andreas thought. Your arrogance will get you thrown out of the yard. *Blood kin or not.*

He wished he'd never influenced the foreman to hire Thor in the first place. It had been a definite mistake. Thor's tardiness had become routine as had his cocky attitude.

Andreas bristled all the way back to the station. A confrontation with the men was all he needed, especially now when the eastern lines were cutting trainmen's wages. The Pennsylvania Railroad had already announced a ten percent wage cut. Rumors, like rabid mice, scuttled back and forth among the men.

When Andreas arrived home, tired and irritable, the first person he laid eyes on was Dagmar. Poised on the parlor threshold, swathed in an iridescent green Oriental wrapper, she peered at him devilishly.

"The whipped Viking returns from the war," she taunted. "How goes it, Andreas? You do look the worse for wear."

He gave her a withering look.

With a huff Dagmar spun on her heel, turning her back to him.

Disgruntled, he went down the hall to the library and made himself a stiff drink.

Immediately following dinner, Andreas escaped upstairs to closet himself behind his bedroom door.

His mood was one of discontent. It would be easy to blame Dagmar's puzzling behavior. Since his return to the city last evening, she'd baffled him. One minute the girl pranced like a coquette; another, she openly glared at him, her eyes piercing. At dinner he'd felt if he were a dart board, she would have taken delight in hitting the bull's eye. His back tingled from the penetration of her stare from around door frames and hallway corners.

Just give me some peace! he wanted to shout at her.

He still suspected that Dagmar, in her strange need to control his life, had kept Ingrid's letter from him. His blood simmered recalling the night he'd missed seeing Ingrid off at the station. Ever since, at his request, Gertrude checked each day's mail delivery as soon as it arrived.

In the room's sepia light, he paced the floor and thought of Ingrid. The pain of not being near her the past four months lay heavy upon his heart. His memories of her were still fresh, still warm, still magnetic.

Despite the promise he'd made to his father to help rebuild the struggling St. Paul & Pacific, he must visit her at the earliest opportunity.

He went to the window and looked out onto the empty street. Railroad dissension brewed in Chicago. Certainly his supervisor would think it wise for him to confer with officials there. Tomorrow he would make reservations to go to Chicago.

The driver clicked his tongue and guided the horse down Madison Avenue. From the front seat of the hansom cab, Andreas patted his coat pocket where he'd placed Ingrid's address. He hoped his telegram, telling of his imminent arrival, had reached her.

The cab turned onto Market Street. Andreas looked out in amazement at the milling throngs congesting the intersection. A surly group of men wearing caps pulled down over their foreheads edged near the horse's right flank.

One man darted a scathing look up at him, his lower lip curling in disgust. "Bloody rich bastard," he snarled, his shadowed eyes filled with venom.

Some of Chicago's citizens weren't in a welcoming mood this hot July afternoon, he thought wryly, and ignored the insult.

Uncomfortable in his boiled shirt and stiff collar, Andreas found his handkerchief in a jacket pocket and wiped beads of sweat from his face. Ahead, a crowd of hundreds gathered in Market Square. Mostly men, they gravitated to a central makeshift podium draped with a hand-lettered banner that read WORKINGMEN'S PARTY OF THE UNITED STATES. A bearded man, hatless and roughly attired, stood waving his arms and projecting a rasping oratory in a German dialect.

The carriage came to a halt in the clotted street behind other stranded conveyances. Andreas spoke to the driver through the open trapdoor in the roof. "Is this one of the anarchists' meetings?" he asked, already suspecting it was.

From the minute he'd got off the morning train in the Chicago depot, all he'd heard about was the impending rail strike and the socialists and anarchists who were fueling it.

"Yes sir," the driver answered, "and they're boilin'. Look at their signs."

Placards wagged above the crowd. ROBBER BARONS STEAL OUR BREAD. WORKERS REVOLT!

Andreas had picked up a copy of the Chicago Daily News on his way to the hotel. STRIKE FEVER! the headlines had screamed. RAILROADS SLASH WAGES! Subtitles reported Chicago's railroad owners were following eastern lines by cutting ten percent from the rail men's pay.

Baltimore and Ohio workers had reacted first, their firemen and brakemen refusing to work on freight trains heading west. Last week, Pittsburgh had protested violently. Would Chicago be next? From the long meeting he had attended today with the board of the Chicago, Milwaukee & St. Paul line, he'd not been reassured otherwise.

Neither were the faces in the crowd reassuring. "Come on, man," Andreas urged the driver. "Get this rig moving!" Then he cursed to himself, knowing they wouldn't be going anywhere in a hurry surrounded by this mob.

He drew the folded paper with Ingrid's address from his inside pocket. According to the hotel concierge, she lived off Market in the direction of the river.

His throat constricted. He'd been forced to wait so long to find Ingrid, and finally she was so close. How would she greet him after these months of separation?

The carriage inched along Market like a sluggish snail amid the jostling masses of pedestrians. Andreas shifted his weight on the leather upholstery, tempted to leap to the street and make his way on foot. But at the corner of Adams, a squad of stone-faced soldiers carrying rifles on their shoulders marched by, and he relinquished the thought of going it on his own.

As the horse shambled behind a delivery wagon approaching Van Buren, Andreas saw a willowy young woman walking ahead at an unhurried pace. She wore the prim clothes of a shop girl. Wisps of blonde hair slipped from beneath her topknot and fluttered out around her small straw hat.

Andreas' breath caught in his throat. Ingrid! He knew it was her. Her walk, the familiar angle of her head. He leaned forward, straining to see the young woman's face, but she moved along just ahead of the carriage and out of earshot among the work-force emerging from every door.

A rush of emotion careened through his veins. Joy—he had found her! Anxiety—what if she no longer cared to see him? Fear—what would he do then? His chest tightened until he thought it would burst.

The young woman proceeded across the wide intersection. In a moment, she would be lost in the sea of humanity.

"I'm going ahead on foot," Andreas called to the driver. "Follow me across the street."

He jumped to the ground and leaped onto the boardwalk. Elbowing his way among pedestrians, he maneuvered across the intersection then cut in front of a dappled pair of drays before coming to the other side of the street.

Halfway down the block, he saw her shapely frame swaying between pedestrians. His heart skipped when she glanced toward the street, her features: brow, nose, chin, in clean profile. Yes, it was Ingrid. More beautiful than he remembered her.

He broke into double stride, almost running. He must catch

her—stop her, touch her, hold her.

The back of her neck was visible, creamy smooth above her lace collar.

His throat dry, he called her name.

She walked on.

"Ingrid," he called, louder.

Her back stiffened. She stopped in the middle of the planked walk. And turned abruptly. Her eyes searched the oncoming faces before they focused on his.

One hand flew to her breast then reached toward him.

Blood pounded at his temples as he closed the distance between them. He grasped her firmly by the shoulders, his eyes rejoicing in her face. "Ingrid. At last, I found you."

She stared up at him, her eyes luminous, burning sapphires. Her heart-shaped lips formed his name. "Andreas. Is it really you?"

He smiled, drawing her close, kissing her forehead her cheeks, her sweet mouth. Passersby jostled them. He didn't care.

"Dear Andreas," she said, returning his kisses, her voice breathless. "I've missed you so. But, what are you doing here?"

"Didn't you get my telegram?"

She stepped back. "No. When did you send it?"

"It doesn't matter." He took her elbow and maneuvered her away from the passing pedestrians, toward a store front. "My carriage is coming to pick us up and . . ."

His voice was drowned out by the ragged group of men darting from a side alley just ahead. They carried the gritty smell of the rail yard with them. And a look of desperation in their eyes. On the heels of the men came a squad of uniformed police, brandishing nightsticks over their heads.

One of the toughs stopped in flight and grabbed a storage barrel in front of a livery shop. He kicked the barrel into the path of the police. It knocked the legs out from under one of the officers. Another roughneck snatched a horseshoe from the top of a crate and sent it flying in the direction of the officer's partner.

"Watch out!" someone hollered.

The second officer ducked, then swinging his nightstick in a wild circle, charged toward the men.

Andreas caught hold of Ingrid and they scrambled to get out of the way. He heard her startled cry as she tripped over a bystander behind them. She jolted backward out of his arms. Her hat was knocked askew. Her skull made a loud thumping sound as she fell against the corner of the brick building.

Andreas dropped to his knees beside her. Fear twisting his gut, he yelled to the remaining officers. "We need a doctor here!"

Ingrid moaned. Blood had begun to trickle from the back of her head. Wincing, Andreas pulled out his handkerchief and used it to blot the wound.

Thunder rumbled from a clouded sky. Raindrops spattered the boardwalk and glanced off Andreas' hat and coat. The rain smell, filled with dust and blood, grew thick in his nostrils.

A burly officer ran over to him. "We'll get her a doctor, sir," he panted.

Andreas acknowledged him with a nod. He saw his driver and carriage pull up across the street. "My driver's here now. Tell me how to reach the nearest hospital."

"Just follow us, sir."

Andreas breathed a small sigh of relief. But as he lifted Ingrid in his arms, her eyelashes lying still upon her ashen cheeks, he stared in horror at the widening patch of blood seeping from the back of her head onto his coat sleeve.

"Dear Ingrid," he cried into her soft, tousled hair. "I've just found you. Don't leave me now."

CHAPTER TWENTY

A ringing started in her ears. Her throat was parched. Sandpaper dry. She blinked, trying to focus her eyes in the dim light.

"Ingrid. Are you awake?"

She strained upward toward the familiar-timbered voice.

From the foot of the hospital bed, Andreas moved to her side. Although lines of weariness etched his face, he smiled. "You took a fall and got a nasty cut, but the doctor stitched you up very neatly."

Ingrid's hand went to the bulky bandage swathing her forehead. Her tongue felt thick, foreign to her mouth. "I'm so thirsty."

He held a cup of water to her dry lips. She drank a small amount.

"Are you hungry?"

She shook her head. The effort caused the room to whirl. She groaned. "Could you make the room stop turning?"

Andreas took her hand in both of his. "I feel I'm to blame for all of this. I should have gotten you away from the confrontation."

Ingrid gazed up at him. His hair, dark and ruffled, needed combing. His eyes shone with untold emotion. "You tried."

Tenderly, he kissed her hand.

Hot tears welled in her eyes. "You're here at last." Making words was so difficult. Fatigue settled over her like a leaden shroud. Her eyelids closed wearily. "So many questions . . ."

Andreas' breath fell warm across her cheek. "Sleep, my love," he whispered. "I'll be here when you awake."

Someone patted his shoulder. "Mr. Eriksen."

He looked into compassionate female eyes. A gray-haired nurse in a starched white uniform stood next to him. "You should have a good hot breakfast and find a better place to rest."

Andreas ran his hand through his hair and shook himself awake. His back ached from sitting all night in the high-backed hospital chair. He sighed. "I suppose I should."

The nurse moved to Ingrid's bedside and felt her face. "She'll sleep most of today. The doctor won't be in to see her until this afternoon."

Andreas pushed up from the chair. His eyes and mouth were gritty. He looked upon Ingrid resting peacefully.

"You're right. I'll go to my hotel and clean up. I can be back in a few hours."

The nurse smiled. "I'll bathe her after you leave. She'll feel much better when you return."

As the nurse left the room to get fresh water, Andreas went to Ingrid's side. Her coloring was as pale as the early light slanting in from the single window. Something wrenched tightly inside his chest.

He remembered the peach-glow of her laughing face the day they raced to the boathouse in the park. Last autumn when the leaves were at their peak.

He bent over Ingrid's sleeping form. Leaning into her, he brushed her slightly parted lips with his own. Somewhere in her dreams, she sighed.

"Dearest Ingrid," he murmured. "Be well soon, my heart."

Choking back a rush of emotion, he pulled away from her and left the room.

At the administrator's office, he stopped and made arrangements to have Ingrid's bill forwarded to his St. Paul address. He left his card with the clerk.

State Street traffic was in chaos. Andreas had forgotten Chicago hovered on the brink of a major rail strike. Once again riding in a hired hansom cab, he was plunged back into the city's cauldron.

Up ahead, a gang of men wielding clubs and sticks broke out from a side street. They forced their way into the thoroughfare, bringing traffic to a halt in both directions.

With mounting anger, Andreas watched the street toughs smash the front window of Remington's gun store in the next block.

He leaned out of his carriage. "What the devil!"

But before the mob could make off with any merchandise, a band of police officers intervened. They shuffled the ringleaders over to a nearby police wagon.

The horse car in front of his carriage inched ahead. Andreas exhaled deeply. The longer it took to get back to the hotel, the longer it would take to return to Ingrid.

It was midmorning when he finally arrived uptown at the St. James Hotel. His once-crisp white shirt clung to him in the July humidity. He was ravenous. All he wanted was to rush to his room, order an immense breakfast, and soak in a deep tub.

A uniformed clerk at the front desk handed him his key and a telegram. "It arrived just this morning, sir."

Warily Andreas accepted the telegram and placed it in his inside coat pocket. As soon as he closed the door to his room, he ripped open the envelope.

It was from Delaney, the St. Paul & Pacific superintendent. He read the brief, urgent message, a hot poker prodding his empty gut.

Strike imminent! Get back here—now.

"Damn!" Andreas crumpled the telegram and threw it on the carpet. Damn. Not now, not when he'd finally found Ingrid.

He paced the room, frantic with indecision. He wouldn't go. He'd telegram Delaney that he had important family business here in Chicago.

No. It wasn't good enough. He could see his no-nonsense boss fume when he read that. What could be more important than an imminent rail strike?

Delaney needed him to quell the men's anger, dissipate their fears. Reassure them their wages would not be cut.

But Ingrid needed him. She was helpless, lying in a hospital bed. He had promised her he would be there when she woke.

Andreas sank down in a high-backed chair next to the bed. What was he to do? His conscience roiled.

A cold sweat broke out over his body. If he left now, he might lose Ingrid forever. If he didn't oblige his boss, and the railmen went out on strike, he'd surely be fired. Worse, he would feel responsible for their actions.

For several minutes, he sat in the chair, head resting heavily in his hands. The irritating clock on the bureau ticked in his ears, forcing him to make a decision.

Finally Andreas rose and went to the window. The street traffic below moved in a frenetic blur. His mind reeled from worry and lack of sleep. He gritted his teeth against the decision he felt compelled to make. He must return to St. Paul.

At the mahogany writing desk in the corner, he pulled open a drawer and found some hotel stationery. He wrote:

Dearest Ingrid,

   It is with deepest regret that I must return home immediately. My superior informs me that the men of the St. P & P are on the verge of joining the national train strike.

I will come back to Chicago and call upon you as soon as the way is clear. Please get well soon. I can only leave believing you are in caring hands.

Have patience and know that I miss you greatly.

With my deepest love,
Andreas

He stood and glanced at the clock. It was noon. Maybe, maybe he had enough time to cross the city to the hospital.

He folded the letter, sealed it inside a hotel envelope, and rushed downstairs. Once outside, he raced up to the corner to hale a driver. State Street stretched ahead in an unending traffic tie-up. A traveler's nightmare. Up the block, he saw police arresting more hoodlums, dragging them out of a businessman's carriage.

Andreas cursed, pivoted on his heel, and returned to the hotel. He hurried through the lobby. With detailed delivery instructions, he left the letter with the desk clerk. The bitter thought that he wouldn't be there when Ingrid woke mocked him.

By midafternoon, he had hired a driver to take him to Milwaukee, where he thought he could catch a late train for St. Paul. All train departures from Chicago had come to a standstill.

In the distance, he could see patches of gray smoke rising insidiously over the city. On his way out of town he'd heard that roving, unemployed gangs were attacking railroad stations. The thought of it made him seethe.

If this madness could not be contained soon, Chicago would erupt in civil war.

Were the men of the St. Paul & Pacific planning the same actions? Andreas urged the driver to give the horse full rein.

My lovely Ingrid. May God protect you.

★   ★   ★   ★   ★

A loud clatter made Ingrid come awake with a jolt. Someone had dropped a metal object out in the hall. Its reverberation echoed off the walls.

She tried to sit up but her head throbbed at the effort. She lay back onto the pillows. The room surrounded her. Sterile. Empty.

"Andreas?" she said aloud.

Where was he? Had he stepped out for a minute? She had so many questions, she didn't know where to begin. How she had missed him in every way. At least he was here now. They could repair past disagreements and begin anew.

A young nurse came into the room. "Miss Johansson?"

Ingrid turned her head slightly. "Yes?"

"This came for you a little while ago."

Ingrid accepted the envelope and focused on the familiar masculine handwriting. Andreas.

She tore open the envelope and removed the letter. Her eyes read the words, but her brain did not make sense of them.

"He is returning to St. Paul?" she cried out to the empty corners of the room. "But he will 'come back as soon as the way is clear'?" Ingrid reread the letter, hot tears pricking her eyelids and blurring his words.

A drumbeat of pain pulsed in her head. She stared out the window at Lake Michigan beneath a gray, overcast sky. All the months she'd spent separated from Andreas and her family, in pursuit of an education, living from hand to mouth, tumbled across her mind. Now, in a bright flash, Andreas had found her only to leave her.

" 'Have patience . . . I miss you greatly.' " She laughed with scorn. "The railroad is always more important."

She threw the note and its envelope across the bed. "Then go take care of your damn railroad!" Vertigo seized her. She grasped the edge of the bed, the room whirling maddeningly around her.

"You're recovering well after your injury, Miss Johansson," her doctor pronounced, after examining her eyes and finding no dilation. "But you have sustained a mild concussion, and I would suggest further bed rest."

"I cannot stay here any longer," she replied. "I must get back to my apartment and back to my job."

"There's a volatile strike going on outside these walls," he warned. "A young woman should not venture out on the street."

She lifted her chin, determined. "I appreciate your help, sir. I can take care of myself."

Against her doctor's advice, Ingrid left the hospital that afternoon.

At the front office, she was told that her hospital bill had been paid by a Mr. Eriksen. It was a kind gesture. But then an ornery thought replaced the first. He can afford to pay it.

As she descended the hospital steps, she breathed a sigh of relief. At least she was saved the embarrassment of having to tell the clerk she had scant means of payment.

Ingrid spied a cab for hire parked on the hospital grounds. The driver didn't like the idea of having to take her over by the river, past the rail yards.

"Look at the headlines fer yerself, lady." He pointed to a newsboy hawking the daily *Chicago Tribune* a few yards away.

The boy's chanting echoed bold front page headlines:

CITY UNDER SIEGE

MAYOR HEATH CALLS IN HUNDREDS OF RIOT PO-LICE

Ingrid's heart leaped. She thought of Meg and Paddy. They must be worried about her. By now they would fear the worst.

She had to get back and explain where she'd been the last two nights.

After some persuasion and agreement to a higher fare, the driver reluctantly agreed. "Please, take the shortest route you can," she urged.

As they approached the river, the streets were nearly vacant. Nearby rail yards were deserted. Freight cars stood idle beneath the stark afternoon sun, an acrid smell of distant smoke filling the air.

Only men moved along the thoroughfares, hat brims yanked down over their furtive eyes. Fear, like an eerie beast, crept over her.

Ingrid closed her eyes to shut out the beast and leaned back against the upholstered cushion. She blotted perspiration from her face and neck. Free of the cumbersome hospital bandage, her head felt light, almost weightless.

Without warning, three ragged men darted into the street directly in front of the carriage.

One of the toughs snarled and raised a club he was carrying, as if to strike the animal. The startled horse whinnied and reared back on his hind legs.

Ingrid screamed in fright. *Andreas, where are you now when I need you?*

A sharp, cracking sound rent the air above the coach. "Out of the road, you swine!" the driver shouted, snapping his whip again.

The horse lunged forward into a dead run, leaving the hoodlums behind in a plume of dust.

The carriage swerved around the next corner. Thrown to the opposite side of the cab, Ingrid's neck snapped to the left. She cried out at the sudden arrow of pain shooting upward to her head. With white-knuckled fingers, she hung onto the edge of the seat cushion.

Please—get me home!

The apartment door flung open. "Saints preserve us. Thank God, yer alive!"

Exhausted from her harrowing ride and climbing the two flights of stairs, Ingrid fell into Meg's welcoming arms. "I'm so glad to be here," she cried, choking over the lump in her throat.

"Girl, ye look like a ghost. Where in the devil have ye been for the last two days?"

Ingrid's legs threatened to collapse under her. "I will tell you all of it, but I have to sit down first."

Meg brushed a swirl of red hair from her face and started for the small kitchen. "Then sit yer body down and I'll make us a good hot cup o' tea."

Ingrid sank wearily into the frayed sofa. "Oh, yes," she sighed. "Hot tea would be best."

Minutes later, sipping her tea and nibbling on a stale biscuit, she related the past days' tumultuous events.

Meg's brows flew up at the mention of Andreas. "He came all the way to Chicago? And he took ye to the hospital?"

"Where he left me . . . again." Ingrid's head drooped.

Meg waved her hand impatiently. "He said it was an emergency, didn't he?"

"I know he had to go back . . . It's just that we had such a short time together."

Meg came over to Ingrid and scooped her up from the sofa. "Come now, ye should lay yerself down for a wee nap. There are clean sheets on the bed."

Ingrid made an effort to smile. "That sounds inviting."

Meg chuckled. "I've had nothin' else to do but the washin' since the mayor announced he don't want us women out on the streets."

Gratefully, Ingrid let Meg remove her high-button shoes and

help her off with her dress. Still in her shift, she fell back onto the clean bedsheets. The familiar lumpy mattress encompassed her. Pulling the top sheet up to her chin, she exhaled deeply, wiggling her toes in sheer relief. She was home. Be it humble, it was the only home she knew.

Right after Ingrid and Meg had finished their dinner stew, Paddy burst through the door, his wide-set eyes blazing.

"I've killed a copper!"

The crockery bowl Meg was washing slipped from her hand and crashed to the floor, splitting into half a dozen pieces.

Ingrid's mouth dropped open, a frightening chill shivering down her spine.

In the center of the room, Paddy quaked like a cornered alley dog. "I killed a bloody copper! I know I did!"

"No, Paddy." Meg rushed over to him. "You couldn't do such a thing."

His eyes glistened with fire and fear in his bulldog face. "I can't believe it m'self." His beefy hand slid into his trouser pocket and withdrew a pistol. "But I did—with this."

At the sight of the gun, Ingrid's skin prickled all over. Meg's face flushed scarlet beneath her freckles. "Dear Lord. Where did this happen?"

Paddy prowled the room, sweat breaking out on his forehead. "At the Burlington Railroad yard—about fifteen minutes ago. I was hangin' around with them other strikers. We was doin' some business and these police rode up in their wagons. Lots of 'em." He stopped, slanting a look at the window.

Meg's gaze followed his. "Quick, Ingrid," she said, "pull the shade."

A tight fist of fear closing around her chest, Ingrid drew down the shade. "After the police arrived, what happened?"

Paddy's voice rose to a high-pitched whine in the hushed

room. "Some of the mob was tryin' to burn one of the buildin's and the officers run up to stop 'em."

Meg leaned closer. "And then . . ."

Paddy's thick fingers drove paths through his grimy hair. "They started shootin' into the crowd. Everyone went wild, scatterin' in all directions." He released a ragged breath. "I—I saw this copper point his pistol at a young lad, and I went crazy."

Ingrid's knees went limp under her, and she slumped into a kitchen chair.

"I grabbed the gun," Paddy continued. "We struggled—and I shot him, in the chest." He looked from Meg to Ingrid, his face dirt-streaked, his eyes brimming with tears. "The bloke spouted blood like a geyser."

In shock, Ingrid shook her head. "Why were you in such a place? Why did you go there?"

"I got fired from me delivery job last Friday. The boss said I was one of them 'agitators,' always goin' to the Workingman's meetin's."

"You didn't tell me," Meg cried.

Paddy rubbed his knuckles together. "I had a right to sympathize with the railmen. Hell, we're all bein' worked to death to make the company owners rich."

"Do ye think they know who you are?" Ingrid asked.

"I don't think so. But if that copper's dead—you can be sure they'll be askin'."

Meg's green eyes grew round. "And they'll be comin' here."

Paddy wiped his forehead with his sleeve. "We've got to get out of this place. Find another."

"But where? We have no money."

"I don't know." He continued to pace. "Let me think."

Meg burst into sobs. Ingrid went to comfort her and felt her own body tremble against Meg's. Her mind spun in circles at the unraveling events. Where could they go but out on the street?

In the midst of roving thugs and hell-bent strikers.

They ranted and paced until Ingrid's head was splitting. She knew of no way to help them. Finally she crept into the bedroom, hoping to get some rest before having to rise for her morning class.

What seemed minutes later, Ingrid was shaken from a restless sleep. "Ingrid, wake up!"

Silhouetted in the doorway to the front room, Meg's hair encircled her face like a wild flame. Her voice knifed into Ingrid's consciousness. "We're leavin' now. But we've got to talk to ye first."

Her heartbeat pumping into her throat, Ingrid bolted upright in bed. "You're leaving?"

"We've found a place, Paddy and me, where we can hide for awhile. Until this is over."

Holding a lighted lamp, Paddy entered the room behind Meg. The dim flame cast his face in eerie shadow. "You can stay here 'til the end of the month if ye like. The rent's paid up."

"But if anyone comes to the door . . . anyone askin' about Paddy," Meg warned, "you've got to promise you'll tell 'em you haven't seen 'im."

Ingrid started to shake. "If the police come . . ."

Meg placed her hands firmly on Ingrid's shoulders. "Promise. You'll tell them nothin'!"

The glare of their eyes and the intensity of Meg's words made Ingrid break out in a cold sweat. She hugged the thin sheet to her chest. "I . . . promise."

Meg uttered a relieved sigh. "That's a girl." She gave Ingrid a quick hug. "Goodbye, then. And God be with ye."

Ingrid stared after them. Her voice cracked as she said, "Goodbye and good luck."

Meg turned at the threshold. She pulled herself up to full height and tossed back her tangled hair. "Remember, girl. There 's no cure for grief but to put it under yer foot."

Footsteps retreated across the front room, and the apartment door closed with finality. Ingrid crawled from her rumpled bed. Meg and Paddy were gone. The flat surrounded her like a silent tomb.

She washed and dressed, fighting back a tide of loneliness. Feeling lightheaded, she fixed herself a cup of tea. At least bells no longer rang in her ears.

Before the bureau mirror, Ingrid brushed and pinned back her hair, then put on her straw bonnet. Its brim would shield her face.

Picking up her purse from the corner chair, she started for the door. Something made her stop. The purse felt awkward, heavier. She opened it and looked inside. An object, dark and shiny, lay at the bottom. A prickling fear darted through her. The pistol. *The officer's pistol!*

She stared in horror at this last, despicable, thing Paddy had done. "Oh, Paddy, how could you?"

Now she was laden with the gun and her promise not to reveal anything of the officer's murder. Murder. The word caused a wave of nausea to roll over her.

Andreas, if only I could run to you now and find refuge in your arms.

She stood in the middle of the room clutching her purse. Questions rolled over and over in her mind. Should she go to the police? If she did, would they accuse her of being an accomplice? They would track down Paddy and Meg. How could Paddy ever get a fair trial?

STRIKE AGITATOR! the newspaper headlines would scream. POLICE KILLER!

Ingrid gulped down a ragged breath. Meg had said she could stay here until the end of the month—that was only a week away. The police could knock down the door at any time before then!

She cringed at the fearful premonition. Where would she find another place to live? She had to get to the millinery shop before Madame Larousse replaced her. Her classes would have to wait. She hastily left the apartment.

As Ingrid turned east on Van Buren, government troops filled the street. Wearing cartridge belts at their waists and rifles on their shoulders, they made an imposing sight. Pedestrians, the majority businessmen, cheered the marching soldiers.

One man called out to the dust-covered troops as they passed. "Stop the bloody rioters, men!"

Her breathing becoming more difficult, she hovered near a shaded doorway. With hundreds, maybe thousands, of soldiers to protect the city, local police would be freer to hunt down lawbreakers. Her fingers felt the cold butt of the gun through the soft fabric of her purse. She swallowed hard. How could she get rid of the weapon without being seen?

On the next block, a street sweeper with his back to her cleaned the front gutter. His trash barrel stood next to the alley.

Ingrid approached him, her heart thumping against her rib cage. Discreetly she opened her purse and held it over the barrel. And then froze.

She was alone now, in this strife-torn city. Why should she dispose of the gun when she might need it to protect herself? She snapped the purse shut.

Angling her head away from the street, Ingrid hurriedly maneuvered along the boardwalk. She must get to Madame Larousse's shop. She walked faster, her heartbeat drumming in her throat with each step.

From behind, something cold prodded Ingrid's right arm. *Dear God.* A police officer must have observed her strange behavior, even been following her, and now would arrest her.

Quaking inside, she looked over her shoulder.

"Excuse me, miss." A young woman, dressed in a plain shop girl's dress, pulled in the handle of her parasol and scurried past.

Feeling dizzy, Ingrid braced herself against the front of a building for a moment before continuing on to State Street.

" 'Put grief under yer foot,' " Meg had told her.

She would try, but could she find a safe haven before the authorities found her?

CHAPTER TWENTY-ONE

"Where have you been, mademoiselle?" Madame Larousse called out to Ingrid when she entered the nearly empty millinery shop. "I've been going crazy with no one here to help me." Her employer's black lashes fluttered like a nervous bird's wings.

"I am so sorry, Madame. I was injured and just got out of the hospital—"

"Ze hospital? How terrible. This strike has made ze streets dangerous." She stared out the front window at the chaos outside.

"It was only a slight concussion." Ingrid untied the ribbons beneath her chin. "I can work today."

Madame clutched the sheer window curtain. "Ze soldiers are coming. *Mon Dieu!* No one wants to buy ze *chapeau* when ze terrible strike goes on and on." She whirled, her dark eyes flaring. "Mad men with guns run in ze streets! Break ze windows. I must close ze shop."

Ingrid flinched. "But, my job . . ."

A tall, elegant customer, seemingly undisturbed by the strikers, politely interrupted their conversation. "I would like to purchase this hat, please."

Madame Larousse threw up her manicured hands. "Ah, *oui*, Madame." She turned to Ingrid. "I am sorry," she said. "I wait on this patron and then I close ze shop."

Taken aback by her sudden dismissal, Ingrid lingered on the Persian carpet. What would she do now? She soon would have no roof over her head nor means to pay for another.

She glanced across the salon, recognizing the attractive patron making the purchase. A woman of about thirty-five whose ginger brown hair had been upswept into a mass of curls and anchored by apricot tea roses. Mrs. Cramer Justin, wife of an English fine arts dealer. And, a socialite in high Chicago circles, she'd heard.

"I'd also like a yard of that lovely yellow grosgrain ribbon," Mrs. Justin added.

"*Oui.* For your petite daughter?"

Mrs. Justin smiled. "Yes, Beth loves ribbons for her hair."

When the patron left the shop, Ingrid followed her outside.

"Excuse me, ma'am. I believe I have waited on you before in the salon."

"Yes, isn't it Ingrid?"

"I overheard you mention your young daughter . . . and I wondered. Would she need a nanny? I am very good with children."

Ingrid stood at the open window of her second-story quarters at her new residence, gazing down at the side garden. The faint sweet fragrance of dianthus rose on the golden afternoon air; Chicago's violent strike of a few weeks ago a fading nightmare.

How fortunate she had been to gain employment in the Justin household.

She had just put Beth, her four-year-old charge, down for her nap and was supposed to be changing into a white serving costume. Downstairs, meticulous preparations were afoot for Mrs. Justin's guest at high tea. A social matron, the mention of whose name set tongues wagging.

Ingrid had laid the crisply starched uniform on her four-poster bed earlier so she could quickly climb into it. But now that she should be hurrying to change, she only glanced at the uniform lethargically.

She continued to stare out the window, something Beth had said earlier during today's lesson in the gazebo surfacing in her mind. The child had looked up earnestly into Ingrid's face with concern beyond her tender years. "You look so sad, Miss Ingrid. Are you sad because your young man went away?"

Ingrid had stopped short, her voice catching in her throat. "Who told you that, dear?"

"Cook told me. She said your young man went away—and that's why you cry."

Embarrassed and touched at Beth's comment, Ingrid had dabbed at the corners of her eyes. Cook must have noticed her melancholy mood and teary moments since she'd arrived, although she had tried to hide them. Ingrid had swallowed over the achy lump in her throat and put her arm around Beth, giving her a squeeze. "Don't worry. I promise I will be cheerful very soon."

Surely she would be when Andreas replied to her recent letter giving him her new employer's address.

A knock at the door made her jump.

"Miss Johansson. You're wanted downstairs immediately," one of the downstairs maids called. "Mrs. Justin wants all of us to join her in the front hall for instructions."

Ingrid hastily grabbed up her serving costume, answering, "Yes, I'll be right there."

Several frantic minutes later, Ingrid found ten female servants gathered at attention in the front hall. They stood in a semicircle before their mistress, dressed in spotless uniforms with starched white aprons. Ingrid slipped quietly into place at one end of the half circle.

Mrs. Justin smiled down her distinguished English nose at them and proceeded to give each servant individual instructions.

"Frieda," she addressed the head downstairs maid, "you will

oversee the buffet table, making sure the trays are always full. Ingrid will assist you and your staff."

The stout woman darted a glance at Ingrid. "Yes, ma'am." They each made a small curtsy.

Mrs. Justin cocked her head toward the butler. "Chambers, please show our guests directly to the sun parlor when they arrive. Don't let them linger in the foyer."

As if in a salute, the butler touched his white gloved hand to his silver brow. "Certainly, madam."

Mrs. Justin gave them a last sweeping glance. "Well then. The ladies should start arriving in fifteen minutes. Let's show them our best hospitality." She moved away down the hall, her white organza skirts flowing around her slim frame.

Ingrid let out a momentary sigh and rushed toward the hall mirror in hopes of adjusting her drooping topknot.

Frieda bustled along behind her, admonishing loudly, "You were late. No time for primping now." The large woman hitched past Ingrid, her wide hips swaying. "Help me at the refreshment table."

In the rear sun parlor, a high-ceilinged room with French doors opening onto the veranda, the refreshment table dwarfed everything else. Swathed in a cream lace cloth, it extended twenty feet. Beneath a canopy of white camellias, lemon jasmine, and ivory carnations lay an assortment of food fit for royalty. The blended aromas of flowers and exquisite cuisine was intoxicating.

As Ingrid followed Frieda across the pastel Oriental carpet, her gaze fell longingly over trays of delicate finger sandwiches, plump scones, and lavish tea cakes. "What a smorgasbord!" she exclaimed.

Frieda came to a halt and wheeled abruptly, nearly causing Ingrid to bump into her. The woman's double chin quivered with indignation. "Don't talk Swedish, Ingrid! Madam prefers us to use only English—especially in front of her guests."

Ingrid's cheeks smarted hotly as if they'd been slapped. But she threw her shoulders back and replied, "Of course." Inwardly, she resented the housemaid for the reprimand over a mere slip of the tongue. She would be on guard not to let it happen again.

At half past four, the sun parlor began to fill with chattering, fashionable matrons of Chicago society. From her post at mid-table, Ingrid had a full view of every dazzling gown and coiffure parading past. She began to fantasize, while keeping watch over the center trays, about what it would be like to be one of these ladies, so self-assured and married to a prosperous business entrepreneur.

You had such an opportunity to marry Andreas if you hadn't run off to Chicago and fallen in with a police killer, a voice sniped inside her head. A recent newspaper article she'd read reported the slain police officer had left a widow and three children. Grief and sympathy had filled her heart. She was guilty of keeping the murder weapon and the name of the officer's killer. What would Andreas think of her if he knew?

Her palms began to sweat, and her throat constricted. She stepped back against the wall between two potted ferns.

At her elbow, Mrs. Justin asked, "Are you all right, dear? You look rather pale."

"I think I need some air."

Mrs. Justin led her outside to the veranda. "The breeze here will perk you up." Before she left, she added, smiling, "Seat the ladies up front. Mrs. Palmer likes to have a close rapport with her audience."

"Yes, ma'am." Ingrid nodded, happy to be released from the confines of the parlor and her secret fears.

Momentarily, a cluster of women flowed from the French doors, and she showed them to the first few rows of chairs. Soon after, a stunning woman wearing a canary yellow gown glided onto the veranda accompanied by Mrs. Justin. From the woman's assured demeanor, Ingrid knew she must be the featured speaker. All eyes appeared to swivel toward this elegant creature, her upswept dark hair, her complement of pearl and jade jewelry.

"Potter Palmer's wife," someone whispered. "He's the developer of State Street . . . built the Palmer House just for her."

After a glowing introduction by Mrs. Justin, the graceful Mrs. Palmer took her place at the podium. Ingrid watched with interest. What could this woman from another world have to say to her?

With a clear and confident voice, Mrs. Palmer began. "You've all heard of the rise of the feminist movement. The new woman of our century is emerging. As you must also know, I am a vigorous advocate of greater education for women—all women."

For all women. Ingrid perked up her ears. This was not to be a simple tea party speech.

"Men do not really admire the superficial fools they have trained us to be," she added. "Men must admire and love us for who we really are. Who we may become."

Mrs. Palmer stepped from behind the podium and moved closer to the guests seated in the front row. All eyes followed her.

With distinctive poise, she continued. "Through self-control and self-discipline, I believe anything can be accomplished."

Self-control and self-discipline. A small flame ignited within Ingrid. She vowed to adopt both. No matter the obstacles, she would continue her education and eventually reach her goal of becoming a teacher.

After returning from her classes the following afternoon, Ingrid put Beth down for her nap, then ventured up the hall to her mistress's bedroom. She found the door ajar, a slight breeze wafting to the hall from an open window. She knocked.

"Yes. Come in."

Ingrid pushed the door open and entered. She found Mrs. Justin reclining on a blue satin chaise, an open book in her lap. "Excuse me, ma'am. I just wanted to say how much I enjoyed the tea yesterday, and Mrs. Palmer's lecture."

Mrs. Justin sat taller and set her book on a mahogany end table. "Why, Ingrid, I'm glad you did."

"When I was studying to become a teacher in Minneapolis, I didn't have time to read anything but textbooks." Ingrid paused, staring down at her hands. "I wondered . . ."

Mrs. Justin inclined her head curiously. "Yes?"

"I wondered if you could suggest some books I might read," Ingrid blurted. "To—to better my education."

"Of course, dear." The woman slipped off the chaise and moved toward open pocket doors leading to another room. "Come into the library, and we'll see what we can find."

Ingrid's heart swelled. She followed on Mrs. Justin's heels through the open doors. Before her, on three sides of the room, were shelves of books. She inhaled deeply, smelling the rich leather bindings.

Mrs. Justin walked along the shelves, pulling books at intervals. "Here's Charlotte Brontë's *Jane Eyre* and, oh yes . . . an exciting adventure, *Moby Dick.*" She stood on tiptoe to reach another book. "We mustn't forget Louisa May Alcott. Here," she offered the book to Ingrid. "You'll love *Little Women.*"

Ingrid's pulse raced with anticipation. "Thank you, ma'am. There are so many."

Mrs. Justin laughed. "Hundreds, I'm sure." She extricated another slim book from a lower shelf. "Not to forget Mr. Emerson—one of his collections on nature."

When Ingrid made her way back to her quarters, an armload of books tucked under her chin, her heart sang. An empty void would now be filled. While waiting for Andreas' reply to her last letter, she would enter new worlds and other lives.

Ingrid descended the horse car into the hustle of State Street. Mrs. Justin had sent her on several errands early this Saturday morning, the most important of which was to pick up two new hats from Madame Larousse's millinery shop. Ingrid put a little lilt to her step, knowing she would return to her former employer's shop as a patroness instead of a mere shop clerk. Well, not exactly a patroness, but employed by one. Close enough for today.

Of course, she owed Madame Larousse a debt of gratitude for introducing her to one of Madame's most prominent clients.

Coming to the next intersection, Ingrid paused. At the signal from the traffic officer, she carefully lifted the skirts of her new cream faille gown, fashioned at bustle and overskirt with cardinal red bows, and stepped off the boardwalk.

The sound of a low whistle caught her attention. She glanced to her right and into the cocky grin of a carriage driver watching her pass.

Ordinarily she would have blushed to her roots at such flirtation, but not today. Today she merely continued on her course, drawing herself up to full measure, and smiled with self confidence. She was nineteen now, a governess and a young lady. No longer a naive girl fresh off the farm.

But as she reached the other side of the intersection, the sight of a young female rushing toward her gave Ingrid's self-composure a jolt. The young woman wore a colorless straw hat and a drab gray frock in too heavy a fabric for the day's eventual heat. She kept her head down, eyes fixed on the boardwalk as she hurried along. Her hair gave her identity away—that familiar flame-red mane.

Ingrid rushed toward the young woman, her heart skipping.

"Meg?" she called. "Meg."

Green eyes glanced upward, looked straight into hers. Ingrid recognized their expression: surprise mixed with fear.

She reached out and placed her white-gloved hand on Megan Killeen's arm. "I thought I would never see you again."

Meg glanced at Ingrid's hand on her arm then shrugged. "Aye, and 'tis Ingrid," she replied, looking her up and down. "Looks like the fates have been good to ye."

Ingrid smiled. "Can we have a cup of tea somewhere?"

Meg shook her head, her red hair tangled below her straw hat. "I'm on me way to a new job a few blocks from here. Me boss is a tyrant."

Ingrid held tight to Meg's arm. "I have so much to tell you—"

Meg pulled away. "Sorry, me girl. Time's wastin'." She turned to go. Two businessmen brushed past, one rudely bumping her.

"But—you must tell me what's happened to Paddy," Ingrid pleaded.

A wary look passed over Meg's face. She motioned to a storefront out of the way of pedestrians. Ingrid followed her.

Once there, Meg muttered under her breath, "Paddy's skipped town. You remember Sean Slattery?" she asked, a hint of the old Meg twinkling in her eye.

Ingrid nodded. "How could I forget him? That slick trickster."

"Well, he got Paddy a place to stay with a friend in New York City. I think he's workin' in some bar."

"You know, after you both left the apartment, I found the gun in my purse," Ingrid blurted, anger kindling inside her at the memory. "Paddy must have put it there."

Meg blanched. "The gun?"

"The gun that killed the police officer!"

Meg's hand flew upward to press on Ingrid's lips. She looked around nervously. "Dear God! Me brother's a bastard," she spat out.

"I ended up keeping it for my protection."

Meg cocked her brow. "Aye—but be wary—the gun has a curse on it." She glanced up the street. "Sorry, I have to go, or I'll be sacked for sure." She took a few steps and looked back, a flash of a smile lifting her freckled cheeks. Then Meg Killeen disappeared into the thickening crowd.

Ingrid swallowed over tears in her throat. "Goodbye, Meg," she said softly.

With a saddened heart, Ingrid continued up State Street. How fast her life had changed. It seemed only yesterday that she and Meg had laughed at girlish things and washed their hair in early summer up on the roof. Before the rail strike. Before Paddy had killed the officer.

A chill cascaded over her body. The officer's death had been an accident. Paddy had run away to New York, leaving misery behind. But didn't life have a way of catching up to you? As Ingrid drew closer to the millinery shop, she released a fatalistic thought. Sure as Paddy had an impulsive nature, trouble would find him again one day.

Later when Ingrid returned to the Justin residence, she saw Beth wave from a parlor window. The child raced to meet her at the front door. Jumping up and down as if on springs, she begged, "What did you bring me?"

Ingrid unloaded her bundles into Chambers' capable hands. "Just a minute, Miss Kangaroo." She retrieved a small parcel and gave it to her ward.

Beth giggled at her new name then tore open the package. "Peppermint sticks!"

Frieda appeared from down the hall. "The child's been waiting and fretting under our feet ever since you left." The stout woman pulled a slim brown envelope from her apron pocket. "This came for you early afternoon."

Ingrid accepted the telegram. The return address was posted

Lake Park Station, Minnesota. It was from home. A twinge of fear started at the pit of her stomach. What news was this?

After leaving Beth in the nursery with an upstairs maid, she hurried down the hall to her room. Closing the door behind her, she ripped open the envelope.

Chapter Twenty-Two

Dagmar Eriksen strode into the drawing room and planted herself in front of the sofa where her mother sat reading the *St. Paul Daily Globe*. "Mother, I must talk with you."

Tilting backward, Emma Eriksen peered over her reading glasses. "Please don't come up on a person so suddenly, dear. You could give them apoplexy."

With an impatient wave of her hand, Dagmar dropped down on the sofa next to her. "But you should hear what Mr. Upman told me at the bank today, concerning the future of our . . . of the family's railroad bonds."

Emma's dark eyebrows lifted an inch above her frames. "The railroad bonds?" She shook her head, not a hair straying from her upswept coiffure. "This horrid strike has probably sent them plummeting. Is that what he told you?"

Dagmar leaned toward her mother, her demeanor confidential. "Oh, no. He talked about the future of the bonds—how much they'll be worth when Mr. Hill extends the railroad to Canada and the Northwest."

Emma's ears seemed to perk up like tiny antennas. She laid the newspaper aside.

Dagmar continued with serious demeanor. "Mr. Upman stressed the importance of keeping the bonds under our roof." She paused a moment for emphasis. "I guess he meant that Andreas and I will inherit them one day."

"Well, of course you will."

Too enthused to sit still, Dagmar hopped to her feet. "That's just it, Mother. Andreas has been so distant to me lately. Running off to Chicago like that He could have been killed by one of those wild mobs."

Emma shifted her skirts on the sofa. "I don't quite follow you, dear."

Dagmar's face burned with fierce determination. "I'm saying that Andreas and I should be closer. Matrimony would consolidate the family's bond holdings." Her plan to wed Andreas must go forward, even if she loathed him now. If he should die suddenly, as his widow, she was certain to obtain his shares. What financial and social power they would grant her.

"Matrimony?" Emma's pale forehead furrowed. "You still have these feelings for him. But how does he feel?"

Dagmar tapped her foot. "He seems to be . . . confused. That's why I need your help. The Holmquists are having their annual regatta at White Bear Lake next weekend . . ."

Her mother pursed her lips.

The front door closed, and the sound of a man's footsteps in the entryway reached them. Dagmar snapped to attention. "That's Andreas now." She flashed Emma a conspiratorial glance and glided across the carpet to the threshold.

"Andreas," Dagmar called invitingly, "won't you join us?"

Andreas turned his head at the sound of Dagmar's voice. Her compelling gaze locked with his. Damn. She was the last person he wanted to talk to right now, grimy and bone-tired as he was from the day's raucous confrontation at the train yard. But beyond her, he glimpsed his stepmother seated on the drawing room sofa, and he relinquished the idea of brushing Dagmar off.

He released a weary breath and followed his stepsister into the room.

"Hello, Emma." He forced a smile at both of the women and

leaned up against the fireplace mantel.

"Andreas. You do look the worse for wear." Emma removed her reading glasses. "How are things going at the rail yard?"

He shrugged. "We had to call the police in today to remove a few agitators. But the rest of the men calmed down after I talked with them."

"Then they aren't going to strike here like they did back east?" Dagmar piped in.

Andreas raked his fingers through his disheveled hair. "We're hoping they won't."

Emma gestured to the wing-backed chair opposite her. "Sit down, Dagmar."

Dagmar pinched up her skirts and seated herself next to Emma. "We want to talk to you about the Holmquist's regatta next weekend." She flapped her dark eyelashes flirtatiously at him.

Andreas stood frozen in place. The Holmquist's regatta was not on his agenda. "I'd like to . . . but any social events will have to wait until the threat of the strike is over." He started for the door. "If you'll excuse me."

With long strides, Andreas moved across the room and stepped into the hall. To his annoyance, Dagmar followed directly on his heels.

"Wait, Andreas."

He looked over his shoulder, impatient to bolt up the stairs to his room and a hot bath.

"We really should talk about this. Maybe after dinner tonight?" Her thin arm reached toward him.

He regarded it as he would a spider's tentacle, recalling her previous seduction attempt. "I don't think so. If things calm down in the yard, I'll be leaving for Chicago by the end of the week."

Her dark brows flew up. "Not again!"

He released an irritated breath. "Dagmar, my comings and goings are none of your concern." Ascending the stairs, he left her staring up at him, her mouth agape.

Ingrid scanned the telegram, the printed words leaping from the page.

Urgent Stop Family sick Stop Summer fever Stop
Briget is worse Stop Mama needs you Stop Money
order for train Stop

Love, Papa

A prickling fear traveled down Ingrid's body. "Briget," she whispered. The thought of her baby sister lying ill, possibly near death, paralyzed her.

She stared at the fluttering curtains at her bedroom window, her mind far away on the farm. She saw the children playing down by the lake. The mosquitoes were as thick as flies this time of year.

She shook her head, trying to collect her thoughts. She must explain her dilemma to Mrs. Justin. Her two class instructors at the academy would have to be notified. Then she would take the earliest train home.

With a racing pulse, Ingrid went to the closet, stood on tiptoe to pull her travel bag from the shelf, and tossed it on the bed. Reaching into a dresser drawer, she scooped up some underclothes and started to put them into the bag. Her eyes popped wide when a heavy metal object flopped onto the floral embroidered coverlet.

She gasped, realizing a shiver of panic. The gun! Almost forgotten in its hiding place.

Curling her fingers around its cool handle, she lifted the loaded gun carefully. When she had first arrived at her new employment, she'd been tempted to throw the pistol away, but she was afraid one of the snooping house maids might find it in the trash bin. She couldn't afford to answer resulting questions. Hiding the gun had seemed the best choice until a better means of disposal presented itself.

Now a renewed need for protection filled her when she thought of the unemployed, roaming vagabonds who loitered in the train yards and sometimes robbed single women travelers. Memories of the recent rail strike still traumatized her.

She stuffed her underclothing, the gun, and an everyday dress into the leather bag, added her brush and hand mirror, and snapped it shut. The packed bag she shoved beneath the bed's eyelet dust ruffle, its new hiding place until she left.

In one corner of the room sat her old trunk. She sighed resignedly. The trunk would have to be sent for later. She collected all the money she'd saved, a mere week's pay of three dollars, and the money order, and slipped them into her purse.

Glancing up, she saw the books Mrs. Justin had loaned her, pressed between bookends on the shelf, next to the tall window overlooking the vast garden. A tug of regret pulled at her. She doubted if she would ever finish the revered books or return to this life of comfort. But she could take what she had gleaned here, tuck it away in her memory. Her family needed her now. There was no other choice.

Ingrid opened the door and dashed downstairs to find Mrs. Justin.

Before she could reach her employer, she overheard Chambers in the entryway speaking with a mail messenger. The butler caught her as she turned down the main hall. "Miss Johansson, you have a letter."

The letter was from Andreas. He had just arrived in the city. He wanted to see her first thing tomorrow morning.

Tomorrow? It wasn't possible.

Torn by conflicting emotions, she fought back a wave of

panic. The one she most wanted to see, she could not. How unfair fate could be. Painful tears pricked her eyelids. If she postponed her return home and Briget's condition worsened, she would never forgive herself.

Andreas arrived back in Chicago on the late afternoon train. The city welcomed him with the big-town bustle one might expect from a thriving metropolis. No picketers. No agitators. No strike. The bedlam of dangerous streets and burning rail yards several weeks before were now only a discomforting memory.

The national rail strike had lasted only a week, but Andreas knew it had set the stage for future confrontations between owners and trainmen. Minneapolis and St. Paul had been spared the terror and violence of larger cities. Andreas liked to think he'd played a part in cooling frayed tempers.

His main objective now was to find Ingrid among the ruins of yesterday's promise. There was no reason they could not begin anew. Her education here would be finished at year's end. She would return to Minneapolis, and they could build a future together.

Early the next morning, his hired carriage rounded the corner onto Michigan Avenue. Andreas looked out at towered mansions with great bay windows and spacious lawns. So this was "Millionaire's Row." Even the air smelled rich here.

I am working as a governess for a wealthy English family, Ingrid had written in her last brief letter.

In the middle of the block, Andreas instructed the driver to pull into a wide circular driveway. The carriage halted beneath the wide portico. Picking up a bouquet of long-stemmed red roses on the seat beside him, Andreas stepped down to the gravel drive. A gray stone mansion, resplendent in the sun-washed August day with its dozen chimneys and flourishing side garden, rose before him. Could Ingrid really be living here?

Nearly a month had passed since he had found her amidst the violent strikers and lost her again to circumstances beyond his control. Now, recovered from her injuries and beginning a new life, would she still want to see him after he'd left so abruptly? Even for such an urgent reason?

He swallowed against his starched white shirt collar, straightened his tie, and climbed the stairs to the arched front doors.

In her room, Ingrid finished packing a few toiletries into her travel bag. She had just said her farewells to Mrs. Justin and Beth at breakfast. Both she and Mrs. Justin had agreed it would be too distressing for Beth to see her off at the station. Sadness had welled up inside Ingrid when she gave Beth a last hug and came upstairs. It seemed she was always saying goodbye to a loved one.

The downstairs maid appeared at the threshold to her room. "A gentleman by the name of Mr. Eriksen is asking to see you, miss."

Ingrid's pulse quickened. He was here. "Mr. Eriksen?"

"Yes, miss," the maid repeated, "a handsome young gentleman. He brought a huge bouquet of roses for you, and I put them in a vase." The maid's tone turned imploring. "He's waiting in the front parlor—he's looking rather nervous."

Her mind raced. He was actually here in the house, in the flesh, after all the days that had separated them. Across the room, the mantel clock's hands read eight forty-five. Her train home would leave in an hour.

"Tell him . . . tell him I'll receive him in the side garden."

Yes, the garden would offer the most privacy.

The maid went back down the hall, her footfalls disappearing on the carpeted stairs. Now that he was here, what would she say to him?

With trembling fingers, she finished tucking loose tendrils into her braided coronet. She must see Andreas if only to tell him she could make no promises. Her family's needs came first. And, there was something she could not tell him. She was unwittingly bound to her secret past in a way that he could not understand.

Grasping the travel bag, Ingrid bolstered her resolve and left her room. Once downstairs, she dropped the bag in the entryway, half-ran down the hall past the pantry, and slipped out the door to the side garden. There she took a deep breath and moved along the row of pear trees to where Andreas stood waiting.

When he saw her, he removed his hat, his fine dark hair illumined in the morning light. Ingrid's heartbeat surged upward, leaving her breathless.

Clean-shaven and tanned, Andreas was even more attractive than she had remembered. Before, his beard had hidden his cleft chin. He wore a cream-colored, two-piece suit that emphasized his tall stature, his broad shoulders. His sea-blue gaze met hers.

She thought she would faint.

"Ingrid," he said in a low throaty voice. Removing his hat, he smiled and stepped forward. "How are you? Please accept my apology for ever having to leave you."

Her heart fluttered inside the stays of her corset as he took her hand in his. "Hello, Andreas. I'm fine now. Thank you for the roses."

"They're not nearly as beautiful as you."

"You look handsome as ever," she said, her knees weak beneath her.

He moved closer, gazing down into her face. Her mouth was so dry she could hardly swallow. First, he kissed her with his eyes. Then, leaning over, he brushed his lips across her cheek. "I know you must think I'm . . . a crazy fool to come here like this, without giving more notice. But I had to see you in person to explain that terrible day of the strike when I was forced to leave."

"You already did, in your letter. Those were terrible circumstances for all of us," she said. "Thank you again for paying my hospital bill."

An angry expression crossed his face. "I'd like to horsewhip the devils who caused your fall. Those worthless strike agitators!"

A sudden fear tingled her skin. "It . . . it was an accident."

Holding his hat in front of him as though it were a weapon, he cursed. "There is no excuse for their actions. They fueled the strike and crippled the country for days!"

Ingrid felt the hair raise on the back of her neck. Even if some thugs went too far in their protests, she couldn't blame the striking rail workers. "From what I heard, they had good reason."

As if she'd thrown a blow to his jaw, Andreas reared back. "How would you know? They didn't give their employers a chance at the bargaining table. Anyone supporting that heinous strike should be tarred and feathered."

His harsh glare and threatening words made the nearness of him unbearable, almost overwhelming. How could he ever understand her recent past? She had lived with a rail strike agitator. A cop killer! She still had the murder weapon. Her hands were stained. What would he think of that?

He was a different person than she had known last autumn, when they strolled through the park, recited poetry, and kissed fervently behind the boathouse. More cynical than the young man she had been intimate with on New Year's Eve.

And time was too limited now to revive the past.

Glancing toward the stables, she saw the coachman drive a

horse-drawn carriage up to the front of the house. "What time is it, Andreas? I'm afraid I have to catch a train—"

Andreas tossed his hat on the nearby hedge lining the walk, placed his large hands on her arms, and fairly lifted her to him. "You can't leave now." His gaze burned into hers, taking her breath away. "You don't know how much I've missed you these past months. How I've longed to see you. There's nothing to keep us apart."

She shook her head sadly. "You're wrong. My sister Briget has fallen ill with fever. Papa sent a telegram just yesterday. I must take the next train home."

Surprise flashed across his features. "I'm sorry. That is bad news. Can I take you to the station?"

She half-turned toward the house. "No. My carriage is waiting." She forced herself to speak firmly. "I am so glad you came to see me, Andreas. But I can see that our lives have changed. I think . . . we must go our separate ways."

"You can't mean that." Andreas raised his hand and cupped her chin. "Let me see the light in your eyes, Ingrid, the way it's shone for me before."

Her body tensed. Tears stung her eyelids. "I—I can't."

He moaned as if she had pierced his very core. His mouth came down on hers, longing, seeking, demanding. Longing as she had longed. Demanding what she was unable to give.

Her heart hammered so loudly in her breast, she was afraid he would hear it. Ingrid splayed her hands on either side of his broad chest and pushed herself away. "Please. Let me leave."

Whirling, she rushed back up the walk. It had never been so long. A part of her begged to turn and throw herself into his arms . . . another part forced her ahead, away from the pain of his world.

Andreas caught up with her, spinning her around to face him. "Why are you running away from me, Ingrid? Why are you acting this way?"

Ingrid looked up into his questioning eyes, past his pain. She could still feel the pistol, cold and hard, inside her purse. She could not imagine confessing her secret to him: *I aided a lawbreaker in Chicago, a police killer!* If they were engaged and word got out, his railroad career would be ruined. He would never forgive her.

Ingrid choked back a sob. "Nothing is the same." With each word, her stomach twisted like a knotted rope. "We do not belong together."

Andreas angled his head as if he wasn't hearing clearly. His gaze captured hers. "I love you."

Ingrid winced beneath the strength of his declaration. "No, Andreas. You love my memory." She held her hand in front of her to keep him from following her. "Forgive me. Forget me."

She could not escape his distraught face. Nor his broken voice. "I'll never forget you, Ingrid."

Shaking from head to toe, she entered the side door and nearly collapsed against the wall. Tears streamed down her face and onto her gown. What had she done? Her heart split in two, as sharply as if someone had rent it with a knife.

"Andreas," she cried. "Andreas."

CHAPTER TWENTY-THREE

From the driveway, Andreas looked up at the darkened house. Moths flickered against the two globe lights on either side of the front door. "Welcome home," he muttered under his breath. Hoisting his luggage, he climbed the steps to the wide front porch.

His body was weary after the long train ride from Chicago and lack of sleep. Myriad questions still plagued him. Why had Ingrid rejected him? Why hadn't he pressed her for more answers? What good would it have done? She'd been adamant: *We've changed. Nothing is the same.*

Then she had rushed inside that impenetrable mansion.

He turned his key in the lock, pushed the front door open, and crossed the dim foyer. How could her love for him have changed since they last met? He trudged upstairs. Yet again, driven by Ingrid's immediate concern for her stricken sister, he could understand her inability to think clearly. He must think of something to win her back.

A familiar pungent perfume assaulted his senses as he approached his room. "Andreas, you are dragging in late."

Focusing his eyes in the dimly lit hallway, he regarded Dagmar coming toward him. "I could say the same for you," he replied curtly. "It's after one o'clock."

She wore a low-cut party gown, her bodice trussed up narrow as a pipe cleaner. Her lips wore a little smirk. "Thor just brought me home from the hospital charity ball."

"Thor?" He paused for a moment, observing her through gritty eyes. "I can't picture it." His cousin must be changing his ways, climbing the social ladder. Whatever did these two see in each other?

Attempting to avoid further conversation with his stepsister, he entered his room and turned to close the door.

"Well, of course, we're just friends." Dagmar slipped over the threshold and boldly moved to within inches of him. Her thin lips curled upward. "I have an important matter to discuss with you."

Andreas set his suitcase on a chair, his shoulders sagging in the cloying nearness of her. "Not tonight, Dagmar."

She lifted her chin a millimeter, that familiar haughtiness surfacing in her jet eyes. "This is something that can't wait." She swished into the center of the dark room, her repulsive perfume surrounding him.

Uncomfortable with her in the darkness, Andreas lit a wall sconce. "Make it short. I'm tired."

She shrugged a thin shoulder. "Very well. You know that mother's estate is considerable . . ."

Frowning, Andreas cocked his head. "And—?"

"Well, Mother knows that we are . . . attracted to each other. I told her about the night you came to my room and tried to win over my affections."

"That is an outright lie," he snarled, "and you know it."

Dagmar's winged brows jumped. "I suppose you're still mooning over that farm cow."

"I've warned you before—never call her that," he demanded through clenched teeth.

"She isn't your kind," she rasped. "You could do far better than her." She came nearer, her lips pulled back in a near-manic grin. "You can have me—and together we will inherit a controlling interest in the railroad!"

Andreas threw back his head and emitted a roar of laughter. "You're crazy!"

She pounced on him, grasping his coat lapels. "No, I'm not crazy. I'm smart. Andreas, why won't you listen to me?"

He peeled her off his chest, but grasped her narrow wrist. "You listen to me, because I won't repeat this. I promised Father I would stay and take care of you and Emma. But I'll have no part of your schemes. Your behavior forces me to leave this house. Stay away from me, Dagmar. I won't allow you to interfere in my life."

"Let go!" She flailed at him, attempting to free her hand, her eyes flashing up at him. "Have your stupid farm cow, then."

How easy it would be to strangle her right now, he thought.

She jerked her head to the side and pulled away from his grip.

Andreas released her wrist. "Get out."

Her fingers fidgeting like nervous cat claws, Dagmar moved to the door. Her disheveled hair clung in clotted tendrils to her perspiring face. "You will regret this."

"I doubt it." His temper barely under control, he commanded, "Get out of my room—and out of my life."

She shook a pointed finger at him. "You will pay!"

Andreas followed Dagmar to the doorway, glaring at her. "I can't stand the sight of you any longer," he rasped.

"Damnable woman!" he swore under his breath, after closing and locking his door. A hotel room would be heaven compared to living under the same roof with her.

Andreas went directly to his closet and yanked two suits off their hangers. From the upper shelf, he removed a leather garment bag and threw it onto his bed. "Witch of witches!"

From a cherry wood chest of drawers, he grabbed handfuls of underwear and starched shirts. He went to the garment bag on the bed and stuffed the clothing into it. From the top of the chest, he hastily removed a silver comb and mirror and cushioned them between layers of underwear in the bag.

He tossed the suits over his arm and picked up both of his bags. Glancing around the room, he looked for anything he might have forgotten. In the bureau mirror, he caught sight of his reflection. God, he looked like hell. His hair fell in a hank over his forehead and glazed eyes. Dusky beard stubble outlined his jaw.

He was sweating after the exertion of his fury at Dagmar. If he stayed in this house much longer, he would do more than rant at her. He would throttle the deceiving life out of her.

Better to move out right now.

Andreas strode down the gaslit hall to the landing and descended the stairs. He felt Dagmar's eyes watching him from behind her half-closed door. He almost expected her to leap from the shadowy depths, tangled hair flying out around her, and chase him, cackling all the way to the front door.

He crossed the foyer, allowing himself a swift darting glance over his shoulder. No apparition followed in his path down the silent carpeted stairs.

Andreas escaped outside into the humid night. His heart was weary, but his determination set. He had to get away from Dagmar and this house. The sting of Ingrid's earlier rejection was somehow less painful now. He could not stop loving her. Nor feeling disgust for Dagmar. She was like quicksand.

As he strode to the stable behind the house, he thought of Ingrid rushing home to the farm and her stricken sister. Given Ingrid's fear of the dreaded childhood diseases, she must be beside herself with worry.

After finding a room in a downtown hotel, he'd try to get some sleep, then think of a way to help Ingrid and her family.

★ ★ ★ ★ ★

Dagmar was shaking as she entered her room, the pungent smell of her own perfume clinging to her nostrils.

How dare Andreas treat her like this, speak to her in such a humiliating tone?

From down the hall, she heard him banging drawers open and shut. So he was moving out of the house, and away from her. So be it. Good riddance.

She didn't need the arrogant, self-centered dandy in her life. How she detested him! He had ruined her perfect plan to merge their inheritance. If he had been agreeable, she might even have reneged on her secondary plan to dispose of him.

She fought back bitter tears.

Andreas' door opened, and she heard receding footsteps on the carpet. She listened intently then rushed to the window overlooking the stables and backyard. In a few minutes, Andreas appeared in the shadows below. He loaded a carriage and hitched one of the horses to it.

As she watched, an unsated rage filled her. He was leaving for good. Simply turning his back and riding off into the night. Her hopes and plans for them would ride away with him. How could he not have loved her? She'd tried so hard to attract him. Together they could have built a railroad empire.

Now Andreas climbed into the carriage and gave the horse a flick of the reins. A queasiness swirled in her stomach.

"Leave, stupid fool," she snarled, "but you will pay the price. Thor will help me destroy you. I vow it upon my life!"

The train huffed away from the Chicago station. Although Ingrid sat in a window seat, she dared not look back. Too many memories threatened to close in on her. The past few hours, with their rushed and wrenching farewells, had left her emotionally destitute.

Mrs. Justin had naturally been surprised but understanding at her sudden departure. "Of course we shall carry on, but we will miss you," she'd said thoughtfully. "Thank you for what you've done for Beth. She's been so much more . . . vibrant since you came."

And Beth. It had been the most difficult to say goodbye to her. "Dear one," Ingrid had begun, stroking the child's dark curls. "I must return to my own home now. My youngest sister is very sick."

"No," Beth had cried, tears slipping down her flushed face. "You mustn't go."

Ingrid had stooped and wrapped her arms around the delicate child. Pressing her cheek to Beth's, she'd murmured, "Don't cry. You know your mother loves you very much, and she can read to you from all of her wonderful books."

Beth brightened. "When I get bigger, I will learn to read."

Ingrid had nodded. "Yes, love. And I know you want me to help my little sister get well."

Beth had released a huge sigh and looked into Ingrid's eyes. "You will make her better."

"I pray that I will," Ingrid had replied, wiping away her own tears.

Now, leaning back against the upholstered seat, Ingrid closed her eyes and whispered another prayer for Briget. *Please, Lord, let me get home in time to take care of her. Do not take her from us.*

Through the window, the countryside raced by in a repetition of green fields. Unbidden, the image of Andreas waiting in the garden, his cream-colored suit outlined in sunlight, his azure eyes smiling, invaded her view.

He had come for her and she'd been forced to send him away.

But it was the only thing she could have done—to protect him from the repercussions of her complicity—and the most difficult thing she'd ever done. She wished she could stop loving him.

Had he returned home and sought comfort from Dagmar? She would never know.

"I'll never forget you, Ingrid," he'd vowed in the garden.

Never forget you.

She could not bear to think of her future without him.

Restless, Ingrid rummaged in her bag and found the slender book of Emerson essays that Mrs. Justin had insisted she take as a going-away gift.

She opened to a random page and read:

The life of man is a self-evolving circle, which, from a ring imperceptibly small, rushes on all sides outward to new and larger circles, and that without end.

She drew in a deep breath and let it out. Self-evolving circles. Yes, that was her life now, circling faster and faster. Without end.

Over a year ago, she had left home, seeking to fulfill a goal and seeking a new love. She thought she had found both. But she had only been drawn into the middle of a circle of unrealized dreams and pain.

Now she was running back. And Andreas? Would she ever see him again?

"We dare not hurt the ones we love," she'd often heard her mother say. She had never meant to hurt anyone. Squeezing her eyelids shut, she tried to push away the aching memory of her parting with Andreas. But her heart remained raw with anguish.

As the train approached the Lake Park station, Ingrid rubbed her eyes and stared wearily out the window. She hadn't slept well on her overnight ride, fitfully turning in her seat, shaking off troubled dreams.

She worried that her wire home had not been received. What then? Would she have to walk in the scorching heat to the farm? And had her sister's condition worsened? Could she arrive before it was too late?

Finally, the train chugged into the nearly deserted station. Her father stood on the platform, his face shaded by a wide-brimmed straw hat. She gave a sigh of relief, but fought back disappointment not to see Jens or Marie Lisbet with him.

Ingrid leaped from the train when it had barely come to a stop. "Papa!" she cried and ran to enfold herself in his warm, clumsy embrace.

His tawny beard crushed against her cheek, his strong arms girded her in a steely grip. She breathed in the faint smell of pipe tobacco. *"Dotter,"* he said, sounding as if he had a frog in his throat.

Breathless, Ingrid drew away. "How is Briget? And Mama?"

"They are still with us." His eyes clouded. "We can talk about them on the way home."

He took up her bag. "Is this all you brought?"

"My trunk will be shipped later." She followed him to the buggy parked in a small patch of shade. As he helped her up onto the seat, she noticed how worn the leather had become.

Her father climbed aboard on the other side. Before he snapped the reins, he gave her an approving look. "You are a grown-up city woman now." A smile enlivened his tired face. "I am glad you are home."

"I took the first train out of Chicago after I received your telegram." Ingrid placed her hand on her father's arm. "Tell me—how ill is Briget?"

Glancing at her from under his hat brim, he shook his head. "We do not know which way she will go. The fever's been with her for almost two days."

Ingrid's chest tightened with dread. "And how is everyone else?"

"Jens is fine, and Marie Lisbet. Your mater has been also sick, but not so bad as Briget." Her father bent his head. "I had to put old Prince down last week. He had stumbled and was failing."

Ingrid brushed away a tear. "Such a beautiful bay he was."

"*Ja.* He always pulled his share."

When they drew up to the Johansson log house, Ingrid saw her mother standing at the front door. Her work dress hung loosely on her. Ingrid alighted from the buggy and raced to meet her.

"There you are, my girl!" Sigrie exclaimed. "I knew you would come."

Jens appeared in the doorway behind Sigrie. They both hugged Ingrid at once, her mother's thin arms about her shoulders, her brother's wrapped around her waist.

Ingrid's eyes brimmed, while her heart sang. Home at last. "Where's Briget? How is she?"

Marie Lisbet emerged from the back bedroom, her slender frame lifting when she saw Ingrid. "She is the same."

"She has been in your bed," Sigrie said to Ingrid. "She is not so good."

Ingrid removed her hat and set it on top of the piano. "I must see her." She went first to Marie Lisbet and gave her a quick hug, then followed her back to the girls' room opposite her parents'.

Beneath the window, the child lay motionless on the bed. Her pale eyelids opened as Ingrid came near.

"Hello, my sweet girl," Ingrid said in her native Swedish.

Looking up at Ingrid through glazed eyes, Briget smiled. Her lips moved, but only a strained whisper escaped.

"She is too weak to speak," Sigrie said from the foot of the bed.

Ingrid swallowed over the ache in her throat. "I will wash out at the well and change my clothes. Then I will take care of her." She turned to Marie Lisbet and her mother. "You both have worn yourself ragged. You need rest."

In the afternoon, Briget's fever worsened. Her small body seemed racked with pain, and she cried out pitifully. Ingrid was forced to call on Marie Lisbet to fetch pails of water for bathing and boiling her mother's goldenseal herb tea. Briget coughed up most of the bitter-tasting brew, but Ingrid continued her vigil. She remembered her own ordeal over a year ago in this same straw bed, when she had pierced her foot with the pitchfork.

"You will survive this," Ingrid vowed to her young sister as she bathed her. "You are a fighter as I was."

At dusk, after Ingrid had mopped the bedroom floor to keep the room cool, then given Briget another sponge bath and a teaspoon of brandy, she went to sit on the small front porch with her mother. The men were finishing chores in the barn. A slight breeze gave little relief from the cloying humidity.

Ingrid swatted at a mosquito on her arm. "Nasty beast," she muttered.

"They are thick this year," Sigrie said wearily. "When they are so bad like this, they bring the sickness with them. Two of the Grinvold children died last week."

"Oh, no." Ingrid wiped the perspiration from her face with the back of her hand. "If only we had better medicines."

Her mother slumped forward, bowing her head into her work-worn hands. "If we can just keep her from slipping away . . ."

The thought of her twin sisters buried in two tiny graves on the hill gripped Ingrid. They had succumbed to cholera, another common childhood disease, when she had been Marie Lisbet's age. She set her mouth in grim determination.

"Briget will not slip away from us."

Raising her head, Sigric looked at Ingrid, dark smudges of fatigue beneath her eyes. "I want you and Marie Lisbet to sleep in the barn until we can smoke out Briget's bedclothes. Marie Lisbet has been sleeping up in the loft with Jens. She will be glad to join you."

Ingrid nodded reluctantly. "But if you need us . . ."

From the lake road came a horse and rig, plowing up dust around them. Who would be paying a visit at this hour? She hadn't time to step off the porch and receive them.

Just then, Marie Lisbet burst from behind the screen door. "Mama, come quick! Briget—Briget is shaking all over. She is having a fit."

Sigrie jumped to her feet. "Dear God!"

Her heart pounding like a trip-hammer, Ingrid chased after them back into the house.

CHAPTER TWENTY-FOUR

The three of them hurried through the house to the back bedroom. Ingrid was first through the door. "Briget?"

On the narrow bed, Briget wailed, her small body thrashing from side to side. Rushing to her sister, Ingrid placed a hand on her damp forehead. "Her fever is worse."

"Marie Lisbet, get some clean cloths," Sigrie called, "and fresh water from the well." Her face strained with fatigue, Marie Lisbet nodded.

"I will go." Ingrid moved quickly across the planked floor and stepped into the outer room. Her head bowed, she was not aware of the two men standing before her until her hand brushed the shirt sleeve of the taller one. Surprised, she hitched her gaze upward into familiar azure eyes. "Andreas!"

Her knees threatened to buckle beneath her. "What are you doing here?"

A concerned frown creased his dust-streaked face. "We knocked, but no one answered. I've brought someone to help Briget. This is my family physician, Dr. Kristen."

In awe, she looked from Andreas to the bespectacled man next to him. "Dr. Kristen. Thank you for coming." She motioned toward the doorway. "My sister is very ill with fever. She is in here."

Medical bag in hand, the doctor followed her into the small, crowded room. Ingrid introduced him briefly to everyone. Dr. Kristen went to stand by the bed, setting his bag on the bedside table. "I'll need more light. Do you have a large kerosene lamp?"

"I will get one," Marie Lisbet said and left the room.

"First, I'd like to wash my hands. Where is your well?"

"Outside. Come with me," Ingrid said.

When they returned, the doctor ordered everyone out of the room but Sigrie. Hans and Jens came in from the barn, and Ingrid informed them of the doctor's arrival.

His lined face slipping into a humble expression, Hans regarded Andreas for a moment. He extended a calloused hand. "I was wrong about you, railroad man. This is a good thing you have done."

Andreas shook her father's hand in a strong grip. "I only hope we've come in time to help Briget."

New admiration for Andreas stirring inside her, Ingrid asked, "Are you hungry?"

"No. We had dinner on the train." He pulled out a handkerchief and dabbed the sweat and dust from his forehead.

"Would you like to take a walk and get some fresh air?"

His eyes answered before his lips. "If you can be spared for a few minutes."

Papa smiled. "*Ja,* we can spare her for a few minutes."

And then Andreas' large hand was at her elbow and they were stepping out the front door. Despite the worrisome circumstances, Ingrid's feet barely touched the few stairs to the yard. The nectar-sweet fragrance of her mother's roses along the fence filled her senses.

They strolled past the barn, where she lit a lantern and took it off the wall. "You must be thirsty," she said. "And I am too. The well is just over here."

"Let me carry this," he offered, taking the lantern from her. "I know you're tired."

She sighed, grateful that he understood without her having to explain the day of misery it had been. At the well, she filled the tin ladle and handed it to him.

"No. You drink first." He placed his hand on hers and gently pushed the ladle to her.

She drank greedily, the cool water slaking her parched throat, then wiped her mouth with the back of her hand. In the twilight, she felt his quiet gaze observing her.

Refilling the ladle from the well bucket, she passed it to him. He set the lantern on the ground, took the ladle, and drained its contents smoothly. "Thank you."

Much lay unsettled between them, she thought, yet this simple act of sharing a drink of cool water seemed to bind them as kindred spirits for this moment.

"You have come such a long way . . . to help my sister. It is so kind of you, Andreas." She wanted to reach out and touch him, but his nearness, his tender gaze, rendered her immobile. A glance toward the house renewed her fears. "Briget's fever has lasted too long."

He moved closer in the pale light of the lantern. His large hands were warm on her arms. "All that can be done for her is being done. I feel Briget is going to be all right."

Her body welcomed his touch, his warmth, his strength. She tipped her chin to look up at him. "I want to believe that. I must get back to see if I am needed."

When they returned, the doctor was talking with her family in the front room. "My immediate diagnosis would be encephalitis. Do you have any sick horses on the farm?"

Her father's expression sagged. "I had to put down one of our geldings last week."

Dr. Kristen's voice was somber. "This illness is spread by mosquitoes infecting domestic animals, usually horses. Briget's eardrums had swollen and I drained them. There was some blood."

"What does that mean . . . the blood?" Sigrie asked.

"If an eardrum ruptures, it could affect her hearing. Depending on the damage, they can heal on their own. I gave your daughter some paregoric to relieve her pain. It will help her sleep." He patted Sigrie's shoulder. "Your girl has a strong constitution. We'll see what the morning brings."

Her mother's eyes misted, and she patted them with a handkerchief. "*Ja.* We can pray and hope the Lord is merciful."

It was midnight before Ingrid and Marie Lisbet settled into their cots in a far corner of the barn. Near the front barn door, Andreas and the doctor were bedded down with blankets. Just far enough away for muffled voices to carry and close enough to keep her aware of their presence.

Drawing the light bedsheet over her, Ingrid inhaled the sweet fragrance of new-mown hay. She closed her eyes, listening to Flicka, their surviving horse, nicker softly in her stall. And heard the drone of male snoring.

Marie Lisbet rolled over to face her. "Will the doctor make Briget well?"

Ingrid sighed in the dark. "We must keep hoping he will." She reached out and touched her sister's arm. "Say your prayers. Go to sleep."

But Ingrid could not fall asleep. Briget's condition kept her on edge.

Through the small window above them a full harvest moon glowed in the velvet sky. Like a sprinkling of fairy dust, its light shimmered across Ingrid's bedsheet. She breathed deeply, remembering Andreas earlier at the well—his hair curling around his ear, his slow reassuring smile.

He was so near. She longed for the strength of his arms.

Then she shook herself out of the brief reverie. Don't be a fool! She had banished Andreas. Sent him away. Nothing could change that. It was doubtful they would ever find a path to reach each other.

Before the rooster crowed, she left her cot and went around behind the barn to wash at the well. Inside the house, her mother was just leaving Briget's room. Low light from an oil lamp on the bedside table cast an ominous shadow across her face.

"She is the same. In and out of sleep."

"Go lie down, Mama. I will watch her."

She tiptoed into Briget's room and sat down in a chair near the bed. A feeble breeze nudged the edge of the curtains at the open window. Like a limp doll, her sister lay propped up in bed, her breathing a shallow whine.

Ingrid gazed upon her, her heart aching. She was so young, only four. *Don't let her leave us.* Slowly, her heavy lids closed.

Some time later, a sound aroused her.

On the pillow, the blonde head turned slightly. With a weak smile, Briget whispered, "Ingrid."

"Briget?"

Frail arms opened like petals from a small bud.

Ingrid ran to the bed and took her sister up in one sweep of a hug. Her body felt cool to the touch. "You are better," she cried. "Thank God! Mama. Papa. Come now! Briget is much better."

Bare feet scuffed over the floorboards to her side.

They all huddled near the bed, Sigrie wiping her nose with her handkerchief, Hans brushing his eyes. A collective sigh went skyward through the roof.

"I will get some fresh water," Ingrid offered.

"I will go get the doctor." Her father spun around and headed for the barn.

As Ingrid left the room, her mother wrapped her arm around her shoulders. "It is good to have you home." She added, "This afternoon, we will smoke Briget's bedclothes in the sulfur."

Bone-weary, Ingrid agreed. "We want no more sickness in this house."

The path uphill to the crab apple orchard was well traveled. Ingrid's feet followed each familiar turn, each familiar rock. Yet her heart tread on uncharted ground.

Andreas walked behind her in silence. He had arrived not twenty-four hours before, only to be leaving for St. Paul in a short time on the evening train.

She had suggested the late afternoon stroll to have one last moment with him alone, to say goodbye. Although she had told him in Chicago that their lives had changed, that they should go their separate ways, no part of her wanted him to go.

"I had forgotten the steepness of the path," she said, slightly winded as they reached the top of the hill.

Before them lay the orchard, the laden trees burgeoning with ripe fruit. "It was early June, not much more than a year ago, when we met here. The trees were full of blossoms then."

"And we were full of hope," he murmured.

His candid observation made her wistful. She walked farther among the trees. "I remember when you lifted Briget up to a branch and let her pick the pink blossoms." She smiled to herself. "And then, you picked some and tucked them into my braid."

Andreas came to stand behind her. His knuckles grazed her nape, sending tiny chills up her neck. "I would have made a crown of them for you."

She fought back myriad emotions. "You told me of your plan to go up north on the railroad. And you went, even though I hated for you to go," she admonished. "Mama always said, 'A railroad man is never home.' "

"Not when he has to build the railroad." Although she couldn't see his expression, she heard the amusement in Andreas' voice.

Gently, he turned her around and stood before her, undeniably handsome in his white shirt and fitted trousers. "Every minute I could steal, I would be home on your hearth."

Looking up into his sincere gaze, intense feelings surged through her.

"If we could just forget our hasty words in Chicago—" He clasped her arms. "We shouldn't have let our opinions about the rail strike come between us."

She softened beneath his imploring words, his warm touch. He cradled her face in his hands. "Let's not argue any more about this. It tears us apart. My only wish is to put it behind us."

Captivated by him, his compelling nearness, she murmured, "I wish we could."

He pulled her close enough to feel his heart beat against her breast; his lips brushed hers softly. On a sigh, she parted her lips and received his deepening kiss. The masculine taste of him and a delicious sensation strummed along her limbs. She lifted her hands to his muscular shoulders. He let one hand drop below her waist and drew her to him, his thighs pressed hard against hers through the folds of her skirt. "I've wanted to hold you like this from the second I saw you last night."

Her body melted against his, and the world was filled with him. Any remaining effort to divulge more of her past ties to Paddy and their secret ebbed away in her passion for Andreas. "How can I stop you . . . ?" Nor did she want to. His warm kisses covered her cheeks, her neck, her earlobe.

"Come back to the city. We can mend our differences." He buried his face in her hair. "Sweet Ingrid. I need your strength."

She looked up into his intense gaze. "And I yours."

"We've each made promises we must fulfill. But there's no reason why we can't work toward them together."

Her pulse quickened at his compelling offer. "That would be a dream come true. No longer would we be apart." No longer two hearts on the wind.

A broad smile lit up his face. "Then, you'll come back?"

Her eyes misted with hope. "I think I can stay with Nettie again. Perhaps enroll again at St. Agnes, or find another school."

With an enthusiastic squeeze, he lifted her off the ground. "I will see to it that you do."

Hand in hand, they started back down the hill, the sun a brilliant mantle about their shoulders. At last, Ingrid thought, there was room for hope. "I will write you as soon as I hear from Nettie."

A sudden frown shadowed his features. "I almost forgot to tell you. I'm staying at a downtown hotel."

Confused, she paused. "Why a hotel?"

"I couldn't tolerate Dagmar's brazen and unpredictable behavior. When I returned from Chicago, she approached me with a ridiculous offer of marriage—to combine Emma's estate and our railroad inheritance. I moved out in disgust."

Ingrid was astounded. "The woman is unstable! I'm glad you left."

Andreas shoved his fingers through his hair. "I haven't yet thought of how I'm going to explain her antics to Emma. She doesn't deserve such a greedy, ungrateful daughter."

Despite her renewed hope, as they continued downhill unresolved questions surfaced in the corners of Ingrid's mind. How would Andreas have reacted if she had revealed her involvement with Paddy and the officer's death? Would his ambition to build the railroad keep him from caring about the plight of the rail workers?

And, could she devote her life and love to a man who could not?

CHAPTER TWENTY-FIVE

"Would you look at the girls play with those new lambs." Ingrid stood before the small kitchen window several mornings later, watching Marie Lisbet and Briget in the side yard as she and her mother baked bread for the week. Ingrid kneaded the moist dough. The yeasty smell and the feel of the plump round beneath her fingers filled her with satisfaction.

"Briget is almost herself," she said, wiping her floury hands on her apron.

Sigrie's face reflected worry. "But she is still so pale, and her neck looks stiff."

Ingrid placed several dough-filled tins on a metal sheet and slid them into the oven. "I should spend some time with her. Maybe she would like a walk up the hill on this beautiful morning."

"Maybe you would too. Get your mind off that railroad man," Sigrie teased.

"Oh, Mama, I cannot," Ingrid said, pushing away a flicker of apprehension. She had told Sigrie a foreshortened story about the rail strike and Andreas, leaving out the terrible secret involving her complicity with the police officer's death. She'd confided that Andreas had asked her to resume their courtship in the city while she finished her education.

Ingrid's gaze strayed out the window and beyond to the apple orchard. "Andreas is a fine man, in many ways. It is difficult to explain my feelings for him."

"Love is not easy to explain," her mother agreed. Their gaze met in understanding.

"Would you like to join Briget and me for a stroll?"

Sigrie whooshed Ingrid toward the door. "No, no. You go now. I will watch the bread."

In the flash of an owl's wink, Ingrid untied her apron, hung it on a wall peg, and was out the back door.

"Come, Briget!" she called. "Let's go pick some crab apples."

With her back to Ingrid, her sister chased the lambs around the yard.

"Briget!" Ingrid repeated. She came up directly behind her. "Come now, let's go up to the orchard."

Briget grabbed a lamb by the tail and yanked on it. The lamb bleated loudly.

Ingrid caught her by her narrow shoulders and turned her around. "Briget! Don't you hear me?"

Staring up at her, Briget's blue eyes grew round with surprise in her pale, heart-shaped face.

"She's been acting funny lately," Marie Lisbet announced as she corralled one of the lambs. "She does not answer me when I talk to her."

Briget broke away, starting toward the house, holding her hands to the sides of her blonde head. "Mama, Mama," she whined plaintively.

Sigrie appeared in the open doorway, frowning into the sunlight. "What is wrong with my *liten barn*, my little one?"

With a strange pounding in her chest, Ingrid rushed to her sister and enfolded her in her arms. "Briget doesn't respond when I call to her. I think she is deaf."

"Dear God!" Her mother burst from the house and ran to them. "My Briget." She cradled the child's face between her worn hands. "Do you hear me?"

Ingrid kneeled before her. "Tell us what is wrong."

Briget shook her head from side to side as if uncompre-hending.

Midafternoon, her heart saddened and heavy, Ingrid followed the footpath down to the lake. A gust of wind ruffled her skirts, nearly blowing her straw hat from her head. Her thoughts tumbled like the cumulus clouds gathering from the west.

Her heart ached for Briget. Poor child. What would her future hold? If the inflammation had left her permanently deaf, what chance would she have for further education? People would always refer to her as "the deaf girl."

She would have to be accompanied, assisted, kept from harm's way. What man would marry her with such an impair-ment? She would end up a spinster—a solitary soul with no husband, no children. Without education, that would be her fate.

Tears choked Ingrid's throat as she made her way down the rambling path to the water's edge. The smell of rain hung thick on the air.

Fresh tears burned her eyes as she looked out over the lake and the waving golden fields. Gray clouds whipped above her; raindrops stung her face and shoulders.

She raised her arms in a hopeless gesture. Why did this hap-pen to Briget? An innocent child!

The rain fell steadily, giving no answers. Her hands, curled into fists, dropped to her side. What could she do to help her sister?

In the distance, she heard her mother calling her name. Her dress now wetly clinging to her, Ingrid started back along the path. She stumbled once and swiped away her tears.

Lord, let me find a way to help Briget.

The night before she was to leave for the city, Ingrid glanced up from her knitting to see her father and Jens come in from the barn. The screen door slapped shut behind them.

"You finished up early tonight," her mother observed.

Hans' bearded countenance broke into a rare grin. "We thought you would like to play a few tunes for us," he said, a twinkle in his eyes.

Sigrie regarded him from her seat in the old pine rocking chair. Ingrid sensed she was about to object.

"Please do, Mama," Jens entreated.

Before Sigrie could protest, Hans slipped his hand beneath her elbow, and the two men jovially assisted her to the cushioned stool before the piano. Marie Lisbet hovered behind her, waiting to see what she would play.

Sigrie leafed through a ragged music book. "I suppose you would like a Swedish tune to start," she mused.

"*Ja, ja,*" Jens and Marie Lisbet chimed in.

Ingrid watched her mother sit up straight and spread her fingers over the keys. With renewed energy, Sigrie began to play. As the notes sprang forth, Hans clapped his large hands in rhythm.

Ingrid set down her knitting. What a welcome turn of mood from the past few days, when everyone spoke in somber tones of "poor Briget" and what could be done about her deafness.

"Come, Ingrid. Show us a dance you learned in Chicago," Jens teased, pulling her to her feet.

Ingrid chuckled. "Not with your lead foot." But she let her brother give her a twirl around the small planked wood floor.

Briget ran up to them and wrapped her arms around Ingrid's skirts.

Looking down into the sweet uncomprehending face, Ingrid's heart nearly broke. She stepped away from Jens and took Briget's hands, swaying her to-and-fro to the music.

"She does not know how to dance," Marie Lisbet interjected.

"She cannot hear."

Ingrid clasped her sister's small hand. "Come over by the piano, love." She led her to the corner where Papa and Marie Lisbet stood and clapped to the tune Mama played. Briget gazed from one face to another, a vague frown upon her forehead.

Acting on impulse, Ingrid drew her closer to the piano. "Play louder, Mama, as loudly as you can," she pleaded.

Sigrie looked at her, questioning, but leaned over the keyboard and pounded away fervently.

Ingrid held her head close to the side of the piano, then guided Briget over to it and pressed her small head against it. Immediately a light danced in Briget's wide blue eyes. An angelic smile lifted her lips.

"She can hear the vibrations!" Ingrid exclaimed. "She can hear them." It was a small thing, she knew, but it gave a fraction of hope.

Along with the rest of the family, Jens clapped boisterously. "Play 'Little Brown Jug,' Mama. It's my favorite."

Sigrie groaned. "You will wear my fingers off." But she found the familiar page in the music book.

Everyone sang:

> Ah ha ha! You and me,
> Little brown jug, how
> I love thee.

Her cinnamon-brown braids shining in the gaslight, Marie Lisbet took Briget and swung her around until she fell in a heap in the middle of the floor.

Ingrid danced again with Jens, joined in song with the rest, and observed Briget from the corner of her eye, hoping that one day she could teach Briget the skills she would need to live in her silent world.

CHAPTER TWENTY-SIX

Train wheels clicked along the narrow-gauge track.

Andreas. Andreas. Andreas.

No matter how Ingrid tried to tamp her rising anticipation of seeing him again, the sound of the wheels' steady rhythm resounded in her ears, repeating his name. Yet being with him, resuming their courtship, posed a challenge that she would soon have to face. Her hands perspired inside her gloves.

She reached into her handbag, closing her fingers around the steel gun barrel. Strange as it was, she had become attached to the odd comfort the weapon provided. Unlike city girls, she knew how to shoot. Was not afraid to shoot the weapon, if need be.

Somehow she must find a way to tell Andreas about how she came to have the gun. Their future together depended on her honesty. They must settle their differences over the strike and move forward.

Ahead, the St. Paul station came into view. It would not be long before she saw him. Her early arrival would be a surprise.

Since Nettie could not meet her at the station because of a late-afternoon class, Ingrid would hire a rig to the Nelson's with part of her Chicago earnings. Working again half-time for Uncle Nels at the dry goods store would replenish her low funds.

Fortunately, she had been able to enroll in St. Agnes' for fall semester. Papa had even encouraged her this time. "Without an education," he'd said, "you cannot teach the children who need you." She knew he referred to students like her sister Briget. Although she couldn't afford to return to the Chicago academy, she hoped one day to take advanced courses for such children.

Moments later, Ingrid descended the train stairs to the crowded platform. Despite an overcast sky and a gusty wind that furled her skirts about her, Ingrid's mood soared. Andreas would no doubt be at work in his office. She couldn't wait to see the expression on his handsome face when she surprised him.

Inside the station, she maneuvered around a family with unlimited children, all carrying licorice sticks, their mouths and pudgy cheeks smeared a gooey charcoal. Beneath the big entryway clock and down a stuffy-smelling hallway, she came to Andreas' small office.

The lamp on his desk was lit, but he was not there.

Disheartened, she returned to the platform and waited in line for her baggage. She glanced around the rail yard, thinking Andreas might be checking cargo on outgoing trains.

Across the tracks, she spied a workman resembling Thor. Moving quickly, his dusky head swiveled from side to side in a furtive way. Indeed, she was sure it was Thor.

He stumbled briefly then went around behind a parked train car. His behavior was odd, but then, he was odd. From the first time they had met the night of Dagmar's twenty-first birthday party, Ingrid had never felt comfortable around him. His stealthy, deep-set eyes observed the world without revealing his thoughts.

With a shrug, Ingrid turned her attention back to retrieving her luggage.

At the rear of the St. Paul station, Andreas knocked on the solid oak door standing half ajar. The superintendent had directed him to his employer's office. He couldn't imagine why. Certainly he had done nothing to cause the Scotsman's ire. Along the line, stories abounded of Hill's temper when he was riled or when a job had not been performed to his specification.

James J. Hill glanced up from behind a massive desk piled with shipping orders and railroad documents. "Eriksen, come in," he said brusquely, waving to him.

Andreas cleared his dry throat. "Sir, you wanted to see me."

Hill got to his feet and came around the desk. Andreas remembered the man's height as comparable to his own, slightly over six feet. He was clean shaven except for a half beard. His dark eyes glittered with intensity, and Andreas was reminded of the loss of sight Hill had suffered in his left eye in a childhood accident. No matter, he knew this man could see as well with one eye as most men with two.

They shook hands, and Hill motioned to a chair at the side of the desk. "Sit down, Eriksen. I've got a proposition for you."

Andreas seated himself and gave Hill his full attention.

"As you must know, I've raised the necessary funds, along with my Canadian colleagues, and acquired control of the St. Paul & Pacific."

Yes, Andreas knew of the takeover. He recalled the night his father had revealed Hill's plans. The night of Adolph's fatal heart attack.

His employer continued, his face radiant with enthusiasm. "I have great hopes for this railroad. We're going to extend the line to the Canadian border and connect with Winnipeg. And that will only be the beginning."

Andreas listened, his hands gripping the sides of the chair. His pulse quickened, his mind preparing to take a whirlwind cerebral journey along with the man who stood before him.

"We'll make Minneapolis the center of milling in America," Hill said. "Our state is teeming with forests—imagine providing lumber to our eager neighbors to the north and west."

Andreas felt as if his body were rising inches from the floor. "Yes, sir."

Hill moved behind the desk. His large hands splayed against the edge, he leaned forward, gazing intently at Andreas.

"I've heard of your positive attitude, Eriksen, your resourcefulness. You influenced the men not to strike during that very disruptive time this summer. That took leadership."

"Thank you, sir."

"How old are you, if I might ask?"

"I'll be twenty-four next month."

Hill looked at him straight on. "A young man needs responsibility, a future goal. Consider staying on the St. Paul & Pacific. I need an ambitious, honorable man to be my right hand, to help me build this line. I will make it worth your while."

Andreas swallowed hard. He wanted this job. It would fulfill his goal and his promise to his father. "I would be honored, sir."

Hill came around the desk. "I thought you would, Eriksen. I've been watching you since you started here, and I know you have what it takes."

Andreas stood and shook his employer's hand, realizing he was headed for a destiny beyond his wildest dreams.

Hill gave a satisfied smile. "You've just made the right choice, Eriksen."

As Andreas turned toward the door, Hill said with a sparkle in his good eye, "By the time our line reaches farther west to Montana, and then California, they'll be calling it 'the Great Northern.'"

"That would be a worthy name for it, sir."

Andreas emerged into the station, his head spinning with the conversation he'd just had with the dynamic rail baron.

I'm going to be James J. Hill's right-hand man!

The opportunity would not only enable him to secure his own future, but oversee improvements in the earnings and safe environment for the railmen. Andreas had made an unspoken vow to the railmen that cold dreary day they had lowered Nordberg into the ground. The brakeman's death would not be forgotten.

He headed for his own small office, his feet striding on clouds. He wished he could shout his good fortune from the train depot rooftop—break the exciting news to everyone within hearing distance.

He wished he could tell Ingrid. Just ride up in his carriage and whisk her away to some secluded spot where they could be alone and celebrate. He hoped her reaction would be the same as his.

As he stepped over his office threshold, Andreas glanced at his pocket watch. Four-fifteen. By now, he should have been checking incoming cargo. Hurriedly he grabbed his clipboard from the desk and headed for the yard.

A screaming train whistle. Grinding brakes. Shouting voices.

Ingrid's heart leaped to her throat. What had happened? She swiveled on the platform to see plumes of smoke, cinders falling like fireflies, men running from across the yard.

"Get help!" one workman hollered down the track to another. "Eriksen's caught under the wheels."

Her hand flew to her breast. Eriksen? "Oh, no!"

Only moments before, she'd seen Thor ambling over by the train cars. Poor Thor. Without thinking, Ingrid picked up her skirt and sprinted from the platform toward the tracks.

Others merged into the yard. Voices blurred, mingled with the hammering of her heart. Where was Andreas?

Ericksen's caught under the wheels!

Dear God. Could it be Andreas, not Thor, pinned under the wheels?

Sheer black fright darting through her, Ingrid ran faster.

Beyond the nearest parked train cars lay a crazy grid of tracks going in all directions. A mighty engine dwarfed her. A fog of cinders and steam invaded her lungs.

She didn't belong here. A young woman scurrying like a rabbit through a threshing field. But she had to know who had been injured.

Ahead crewmen rounded the caboose of one train, and she followed them.

"He's up here," one called over his shoulder to another.

Throat burning, she approached more rail workers huddled in front of a giant, smoke-billowing engine.

A burly man in blackened coveralls moved toward her, his forehead smudged and grooved with deep frown lines. "You shouldn't be here, miss. You'd better go back."

"What happened?" she demanded. "Who's been hurt?"

His body blocked her view. "Don't know who. A man's trapped under the train. You don't want to see it."

Her heart lurched in her chest. She had to see who it was. Ducking quickly to the side, Ingrid squeezed through the barricade of workmen. Emerging on the other side, she stared ahead and gasped.

Two legs stuck out from between the second and third wheels, the upper body wedged halfway under the train. Dark blood soaked the tracks and pooled near the man's feet. Shards of broken glass from a whiskey bottle glittered on the ground.

Ingrid's stomach roiled, bile rising in her throat. *It is not Andreas—it can't be Andreas.* Her knees threatening to give way beneath her, she drew back.

Over the din, a graveled voice reached her ear. "I thought he heard the warning whistle. But he didn't even look behind him. Next thing, the cowcatcher tossed him into the air . . . he got sucked under the wheels."

Heart pounding, Ingrid rushed to the man's side. "Do you

know who he is?" Her head whirled dizzingly. "Where is the doctor?"

A firm hand grasped her arm. "Ingrid."

Startled, she turned and looked up into familiar eyes. The shock of relief hit her full force. "Andreas! Thank God, you're safe." She threw herself into his arms.

"I'm fine." His gaze caressed her face. "I'm so glad to see you." His hand tensed on her arm. "But Thor—we've got to get him to the hospital."

With his revelation, tears pricked her eyes. "Yes, you must. What can I do?"

"Go back to the station and wait for me." He disappeared into the throng of crewmen.

Still trembling, Ingrid made her way over the steel tracks toward the depot. Her mind could not make any sense of Thor's terrible accident. Why hadn't he heard the warning whistle and the oncoming train? Could he have been distracted? Yet, how relieved she was that Andreas had not been involved in the accident.

What seemed like hours later, Andreas rushed back to his office where she waited. "They're taking Thor to the St. Paul hospital. I'm going to meet them there."

Ingrid stood. "I want to go with you. How bad is Thor?"

His features strained, Andreas took her arm as they left the office. "It doesn't look good."

Ingrid and Andreas had no sooner arrived at the hospital than Dagmar approached them near the entrance. Her demeanor matched her apparel. She wore a dark purple gown, accented by her wild hair and glinting eyes. "I demand to know Thor's condition."

Andreas scowled at her but kept walking, guiding Ingrid toward the reception desk. "That's what we're here to find out."

Dagmar's eyes flashed a fiery jet black. "They won't tell me anything at the desk."

Ignoring his stepsister, Andreas proceeded ahead. Ingrid would like to have avoided Dagmar altogether, but a question loomed before her that she could not hold back. "How did you know Thor was injured?" she asked as Andreas questioned the white-capped nurse.

Dagmar raised her brows. "I dropped by the rail yard to visit Thor and was told about his—what happened—if it's any of your business."

"I see." The last time Ingrid saw Thor, he'd hardly been presentable for a visit from a well-dressed society woman.

Andreas motioned for her. "Thor's in the room at the end of the hall."

All three of them raced down the corridor. Andreas entered the room, pulling a white curtain shut behind him.

Dagmar strutted forward. Ingrid caught her by the arm. "Let him be alone with Thor. He is his only family."

Dagmar's eyes flashed with arrogance. "How dare you." She brushed Ingrid's hand away, but only hovered nearby. "Thor has been as close as family. He's been my companion."

Releasing a weary breath, Ingrid went over and found a wicker chair in the waiting room. She wished Dagmar was not here during this anxious time for Andreas, this desperate time for Thor.

Minutes later, Andreas came out of the room, his face ashen. "Thor has passed away," he told both women. "His injuries and loss of blood made it impossible for the doctors to save him." His voice faltered. "I've made arrangements for them to send him to the funeral home."

Dagmar let out a high-pitched wail. "No! He is not dead." Sparks flew from her glinting eyes. "You're lying."

Astonished at her defiant reaction, Ingrid moved to her.

"Dagmar, you are upset—"

"Leave me alone!" Dagmar pushed Ingrid away, strode purposefully to the white curtain, and yanked it back.

Ingrid's mouth dropped open in surprise. "Let her go," Andreas said. "There's nothing more she can do."

Inside the room, a nurse cleaned up bloody towels from the floor. She rose when Dagmar entered. "I'm family," Dagmar said with authority. The nurse nodded and scurried out of the room with the towels

On a wheeled cot lay a bulky figure, covered by a sheet, one large foot protruding from the end of it. She dared not think what was left of the rest of the body. The sharp smell of alcohol . . . and death . . . filled her nostrils. Made her stomach lurch. She swallowed hard and forced herself to go over to the ghostly bedside.

Gingerly lifting back the sheet, she caught her breath. *Thor.* She hardly recognized him. His face was swollen, bruised; his eyes closed. Beard stubble covered his jaw. No longer the devil-may-care lover, Thor lay still, silent. She could not look further at his mangled remains. Her hand dropped to her side, acute pain and anger boiling up within her.

Thor, what happened? You were supposed to push Andreas under the wheels, not end up there yourself?

How could you have left me like this? We had such plans. The fact that she'd decided to cast him aside after his evil deed escaped Dagmar for the moment. Only disbelief and self-pity prevailed.

The unfairness of it. The lifeless body before her should have been Andreas. It was his fault. If he hadn't rejected her, her beauty, her generous offer of a life of ease and prominence . . . He didn't deserve to go on without her.

It wasn't too late. She could yet persuade him of the ridiculous mistake he'd made. Turning quickly toward the door, she bolted out into the hall. Andreas and that farm girl were gone. Her heart in her throat, Dagmar nipped up her skirts and hurried to the entrance of the hospital. In front, she saw them getting into his carriage.

I'll track them down. They won't get away with this! She rushed out a side door to her hired rig.

CHAPTER TWENTY-SEVEN

Nightfall crept around the clouds overhead as they drove onto the Hennepin Avenue suspension bridge, its towers looming. Ingrid moved closer to Andreas on the carriage seat, the dregs of unease lingering. Thor's tragic death and Dagmar's upsetting behavior at the hospital had left her shaken. "I wish this day had never happened."

A tense expression pulling down at the corners of his mouth, Andreas nodded. "Thor was a wild card. I wish I could say that I knew him." He smiled over at her, his features softening. "At least, you're finally here."

The hard clopping of horses' hooves and the jangle of harness made Ingrid glance over her shoulder. A two-horse-drawn carriage bore down on them. The driver hollered, "Pull over!" and forced Andreas to the side of the bridge, where he cut in front of them.

Andreas reined his horse to a sudden stop.

Before either could make sense of the driver's actions, Dagmar erupted from the carriage and rushed toward them. Her hair escaping in tangled disarray from her cape, she shouted, "I want you to know, Andreas, you are going to pay!"

Andreas tied the reins and alighted to the pavement. Ingrid climbed down on her side. "What is—?"

Dark eyes glittering, Dagmar lunged at him. "I warned you a time would come when you would pay." She shook her finger up at his face. "I'm going to tell everyone Thor's death was your fault. It was no accident. You pushed him in front of the train!"

Before Andreas could answer, Ingrid moved in front of him, facing Dagmar. "That is nonsense. How do we know you don't have something to do with it and are trying to blame Andreas? You have been so eager to get your hands on his inheritance, as well as your own."

Dagmar glared at Ingrid then glanced quickly ahead at her waiting rig. "It was no accident," she insisted.

"Thor was drinking on the job," Andreas stated as he guided Ingrid to his side. "I've caught him before and should have fired him then. He caused his own accident."

"You're lying!" Dagmar shouted and ran back to her carriage. In the flash of a moment, she leaped up on the carriage step and snatched her driver's horse whip from his hand.

Her jaw jutting forward, Dagmar confronted Andreas. "You can't talk about Thor like that and get away with it." She snapped the whip, narrowly missing his face.

Andreas lunged toward her to grab the whip, but she darted backward, the wind billowing her skirts and hair about her like some crazed witch.

Anger and fear for Andreas boiling in her veins, Ingrid grappled for a way to protect him. By a different stroke of fate, Andreas could have been crushed beneath the train wheels instead of Thor. She would not allow him to be placed at risk now by this wild woman's vengeance.

Reaching inside her handbag, she pulled out the gun. Moving to within a few feet of Dagmar, she pointed it at her. "Get away from him—or I'll shoot."

Scowling in surprise, Dagmar held the whip in midair.

At that moment, Andreas seized it, the action sending her stumbling backward.

Immediately reclaiming her footing, Dagmar burst forward, tackling Ingrid from the side. For a heart-tripping second,

Ingrid was caught off guard, but she held fast to the gun. The women struggled in total abandon.

Nothing else mattered but the gun and Ingrid's fight to defend Andreas. Gasping for air, her hair flying about her eyes, she wrestled Dagmar over toward the bridge railing.

"Stop this—both of you!" Andreas demanded. "Before someone gets hurt."

His words faded in the heat of the scuffle.

If I can get her backed up against the railing, Ingrid thought, *maybe we can talk some sense into her.* But Dagmar wasn't cooperating. When her teeth sank into Ingrid's right wrist, Ingrid gasped in pain.

A shot exploded from the gun—the bullet pinging against a steel girder. The jolt of its report sent shock currents down to Ingrid's knees. Slipping from her hand, the firearm clattered to the bridge floor.

Dagmar started to dive for it, but Andreas kicked the weapon yards beyond her reach. She swung toward him, her cheeks a mottled purple, the same shade as her gown. "I'll tell everyone you tried to kill me. I'll tell Mother!"

Andreas grasped her arms, fairly lifting her back over the railing. "You'll do nothing of the sort. Say nothing. Your name is not worth protecting, but Emma's is. And you wouldn't want to put your inheritance at risk." A harsh laugh escaped his clenched jaw. "After the way you've treated your mother, and both of us, I don't see how she'll leave you anything."

Dagmar thrashed furiously against him. "Let me go!"

"Andreas is an honorable man. You have done nothing but try to disgrace him when he only had your best interests at heart," Ingrid countered, releasing long pent up mistrust and injury.

"You killed Thor," Dagmar spat out at Andreas, her eyes shooting fiery sparks.

"You are wrong, Dagmar," Ingrid called above the wind. "We may never know, but it is far more likely that *you* had something to do with Thor's death."

"You'll never prove it," Dagmar snarled.

Two rigs drove past, one driver gawking at them.

Forcefully, Andreas escorted Dagmar over to her carriage. The disheveled driver made no effort to get down and assist his passenger or retrieve his whip.

"Leave us alone, Dagmar," Andreas demanded, "or you will truly regret it." With a rough push, he shoved her up into the coach's interior and closed the door tightly.

The driver snapped the reins and growled a command to his horses. The coach lurched forward, made a sharp turn around, and headed back toward St. Paul. Her hair a jumbled snarl, Dagmar leaned out the carriage window, spewing further threats and shaking her fist.

Ingrid leaned back against the railing and exhaled a long sigh. Her knees trembled beneath her skirts.

Andreas stood, one hand balled against his hip, staring after the disappearing nightmare coach. "She's gone. Thank God." He looked back at Ingrid. "Are you all right?"

Holding her wrist up to inspection, she nodded. "It looks like she only broke the skin."

Glancing up at his tired features, shadowed in the fading evening light, Ingrid hoped she and Andreas could start fresh. Without Dagmar's twisted ambitions and interference in their lives.

But, as Andreas bent over and picked up the gun, he looked back at her curiously. Her heart stood still. "Where did you get this?"

A chill quaked through her. Andreas held the weapon that had caused pain and death, provided protection, and separated her from him, the man she loved. Her past secret rose to shame her. She could no longer bear the guilt over not reporting the officer's murder and shielding Paddy, even if he'd vowed it was an accident.

"I have something to tell you," she said, moving toward him. Fear clutched at her throat. "I've been meaning to tell you for a long time. It has to do with the rail strike."

His eyes narrowed slightly. "What is it?"

Despite her great wish not to have to hurt him or destroy what love they still held for each other, Ingrid drew herself up. Even if it meant losing Andreas, she must reveal the truth. "During the rail strike, my roommate's brother killed a police officer. It was accidental—"

Andreas' brows drew together in an agonized expression. "It was accidental?"

She let out a frustrated breath. "Yes. Paddy fell in with some of the strikers after he lost his job, and he was involved in a skirmish at the rail yard."

Staring at her in disbelief, Andreas backed away. "He sympathized with the strikers?"

"Yes, he did. We thought he had good reason."

With obvious disgust, Andreas paced along the bridge railing. "How could you justify living with a strike agitator? A police killer?"

"He didn't plan on killing anyone. It was what happened during the strike."

Andreas shook his head. "You became an accomplice to violent actions against the railroad . . . knowing it was my life, my future."

"My last thought was to betray you, Andreas."

He looked down at the gun, still in his hand. "And you kept the gun."

"For protection. I was alone and the streets and railways were not safe." She lowered her gaze to her folded hands. How could he possibly still love her when he believed she'd acted against him? Painful tears stung her eyelids.

"By rights, I could still turn this gun over to the police," Andreas stated, his voice strained.

Girding herself with courage, Ingrid faced him. "Yes. If you feel it is the right thing to do. I know you are an honorable man, and you must follow your conscience."

His lips pressed tightly together, Andreas looked at her then away over the river toward the twinkling lights on a St. Paul hillside. What was he thinking? That he no longer loved her?

She stared at him, her mind a swirling mixture of hope and dread.

Then, to Ingrid's amazement, he lifted the gun and tossed it over the bridge railing. It made a plopping sound as it hit the surface before falling downward into the watery depths.

Her legs nearly crumpled beneath her in relief. His actions had told her everything she needed to know.

With a sudden smile, and in three strides, he came to her. "A gun should never come between a man and the woman he loves."

His arms went round her and drew her to him, full measure, his body flush to hers. "I love you, Ingrid. I don't give a damn what happened in that foul strike." His kisses caressed her face, took her breath away.

She clung to him. "Do you forgive me?"

His lips brushed hers tenderly. "There's nothing to forgive. I respect your loyalty to your roommates during a chaotic time. You told me the truth and took responsibility for your actions."

She shivered in his arms and pressed her face into the shelter of his strong shoulder. His coat smelled of train smoke, a hint of bay rum, and safety.

"Let's get you into the carriage and out of this cold wind."

She smiled up at him. "I don't mind a little wind, as long as you hold me like this."

His lips claimed hers in a velvet-soft kiss. Sparks, like shimmering fireflies, danced through her body.

"I want you to know that today Mr. Hill offered me a higher position on the new Northern Pacific. He asked me to be his assistant manager, his right-hand man."

"Oh, Andreas, that must be what you have always wanted." She paused, averting her gaze.

Looking concerned, he stepped back. "Is something wrong?"

"No, but I can't help wonder if the rail workers will be any better off than they were before the strike?"

"They will be, my darling." His large hand cupped her face and held it gently. "I plan to devote my life's work to improve the workers' future."

"Your father would have been so proud of you," she said. "I will support you in every way that I can."

He cocked one brow, his hair ruffled roguishly about his forehead. "Ah, but I want more than your support . . . I want your strength, courage, and love. As I will freely give to you, as your husband."

Her heart did a somersault. Andreas was proposing to her. As many times as she had imagined him saying these words, from the day of his cousin's wedding when she first saw him striding up the hill, and he had mesmerized her with his city charm, she could never have prepared herself for this exhilaration!

"Will you marry me, Ingrid?"

In the moonlight peeking through the clouds, she thrilled beneath his tender gaze. "I will, Andreas. With great joy."

He gathered her close. "I hope your father won't mind that he's getting a railman for a son-in-law."

She laughed through happy tears. "Papa knows he could do no better." Realizing the late hour and that the Nelsons would be waiting for her, she said, "I cannot wait to tell Nettie."

Swiftly, he lifted her up and carried her to his carriage. On the seat, snug and safe, Ingrid leaned into the shelter of his warmth. Andreas flicked the reins and directed the horse across the bridge toward the lights of Minneapolis.

EPILOGUE

Eden Valley, June 1880

"How glorious the crab apple blossoms are this year!" Ingrid stepped ahead along the path, Andreas' steadying hand on her bare forearm.

"Indeed, Mrs. Eriksen, almost as colorful as the day you first met me on this hill." He pressed her arm tenderly, sending tendrils of heat upward to her shoulder.

A small finger pointed to the fragrant trees as they approached the orchard. "Mama. Mama!" The baby in her arms squirmed to get down. Ingrid bent over and set the fourteen-month-old on her feet, laughing as she tottered away, wisps of blonde hair sticking out from the sides of her miniature sunbonnet.

"Already she has a mind of her own," Ingrid observed.

"So does her sister." Andreas released the other twin, who busied herself waving at a passing butterfly.

Ingrid glanced at him from beneath her straw hat brim. "Did you ever think we would have twins?"

Andreas grinned knowingly. "Guess they run in your family."

Ingrid nodded, gazing toward the family cemetery where her baby sisters were buried. "I pray our children will be healthy."

"They are robust." He moved behind her as they watched the toddlers. "Our little Emily and Anna are beautiful, but they have a way to go before they catch up with their mother." He trailed soft kisses down her neck.

She jumped at the tickling sensation, then turned and looked fondly up into his eyes. "Next time, we will have a son."

"A young railroad man," Andreas said proudly.

Ingrid clamped her lips together and frowned in mock defiance. "We shall see. Maybe he will be a teacher."

Andreas' expression was dubious. "His grandmothers would probably disagree over that."

She picked up one of the babies from the dirt and brushed off her white pinafore. "They will love them for who they are," she declared, adding thoughtfully, "Emma was so generous to give us the majority of her railroad stock."

Andreas chuckled. "Just before Dagmar ran off to New York with her diminished inheritance."

Ingrid shook her head. "Her greed only spawned misery and nearly destroyed her."

"I've heard Dagmar's been seen traipsing around the city with a greasy-haired salon director. A reputed con artist."

Ingrid sighed. "At least she is out of our life. And Emma seems like a new person, so invigorated now that she is no longer dependent on her remedy."

"Fate did work in our favor." Andreas turned and waved to Ingrid's younger sisters dashing up the hill toward them.

Marie Lisbet called, "We've come to take the twins to play with our new litter of kittens!"

Seven-year-old Briget followed close behind. With sun-browned hands, she made the sign of "kittens" to Ingrid.

Pleased, Ingrid smiled. She returned the hand signing, saying, "You can take the girls."

"You are doing wonders with Briget," Andreas commented as they watched her sisters carry the babies back down the hill.

"We've been studying sign language for the deaf. She is a very fast and eager student. There is so much I want to teach her."

Andreas circled her within his arms. "My darling. I brought you up here to tell you my surprise."

She cocked her head, the corners of her mouth lifting. "I love surprises. What is it?"

"A school. A special school. I want to build it just for you and your students."

Momentarily speechless, Ingrid stared at him. "Oh, yes! For children like Briget." She whirled happily, arms outstretched, her periwinkle skirt twirling around her. "And Nettie will want to help teach."

Then she stopped and looked back at him. "I love you so much," she said, joyful tears springing to her eyes.

Andreas beamed. "You will be the headmistress, and a damn fine one."

Ingrid tossed back her head, laughing with the wonder of dreams come true.

He captured her in his arms, enfolding her to him as if he would never let her go. Words were lost, only hearts beating as one, his lips warm on her neck, her cheek, her mouth.

Above them, blossoms floated away on the wind, down over the verdant meadow.

QUESTIONS FOR DISCUSSION

1. Was it selfish of Ingrid Johansson to want to leave the family farm and become a teacher? Do you have female ancestors who overcame societal restraints to accomplish their goals?

2. What were Ingrid's greatest strengths, weaknesses?

3. Did *Hearts on the Wind* entice you to read more about American history? The emergence of the early railroads? Railroad barons—James J. Hill in particular?

4. Great challenges faced Andreas Eriksen throughout the book. Did he make the right decisions? Was he too blind-sided to stepsister Dagmar's devious nature?

5. Did you believe Dagmar capable of carrying out her ambitions with Thor? Did you think her resulting inheritance was just?

6. Was this a satisfying love story? Are you more inclined to read a historical novel if it includes or centers around a romantic relationship? Or not?

7. In this period of American history, the letter was the main form of communication. After reading *Hearts on the Wind*, are

you more likely to research your own family history? Keep a family journal?

ABOUT THE AUTHOR

Leslee Breene creates stories from the heart, depicting heroes and heroines of Western romance. *Leadville Lady* was Ms. Breene's second published novel, for which she received the Rocky Mountain Fiction Writers PEN Award. Her debut novel *Foxfire* (2001/AuthorHouse) was a second-place winner in an annual RWA Valley Forge contest and is available in trade paperback at www.lesleebreene.com.

Her short fiction was serialized in (2005) *Miss Kitty's Journal, Colorado's Official Tea Room Directory*. Other stories have won or placed in the Moonlight & Magnolia international short fiction awards, *Byline* Magazine, and *Writer's Digest* annual competition.

Ms. Breene attended the University of Denver, was awarded a Denver Fashion Group Scholarship, and graduated from the Fashion Institute of Technology, New York City. During leisure time away from her computer, she enjoys scouting for book settings with her husband in the Colorado Rockies and Wyoming, and walking her miniature poodle.

A believer in supporting fellow writers, Ms. Breene is a member of Colorado Romance Writers, Rocky Mountain Fiction Writers, and Women Writing the West.